"Donnie, I need to talk to you about something important."

"What?" my little son inquired. His brows knitted together in their usual way when he was looking perplexed or meditative, or angry, but at the moment, he was looking at me real hard, as if he was steeling himself for something big.

"Donnie, honey, I'm not feeling very good these days. I'm pretty sick." There. It was said. I'd lain awake half the night trying to figure out the best way of telling him and had finally come to the conclusion that I trusted myself enough to know how, when the moment came.

"The doctor didn't make your cold go away? I heard you coughing." His brows remained pinched, worried.

"No, it's not a cold, darlin'. It's something else with a real long name that's hard to say. The doctor wants me to see some other doctors who can help me more than he can. I have to go where they are, and stay for a little while. Remember when we went to Asheville to see that play, *The Nutcracker*, at Christmas?" He nodded. "Well, I have to go to a place that's not too far from there."

"Will you see a play?"

I laughed. His five-year-old world was very small, compartmentalized. "No, honey, I'm not going to the theater, just to a hospital that takes care of people who are sick, like I am."

"Oh." He looked away as he digested this and I knew that suddenly the awfulness of my going away was sinking in. The word "hospital" had done it. "How long will you stay?"

"I'm not sure, but I'm hoping it won't be too long . . ."

Also by Janie DeVos

Beneath a Thousand Apple Trees

The Art of Breathing

Janic DcVos

LYRICAL PRESS
Kensington Publishing Corp.
www.kensingtonbooks.com

LYRICAL PRESS BOOKS are published by

Kensington Publishing Corp.
119 West 40th Street
New York, NY 10018

All Kensington titles, imprints, and distributed lines are available at special quantity discounts for bulk purchases for sales promotion, premiums, fundraising, educational, or institutional use.

Special book excerpts or customized printings can also be created to fit specific needs. For details, write or phone the office of the Kensington Sales Manager: Kensington Publishing Corp., 119 West 40th Street, New York, NY 10018. Attn. Sales Department. Phone: 1-800-221-2647.

Lyrical Press and Lyrical Press logo Reg. U.S. Pat. & TM Off.

First Electronic Edition: February 2017
eISBN-13: 978-1-60183-683-0
eISBN-10: 1-60183-683-X

First Print Edition: February 2017
ISBN-13: 978-1-60183-684-7
ISBN-10: 1-60183-684-8

Printed in the United States of America

This book is dedicated to the memory of my grandmother, Kathryn Flaharty Sandell, who lost her battle with tuberculosis in a Chicago, Illinois sanatorium in 1938, but whose loving spirit was felt throughout the writing of this story. And to my wonderful father, Don "Donnie" Sandell, who lost his mother at age eleven but kept her love alive through his memories of her kindness and gentleness—and amazing fudge cake. *May you two be together again, sharing a heavenly slice.* And finally, to my dear friends Teaky Tollison and Nancy Lindeman, who accompanied me on many field trips as I researched this book: *Thank you for sharing this important journey with me. Until the next one!*

ACKNOWLEDGMENTS

There are many people who must be acknowledged for their time and effort in helping me to bring this story to life. First, I'd like to thank Stacy Merten, Director of the Historic Resources Commission for the City of Asheville, NC, who was able to work a little magic in providing a tour of the home of Dr. Karl Von Ruck, one of Asheville's pioneer physicians dedicated to curing tuberculosis. I'm also grateful to Ms. Merten for taking me on a neighborhood walking tour to study some of Asheville's outstanding architecture of the late nineteenth and early twentieth centuries. Thank you, Stacy, for your time and knowledge. We shall break bread again soon.

I owe a wealth of gratitude to the good people in Chicago, IL, who gave me an in-depth tour of some of the buildings and grounds that were once part of the Chicago Municipal Tuberculosis Sanitarium, but which have been reincarnated into a vast park system. I'm especially grateful to Kiala Moore, Peterson Park Supervisor, and Sean Shaffer, Education Naturalist, at the North Park Village Nature Center, whose generous gifts of time and knowledge of the CMTS painted a much clearer picture as to what my grandmother's life and death must have been like in the sanatorium in 1938. You will never know how much that afternoon meant to me personally; and professionally, it was invaluable in the writing of this book. Thank you, both.

I'm also indebted to Dr. Richard Rhea, Assistant Director at the Black Mountain Neuro-Medical Treatment Center, which at one time had been the Western North Carolina Sanatorium, in Black Mountain, NC. Through his help, I was able to see how drastically things changed for the better in mid-twentieth century sanatorium life, including society's more tolerant attitude toward tuberculars, better quality of institutional care, advancements in progressive medications—most specifically streptomycin—and the use of far fewer radical surgical techniques. At last, the victims of this most formidable harbinger of death found reason to hope. Thank you, Dr. Rhea, for your wonderful insight and vital information in helping to create my character's sanatorium experience.

And finally, I'd like to express my deepest thanks to my husband, Glen DeVos, who let me drag him along on my research trip to Chicago, and who patiently stood by me through my long writing days and nights, while graciously putting up with countless dinners of frozen pizzas and takeout food: I owe you a lot of good home cookin', dear. And to my good friends in Spruce Pine, NC, especially the Spruce Pine Rotary Club, who understood why I disappeared for half a year and welcomed me back when I finally walked out into daylight again.

To all of you, my deepest gratitude, respect, and love. J. D.

PREFACE

The strangling coughs and ineffective rapid breathing of the patients in every bed, on every floor, ward, and separate cottage were the commonality of the patients suffering from tuberculosis. It bound them together and forced each one to witness the slow and painful death of so many around them. Up until the mid–twentieth century and the discovery of streptomycin, only a small percentage recovered, while for the vast majority the wet, rattling cough grew ever more relentless with the passing days. It was the dreaded sign that the patient's lungs were growing weaker as cavities and lesions grew bigger.

One of the earlier names given to the disease was "consumption." Not only did it consume the lungs and other organs, but it consumed the hopes and dreams of its victims. Most patients fought with every cell in their bodies to beat the slim odds of recovery, knowing they had to accomplish just one thing: to keep breathing. For each patient it became a beautiful art form—that easy, even, rhythmic flow of breath that was taken for granted by those who didn't suffer the slow suffocation of tuberculosis. But eventually, the vast majority lost that battle, measuring the progress of their disease by the quality of each measured breath. And the more labored it became, the more obvious it was that patients would soon leave the sanatorium behind for a quiet and gentle place; a haven where the tired, wasted body was replaced by spirit alone, and where the beautiful art of breathing need not be practiced anymore.

PART ONE

CHAPTER 1

April 1954

I was born in the Blue Ridge Mountains of North Carolina, in the small logging town of Howling Cut. And though it was just two hours away from the city of Cabot, where I would live once I was married, the difference between the two places made it hard to believe they were so close. Cabot had grown by leaps and bounds, and social status and wealth were the measuring sticks of success. By contrast, Howling Cut grew at a much slower pace because of its higher elevation and far harsher weather. For the people in my hometown, success was measured by the number of winters and illnesses you were able to survive, and whether or not you could hang on to the family farm for another year.

My parents, Jack and Rachel Harris, built the white two-story house I grew up in on the edge of their enormous apple orchard. My home wasn't far from my great-grandmother's place, which she'd bought as a young woman in the 1880s and where my grandmother and mother had been born. The town was so small that most everyone was related in some way, even if they were "distant, distant somethings," and if they weren't related, then you could bet your last dollar that they knew each other well—well enough to know things about each other that they probably shouldn't have.

I was the first of Jack and Rachel's three children, and I looked like a combined image of the two. My hair was dark brown, like Daddy's, and my nose was the female version of his straight and strong one, but the rest of my facial structure was much like Mama's. We both had light eyes as well, but whereas hers were a true "Carolina blue," just like the sky on an October day, mine were as green as the grass in June.

My brother, Andrew, was sixteen months younger than I, and nearly a carbon copy of me. Though he'd grown into a ruggedly handsome young man, he'd been a beautiful, almost delicate-looking baby. I thought he was pretty and called him such, although my toddler's attempt at saying the word "pretty" came out sounding like "Ditty," and the name stuck.

Our sister, Emily Nell, came into the world two years after Ditty, and she was fierce and fearless from the start. I heard Mama once say that she was startled when she first laid eyes on Emily Nell because she reminded her so much of her own sister, my wayward aunt Merry Beth, whom I'd never met. According to Mama, both had hair as black as the inside of a coal mine, and it grew as fast and wild as a wisteria vine. And apparently, both of their spirits were about as wild, too. I'd questioned Mama about my aunt a few times, but it wasn't a conversation she wanted to get into. She simply said that Merry Beth had ended up going down the wrong road with the wrong ride; then Mama would conveniently find something else to distract us.

When Emily Nell was two years old, she caught a cold that just wouldn't go away. It was early January, and we were experiencing record cold that winter. The house was warm enough, but even so, the north wind crept through every tiny space it could find in the walls, relentlessly working to bring the below-zero temperatures into our home. Daddy kept the kerosene heaters full, and the fireplaces blazed, but even so, Emily Nell developed pneumonia.

For nearly a week, the roads were impassable because of the thick layer of ice that covered them like glaze on a coffeecake, and we stayed frozen in place because of it. The house grew quieter as Emily Nell's ragged breathing grew louder, until all sounds of her began to fade. I felt a certain amount of sympathy for her, as much as I could at my very young age, anyway. But there would come a time when I would have the deepest kind of empathy for her, and not because I was an adult by then but because I was no longer a bystander.

My parents knew that they had no choice if there was any chance of saving my baby sister, so wrapping her as warmly as they could, they took her to the hospital in Marion, slip-sliding down the mountain roads as they did so, all the while praying to God that they would not all die in the attempt.

Though they arrived at the hospital in one piece, and the doctors used every medication and technique available to them at the time, Emily Nell was just too far gone. She died there in Mama's arms three days later. It was the darkest period I've ever seen my family go through, and even though I was only six years old at the time, I'll always remember the black grief that gripped our family as deeply and as painfully as the north wind that winter.

But spring unfailingly returned, as did the cycle of seasons over and over again, and through those years, my parents expanded their apple orchard as often as they could. They had contracts with the Gerber baby food company and with several restaurants in Cabot and nearby Asheville, and every year, it seemed, more of my parents' apples were in demand.

The spring freeze of '44 had damaged many of the trees, and that year my parents were forced to purchase apples from orchards farther south in order to fulfill their contracts. Over the following two years they'd had to purchase more trees as well as more land, leaving less money to help with my college expenses. So I worked long hours as a short-order cook at Woolworth's, in Durham, to help make ends meet.

I'd decided to study nursing at Watts Hospital School of Nursing, just as my father's sister, my Aunt Harriet, had done, and I met my future husband, Geoffrey Cavanaugh, during his final year of law school at Duke. One late frigid January evening in 1948, I had just begun to degrease the grill after a twelve-hour shift when a highly intoxicated Geoffrey, along with several of his fellow law school friends, staggered in. Silently scolding myself for not having locked the door before starting on the grill, I grabbed an order pad and walked to the middle of the counter where the four inebriated men had made themselves at home on the red leather stools.

"What can I get y'all?" I asked, with pencil and pad at the ready. But the men were in their own world, laughing at things that only they found humorous, and slurring any word that had more than one syllable. I waited another minute for the customers to pull themselves together, but when they still couldn't, I firmly told them that I had work to do and asked them to leave. However, one of the men, shorter and stockier than the other three, did not take well to being told what to do and he declared that I had all the telltale signs of being the daughter of an ignorant cabbage farmer.

"Easy there, Tanner." Geoffrey immediately interceded, rising from his stool and moving to stand behind him, then slapping him on the back much too forcefully to have been a friendly gesture. "The poor girl is just trying to get out of here, that's all. No need to insult her. As a matter of fact, you really owe her an apology."

At the same time, he applied just enough pressure that his friend croaked out a very disingenuous and humiliated, "I'm sorry!"

"There now, don't you feel better?" Geoffrey asked the red-faced young man, patting the place he'd squeezed. "Let's go. Let the young lady close up. We'll get a bite over at Dusky's." The four of them started for the door, but not before Geoffrey laid an extravagant tip of five dollars on the counter and said, "Sorry for the trouble, pretty lady. I'll be seeing you." Then, smiling broadly at me, he opened the door and, with a great flourish, bowed while sweeping his hand out before him and allowing the other three to exit before him. When he straightened up, he looked at me and winked, and in return I smiled a soft, grateful smile. Then he, too, walked out.

I quickly went to the door and locked it while my eyes remained on the handsome young man with the dark blond hair as he rejoined his group. Abruptly, I turned away, though, wishing that I'd done so a half second sooner, for Geoffrey had turned around just in time to catch me watching him, as if he was sure I would be. Smiling, he lifted his hand in a wave before he walked out of the circle of light cast by a street lamp, and faded into the darkness.

He came back the following evening, only to find that I had the night off. However, by using his charming, persuasive style, he talked my coworker into divulging my name and address, and showed up at my apartment door. I'd been in the midst of studying my anatomy book when the doorbell rang. Thinking that one of my roommates had forgotten her key again, I opened the door, only to find the handsome man from the night before amusedly assessing me in my faded flannel robe (with one missing pocket), hair tied in rags, and cold cream covering my face. I froze, uncertain whether I should invite him in first; slam the door, clean myself up, and *then* invite him in; or tell him he was rude to show up uninvited, and slam the door on him forever.

Before I could respond in any way, Geoffrey began to laugh and told me that I was the sweetest thing he'd ever seen just as I looked at that very moment. I couldn't help but laugh, too, and I let him in.

He started asking me out after that, and whenever we were together—which wasn't too often, at first—I'd catch him watching me with a mixture of amusement and fascination. I asked him about it once and he told me that he was charmed by the fact that I'd ventured out on my own, and because I wasn't the usual high-society girl that he'd grown up with. I was a rarity to Geoffrey, and trying to figure out how to snare me was a challenge that he just couldn't resist.

Making that challenge more appealing to him was the fact that I resisted. It wasn't that the interest wasn't there, but I just didn't have much time. Almost every hour that wasn't spent on schoolwork was spent behind the counter at Woolworth's. However, the more I said no to going out with him, the more determined he was to see me. He ate more greasy cheeseburgers than probably all of Duke's student body as he waited for me to close up in the evenings. And he spent many late nights and weekend nights sitting in the library with me as I trudged through my anatomy and biology books, while he studied for college finals and then the North Carolina bar exam in preparation for a position within his family's prestigious law firm in Cabot.

He was more than ready to leave his college days behind, but not quite as ready to leave me in the past with them. So, after only six months of dating, he asked me to marry him. I felt like I loved him and wanted to be with him, but I knew that would mean leaving behind my college days, as well. I just couldn't say no. For one thing, he was unlike anyone I'd ever known. He was sophisticated and elegant, and I was more than a little flattered that he took such an interest in me. And I would have been lying if I said that the idea of living a life of prestige and grandeur in the old-moneyed city of Cabot, with a son of the old-moneyed Cavanaugh family, wasn't exciting.

In the end, I decided to put my dreams of finishing nursing school on hold. I told him I'd marry him, while telling myself in no uncertain terms that I'd finish my training after settling into married life. What I found over time, however, was that Geoffrey had very specific ideas as to what his wife should be, and a nurse to the ailing, aging, and disabled did not fit within those parameters. But any remaining pangs of regret I felt at abandoning my career were quickly replaced by a love and happiness that was more whole and complete than any I'd ever imagined when our son, Geoffrey Donald Jr, was born less than a year after we were married.

My son's first few years of life were some of the happiest I'd ever known. But all too soon, I would be made to wonder if there wasn't some cruel law of the universe that prevented a soul from being too happy for too long before it indifferently snuffed that joy out.

CHAPTER 2

Home to Howling Cut

The weak light that softly illuminated the windows of the train depot grew stronger as the early morning sun slowly eroded the darkness. It was just before seven o'clock, and I was headed home to Howling Cut. It was a big occasion for my family: My mother's brother, Prescott, was finally getting married. I'd tried to convince Geoffrey to come with Donnie and me, though I knew it was a waste of time. He was busy at work. As usual.

And wedding or not, Geoffrey disliked the country, and though he did not dislike my family, there was a distance between them that was simply born from not having anything much in common with each other. My father talking apples to Geoffrey was as foreign to him as Geoffrey talking to Daddy about patents, acquisitions, and mergers. Deep inside, I always wondered if Geoffrey was a little embarrassed by my very humble beginnings. Of course, he would never admit that, maybe not even to himself.

As we stood on the train platform, one of the lapels on my fawn-colored wool coat was turned under and Geoffrey straightened it. "I'm sorry I'll miss the wedding, Kathryn," he said softly, looking up from my lapel. There was genuine regret in his eyes and voice. "Your uncle seems like a good man. Give him my congratulations, please." Then, looking down at Donnie, he gently placed his hand on the little blond head and said to his son's upturned face, "Be a good boy, son. Mind your mother and your grandparents, all right?"

"Yes, sir," Donnie replied, then was quickly distracted again by the arrival of another traveler coming through the station door.

"Geoffrey, go on now. We'll see ourselves off. You keep looking at your pocket watch as if you're afraid it's going to up and disappear. I know you have a lot to do, so go on, please. We'll be fine."

"Well . . . all right, then." He leaned down, gave me a quick kiss on the lips and asked me, yet again, if I was sure I had enough money, as he slipped on his overcoat. "Don't forget, they're two-way tickets, Kathryn. They're all paid for, so make sure the conductor gives them back to you after he punches them for this leg of the trip. Donald, take care of your mother, son." Geoffrey awkwardly pulled the boy to him. Donnie hugged him in response but only briefly, for almost immediately Geoffrey released him and headed for the door. We watched the back of him as he exited the station, and glancing down, I saw the longing on our son's face.

"Let's go look at the train we're taking, honey," I said, pulling his attention away from his retreating father, and steering him over to the window opposite the one that looked out over the parking lot where Geoffrey had left his car. "It's been a while since you've been on one. Why, you weren't more than a tiny little fella, and that was when we went to see Grandma and Papa. You've grown so much I bet they won't recognize you. They'll think I accidentally grabbed some other child's hand when I got off the train!" Donnie muttered a distracted "uh-huh" as he watched the porter loading luggage into the storage compartment.

It pained me to see the hurt that the distance between Geoffrey and Donnie caused my little boy, caused them both, really. I saw the attempts our son made to please his father or just to get his attention, but unsurprisingly, Geoffrey was the same sort of father that his own father had been to him.

I knew that for men like Geoffrey, there was no lack of love for their children, but there was confusion about the proper order of life's priorities. Family was a few spots down that list, with career, wealth, and social status topping it. Poor God was even further down in the rankings than the family, and I often prayed that He would be forgiving of His low status in the opinion of my husband and in-laws. Geoffrey once told me that without wealth (which was acquired by the firm), and without good standing in society, they wouldn't have the family they did. It never occurred to him that my own family, which had nothing close to that kind of wealth, had done all right anyway.

It worried me that the older Donnie got, the deeper his pain would be felt, for it was likely that he would be greatly conflicted as he was caught between two worlds: the world of wealth and power versus a world of simple living, where money was not often in abundance, but love was, and it was given generously and without apology.

I knew that Geoffrey wanted to be closer to his son, but I also knew that he felt a deeper, more meaningful relationship would develop through the years, when Donnie was better able to relate to his father. It was as though the childhood years with our son belonged to me, while the adult years would be Geoffrey's, as he groomed him to traverse the same roads that generations of Cavanaughs had navigated so well.

The train belched coal steam as it sat idling impatiently on the tracks. Donnie was getting impatient, too, and started to ask me for the third time when we'd be leaving. Just then the conductor called for all travelers bound for Marion to board. Picking up my purse, a small wicker basket carrying our lunch, and our suitcase, we moved to the back of the small line gathering at the train's open door.

Howling Cut was a half day's train ride away because of the stops we would make through familiar tiny towns sporadically laid out along the line. And as we snaked our way around the foothills, then up into the mountains toward home, I enjoyed seeing the landmarks of my childhood. All of the small towns brought back memories as I recalled trips to those places when I'd accompanied my father or uncle on buying, selling, or trading missions. Their mode of transportation had been slow, as we traveled in their sluggish horse-drawn wagons or buggies instead of a truck. I'd asked Papa why we didn't always use the truck, and he'd told me that if we did, we'd never have time to see the trout in the rivers and the new nests in the budding dogwood trees, and we'd certainly never be able to smell the honeysuckle over the smell of the gasoline. I'd laughed at his assessment, but now that I was older, I had to agree with it.

Today, however, I felt a great urgency to get home. For one thing, I was tired. Unusually so. I knew I'd been busy trying to get us ready for the trip, but this was a different kind of tired. My body felt heavy and sluggish, and had for the past several weeks. *Nothing that sleeping in my old bed can't fix*, I told myself. *That and some of Mama's home cookin'*. But deep inside, I wasn't quite convinced.

I also felt that I needed to get back in order to check my own pulse, my own feelings after being away from Howling Cut for two years. I needed to reassure myself that my own feelings for the place and its people had not been corrupted. I didn't feel as though I'd changed, that I'd become more of a Cavanaugh than a Harris, but I needed to return to confirm that. And I prayed that many of those things that I had loved so much about home had remained the same, including my love for everyone there.

CHAPTER 3

A Very Solid Whole

"They'll sure run ya!" Daddy exclaimed, referring to some hornets that had chased him. He and Mama had picked us up at the station and after much hugging and many exclamations over how big and handsome Donnie had gotten, I noticed that my father had quite a few red blotches on his face. "We hit a hornets' nest in one of the apple trees," he explained. "I was trimming back some dead branches when I knocked that nest. I didn't see the thing as it was covered up with a good bunch of apple blossoms. Those things came flying at me and I went flying from them—all the way into the pond! They'll sure run ya, boy. I'll give 'em that!" We all laughed, Daddy included.

My folks looked good. The years had been kind to them. Both had more gray sprinkled throughout their hair than the last time I'd seen them, giving Daddy's dark hair a true salt-and-pepper look, whereas Mama's hair looked like a mixture of white and brown sugar. Their faces were lightly lined, but it hadn't lessened their looks, rather it had carved their features into more striking, prominent ones. The constant exposure to the sun had turned their skin the color of coffee with a lot of cream in it, which only helped to accentuate my father's beautiful golden eyes, and my mother's bright blue ones. And their constant care of the apple orchard continued to provide them with a youthful agility that belied the fact that the two of them were in their midforties.

We climbed into Daddy's weathered truck and headed for home. Mama and I sat in the backseat, exclaiming over how good we thought the other looked, and after assuring each other that all was well, we briefly talked about the health of the orchard and the relatively mild winter. Much to the relief of my parents, and all who were involved in the orchard in some way or another, the trees had survived the cold months unscathed, and it looked as if they'd bear a good crop come fall.

"How's Geoffrey, Kate?" Mama asked. "And how's his work goin'? It's a shame he couldn't come with y'all for the wedding. As hard as he works, it'd be good for him to relax some and take it easy for a time." She watched my face closely to see if there were any signs of trouble between my husband and me. There was no trouble, just a vague feeling of dissatisfaction with the conventions that were so important to Geoffrey, but I could honestly look her in the eye while answering that he was doing fine and also tell her how busy he was at work. I explained that he'd recently taken on a junior partner, which would eventually help Geoffrey cut back on the six, sometimes seven days a week that he'd been working for the last year.

"Mama, tell me all the news about Ditty, and how Grandma Willa is doing. I want to hear everything about everyone, and, of course, every detail about the wedding. How's Uncle Prescott holding up under the pressure of his upcoming nuptials?" I laughed, picturing him looking as nervous as the fattest turkey in the yard at Thanksgiving.

"Actually, he's been so busy at the mill trying to finish up a large order for some wealthy fellow's mansion down in Miami that he's not gone over the deep end. Thank the good Lord for his work."

There was deep respect for my mother's brother, who had made quite a name for himself with his woodworking skills. And not just in our county, but throughout the country. His God-given talent had saved the family's sawmill from closing years ago. And, according to my mother, Prescott and the mill were still doing very well these days, as were both sides of its business; the timbering and the furniture making.

"What's the name of the lady Uncle Prescott's marrying, Mama?" I asked. "I know you told me but I can't remember."

"Her name's Glory Burke. Prescott met her while he was teaching a woodworking class at Appalachian State last summer. She's an art teacher there but grew up in Banner Elk. She's nearly ten years younger than he is. Seems real nice, from what we can tell, though we haven't spent much time with her."

"She's easy on the eyes, I'll say that about her," my father interjected. He'd obviously been listening, even though he was also carrying on a conversation with Donnie.

"Oh, Lord!" my mother responded, but good-naturedly. My parents were devoted to each other, and had been so since they were teenagers. Even though I was a grown woman with a child of my own, there was something reassuring and comforting in that knowledge. No matter how old I was, I still wanted my parents to be two halves of one very solid whole. "Anyway"—Mama steered us back to the conversation—"your father's gotten it into his head to give 'em a shivaree after the reception!"

"Grandma, what's a shi . . . shiva . . . ?" Donnie had turned around in his seat and was hanging over the back of it.

"A shivaree. It's a kind of surprise party, you might say," Mama answered.

"I'd sure say it is!" Daddy snorted.

Mama, choosing to ignore Daddy, began to describe it. "Honey, a shivaree happens after a wedding takes place to let the bride and groom know that everybody approves of the marriage. We'll sneak up on them at Uncle Prescott's house, after the ceremony, and we'll bang pots and pans, and holler and sing, and make a big ol' ruckus—just to let them know that we're tickled Glory's a part of the family now."

"Sure hope we don't catch 'em in a most compromising position." Daddy snickered. "I can just see it now: We'll be sneaking up to their window, real quiet-like, and before we can make any racket, we'll hear Prescott shouting to the rafters, *Lord, God a'mighty! Glory hallelujah!*"

Daddy and I roared with laughter, while Mama, trying her hardest to be stern, could barely contain herself either. "Oh, for *heaven's* sake, Jack! You behave yourself, you hear me!" Then she couldn't hold back any longer and joined us as we laughed so hard we cried. Oh, it was good to be home!

"Mama . . ." I tried to move on to another subject, but each time I did, we started laughing again. Finally, I was able to ask the question. "What's going on with Ditty? I haven't heard from him since Christmas, and every time I've called his place, there's no answer. I've even left messages with Jean to have him call me, but she'll say something like *Well, I will if I see him*, real mysterious-like. When I ask her if there's something going on with him, she'll say she *doesn't know nothin' about no one.* Says she's just the mill's secretary and that she minds her own business. So, what's going on with him? Is he all right?"

"We don't know," Daddy quietly answered and all the humor suddenly evaporated. "We haven't seen him in weeks. Last we heard he was over in Lost Cove."

"Lost Cove! What in the world is he doing over there?"

Donnie was watching and listening hard to our conversation. Mama knew the subject was one that needed to be discussed without him, so she quickly shifted the conversation. "How 'bout we save this talk for the front porch, later on." Then, "Donnie, after we eat some supper, we'll go do somethin' fun. Sound good?"

I suggested that we go down to the creek and try catching a few trout. "Or would you rather go over to the orchard's shop and get some of those good soft peppermints that your grandma loves more than life itself?"

"Peppermints!" both Donnie and Mama shouted in unison. And though the atmosphere in the truck was light once again, I was fairly certain there was a storm brewing on the horizon and my brother was in the eye of it.

CHAPTER 4

A Glass Half Full

"All right, Mama, tell me about Ditty," I said, as we settled into some rocking chairs on the front porch after finishing the supper dishes. While we'd cleaned up the remains of the country-fried steak and mashed potatoes that Mama had fixed, Donnie had been within earshot at the kitchen table, finishing his chocolate pie, so she whispered that she'd tell me about Ditty after Papa took him out to the orchard. In the meantime, she filled me in on the latest with Grandma Willa as Mama washed and I dried.

Willa Holton Harold was my mother's maternal grandmother, and, according to Mama, she was quickly fading away in a nursing home over in Flat Top, which was the next mountain over. Even at the ripe old age of 92, Grandma Willa had been doing well until she'd slipped off an icy step coming out of her house one early January morning. The fall had broken her pelvis and left elbow. Mama had wanted to bring her back home to the orchard after her stay in the hospital, but Willa hadn't been able to get up and walk because her pelvis wasn't mending properly. Then pneumonia had caused a major setback, and we feared it was only a matter of time before there would be no strength left for her to fight with. With Willa's immobility, the recurrence of pneumonia was almost inevitable, and I knew that when we lost her it would be very deeply felt, but most especially by my mother, for Grandma Willa had been Mama's greatest source of strength growing up.

Willa helped raise Mama, Prescott, and Merry Beth after their unstable mother, Anna, had died when my mother and her siblings were just young teens. Willa had always been there for all of us and we dreaded the day when we'd lose her. But she'd lived a long and full life, and as death stood like a silhouetted sentinel in the doorway, she welcomed it and was unafraid. She knew that crossing that ultimate threshold would release her from all earthly pain and the limitations brought on by age. But more importantly, death would reunite her with her beloved second husband, Sam, who had died two years before and was the reason for my last visit home. The loss of him, Mama explained, had taken much of the wind out of my great-grandmother's sails.

Rocking across from me on the front porch, Mama was just starting to tell me about Ditty when the phone rang. While she answered it, I was left alone to enjoy the quiet and beauty of the place. While I looked out at the fading light of the day as it lengthened the shadows of the trees in the orchard, creating abstract versions of them, a light breeze came up, carrying the scent of apple blossoms on it. It felt good after working in the kitchen. I undid a couple of buttons on the old cotton blouse I'd changed into as soon as we arrived home. Clothes that I'd worn in high school still hung in my closet and filled dresser drawers. I'd taken advantage of one of the blouses and a well-worn pair of dungarees, rolling the legs of the medium-length jeans into cuffs right below the knees. It felt wonderful being in my old, familiar clothing, and I was surprised but pleased to see the old outfit still fit. I had a small frame like my mother's, but I was taller than she. The clothing was not the least bit tight, though it had been the last time I was home. I'd obviously lost a little weight, though I'd not noticed it before. During my time home, I would enjoy rummaging through my old clothes, and putting to good use those pieces that had my history imbedded in their well-worn threads.

Mama returned from her phone call, bringing the iced-tea pitcher with her and telling me that it was Grandma Willa calling from the nursing home, wanting to know if Donnie and I had gotten in all right. Mama had asked her if she wanted to talk to me but the nurse came in just then to check on her, so she'd told Mama to just tell us that she loved us and would see us soon. Mama refilled our tea glasses, then, after taking a long drink from hers, began to tell me about Ditty.

"Well, you know how he was staying in that little apartment over the garage at the mill? He'd usually come down for work about seven thirty in the mornin', after Prescott got in. "Well, after there was no sign of Ditty come late afternoon, Prescott figured maybe he'd tied one on—again—and went up to the apartment to rouse him. But he wasn't there and we haven't seen him since. That was over three weeks ago. We've been fairly worried, but before you ask me why we didn't call you, it's because we figured he'd turn up after a time and that there was no need having you worry yourself to death, too. He's done this before, Kate. It's not the first time. He's always come back, though, just a little the worse for wear." She shook her head in frustration.

"Anyway, we made some phone calls, but no one had seen him. Then, your daddy ran into Ronnie Coons up at the mercantile. Remember? Ronnie's brother, Ray, married your Aunt Merry Beth." I told her I remembered and she continued. "Ronnie told us that Ditty was over in Lost Cove, at least he'd been there the week before."

A near-empty settlement at the Tennessee and North Carolina line, along the Nolichucky River, Lost Cove had been big in timbering at one time, so railroad tracks were laid to it. But when there wasn't enough lumber going out any longer, most of the trains quit coming in. That was the quickest way to kill a place in these parts. Only a handful of its die-hard residents had stayed, and because of its out-of-the-way location, not to mention the fact that the place was thick with rattlesnakes and copperheads, it was the ideal location for getting lost if one wanted to, and also the perfect spot for moonshine making.

"Ronnie said Ditty's working a still up there now," Mama continued. "Looks like he's following in the footsteps of my daddy." Emotion choked her up, and she took another sip of her iced tea. Then she was quiet for a moment as she stared out over the orchard, though I knew she wasn't really focused on the trees.

"Mama, why's he doin' it?" I softly asked. "For what reason? He makes a decent living working at the mill."

"Who knows?! I have to think it's the pull of that damned poison. Some folks just can't quit it. It's not that they don't want to. It's that they can't. You know we have a history of it in this family," Mama finished disgustedly.

I didn't say anything. I just leaned over and squeezed her hand. The soft creaking of our rockers and the arguing of two blue jays somewhere off in the orchard were the only muted sounds as each of us got lost in her own thoughts. Undoubtedly, though, we were both thinking about the same thing: Calvin Guinn.

Mama's father had been a good and honest man for most of his years. He'd provided well for his family through backbreaking work at his timber mill. But long hours and long relationships with customers hadn't been enough to keep the family business going. The Hollis Mill, over at Flat Top, had taken a lot of our family's business through means that were unethical, to say the least, and downright il legal, to say the truth. The end result was that it about ruined our mill, so, out of desperation, my grandfather did what he had to in order to keep food on the table and a roof over the family's head: He started making moonshine with my other grandfather—Daddy's father, Gilbert Harris. It was not a skeleton our family was proud of, but like it or not, it lived in our closet. Both men paid mighty prices for their illegal endeavors: Mama's father was killed in a shootout with the law at the still that was set up right in our own orchard. And Daddy's father was sent to prison, where he died many years later from influenza. Through absolute determination, my father was able to keep the orchard going through hard and honest work. Now, it seemed, the apple didn't fall far from the tree with Ditty making moonshine, too.

I broke the silence. "Has anyone gone over there to look for Ditty?"

"Your father had Ronnie take him back in there, but they didn't get too far. Two men with shotguns, acting as the welcoming committee, saw your father and Ronnie comin'. They stopped them before they could get too far in. The men said that they hadn't seen Ditty in a couple of days, so Ronnie and Jack left. They both knew those guys were lying, though. It was obvious that they just wanted them gone, but there was no sense in arguing with them. So, that was that, at least for the time being, anyway."

"I'll go back over there with Daddy, Mama. Maybe Ditty will come."

"You'll do no such thing, Kathryn, and I mean it! You could go missing just like Ditty, but not because you want to be missing. You stay away from there, you hear me? Promise me you will!"

"All right, Mama, I promise." I didn't want to upset her more than she already was. "Answer me something, though: How was Ditty doing before he took off?"

"Ditty's Ditty, honey. You know he's never taken life too seriously, and work even less so. Your daddy and I are still trying to figure out who he got his ways from. He's always been as carefree as a child in the summertime." She looked away from me, off into the distance. "Reminds me of my sister, Merry Beth. I'll never know what possesses some people to do the worst things they could possibly do, even though they *know* better." Though her voice was low, I could hear the frustration in it. "Rebellion, maybe. I don't know," she continued. "But her runnin' off with that no-good boy Ray Coons was more than just rebellion, I think. It went way beyond that. With your brother, it's a different matter altogether, though. I don't think he's tetched in the head like Merry Beth, or my mama, but still, I don't know . . . I swear . . . I just don't know . . ." Her voice trailed off.

As hard as she and my father had always worked, I knew my brother's attitude frustrated her to no end. I sometimes wondered if she was disappointed in me for dropping out of nursing school to get married. She and Daddy had been so excited and proud when I'd been accepted at Watts. "Mama, I want to ask you something, and I want you to be honest with me. Were you and Daddy disappointed that I dropped out of nursing school to marry Geoffrey?"

"Yes and no," she answered quickly, as though she'd pondered the question herself. "Your father and I understood you wanting to get married, but we were sorry it couldn't wait until after you'd finished school. It's getting so that it's just about as important for a woman to have her education as it is for a man. But mainly we just wanted you to be happy. So, the *no* part of my answer to your question is on account of the fact that you seem to be living a good life, and besides, we got Donnie because of the decision you made."

I smiled at her fair response. Though she liked to point out that a glass was half full, she wouldn't hesitate to remind someone that the glass was also half empty if there was a need to. She had never looked at life through rose-colored glasses, and if you wanted a candy-coated answer, you had to look further than Rachel Harris for it. But she also tried to see things from other people's points of view, rather than judging them. Because of that, she was one of the most logical and fair people I'd ever known. Sitting on the porch with her, I realized how blessed I was to not only have her as a mother, but also as a wise and wonderful adviser.

"You are, right?" Mama asked.

"I am what?"

"Happy. Are you happy, Kate?" Just as she had in the truck on our drive from the train station, she searched my eyes for the truth.

"I am, Mama. We all are. Well, I guess I shouldn't speak for everybody, but I believe we all are. It's just different in Cabot, than here. That doesn't make it bad, though. But, sometimes, I wish Geoffrey would just relax a little more. He's always caught up in work and reaching that next goal he's setting for himself. Even when he's doing something that's supposed to be fun, like playing golf or tennis, he's always got to take more lessons so he can improve his ranking in whatever league he's playing in. You'd think he was playing head to head with the pros. I just wish he wouldn't take life, or himself, quite so seriously.

"Just this past November, our church decided to invite the two other Presbyterian churches in Cabot to have a father-son go-cart race to help raise money for Christmas gifts for the Children's Home. The fathers and their sons would build the go-carts, then race them the day before Thanksgiving. Of course, each cart was sponsored by local businesses, with all of the money going for the Home. Well, you'd think Geoffrey was building a car for the Indy 500! He even went so far as to call that Indy winner, Lee Wallard, who was the guest speaker at one of the firm's big dinners last year, to get advice on making Donnie's go-cart 'aerodynamically superior.' Lord! He had that child dressed up in a miniature race-car driver's getup, and it was so bulky that Donnie could hardly get into the cart, much less drive the thing. Poor little fella. I told Geoffrey that Donnie was *not* wearing that getup on race day, and if he felt so strongly about it being worn, he could do the wearing!"

"Well, did he?" Mama teased.

"I swear he would have if he could have gotten into the outfit— and the cart—and gotten away with it! Anything to ensure another Cavanaugh win." I laughed because I knew the story sounded funny. But it didn't feel quite so funny, and my mother knew it. She always knew what was going on deep down inside of me.

She was well aware that there were things I would have changed in Geoffrey if I could have, but she also realized that I loved him. He had always been good to me, making sure I lacked nothing, in the material sense, anyway. Geoffrey was kind and considerate, as well as generous, but in a more restrained way than I was used to. Like I'd told Mama when I answered her question about being happy, his attention was just different—not wrong, just different. I was much more at ease than he was with being openly affectionate. Holding hands or an impulsive hug when it just felt right never seemed awkward to me, but to Geoffrey, those displays of impulsive affection, no matter how small, made him uncomfortable. However, all inhibition and restraint were quickly forgotten when the lights were turned out at the end of the day, and it was only the two of us. But I wished, for Geoffrey's sake as much for mine, that he could let go of propriety a little more often while the sun was still up.

Our arguments were few and far between, which was unusual given the fact that we came from two very different worlds. Even when there was a disagreement, true to Geoffrey's style of behavior, we settled things with lowered, almost formal voices. Though there may have been a little iciness between us for a day or two, there was never a loud, heated exchange of words. I wondered, at times, if the world would stop spinning if Geoffrey's voice were raised an octave or two, though I doubted I'd ever find out. I believed that another reason we rarely argued was that I had acquiesced to doing those things that a socialite, a wife of a Cavanaugh, was expected to do. Even so, as I stood at the altar promising to honor and cherish Geoffrey for the rest of our lives, I also made a promise to myself never to lose my own identity. And I hadn't.

Though I gave in to his mother and joined the garden club, and I went to the parties and dinners as well as hosted my share of them, I also stayed true to my nature. The gardening around the house was left entirely in my care. Our Italianate-style home took up most of our lot, but I was able to carve out enough room back by the toolshed for tomatoes, cucumbers, and some peppers. Still, I missed having a big garden.

So, one day I drove out to Cabot Children's Home, a place for orphaned and abandoned children. My intention was to sit down with the Home's director, George Eisenhower, and discuss the possibility of putting in a large garden. After spending less than two hours with Mr. Eisenhower, I left with a new sense of purpose and a rough drawing of plans for a large garden to be placed behind the rear dormitory. That had been three years before, and there were now several gardens thriving. They helped to feed over three hundred children residing there, and served other purposes, as well. Gardening taught them a skill, and the discipline of cultivating and caring for plants that could either feed them well, or wither up and die due to neglect. As I told the young gardeners every spring, it was completely up to them. Thus, the children gave the gardens the attention that they themselves so craved and because of that, the gardens flourished.

The only real lack in my life was that I had wanted to bear more children, to give our son a sister or brother. But when Donnie was almost three, I gave birth to a stillborn daughter, and the doctors had warned me that should I get pregnant again, both mother and child could very well be lost. I was tempted to try anyway, but Geoffrey was completely opposed to the risk I'd be taking, and out of fairness to him and to Donnie, I relented, for I didn't want to leave my husband a young widower, and even worse, my son motherless.

Mama's yawning in her rocker across from me brought me back from my deep thoughts. I began to yawn, too. "Lord, yawning is contagious." I chuckled. Darkness had nearly blanketed the orchard, and the night moths were fluttering around the porch light over the door. "Well, I guess that's it for me tonight, Mama." I stood up and stretched, before grabbing my empty iced-tea glass. "I'm worn out. Guess I didn't sleep much last night, excited about the trip 'n' all. I think I'll go ahead and take my shower. When Donnie gets back, would you send him on in and I'll bathe him as soon as I'm done."

"You go on, honey." She followed me to the door. "I'll get Donnie cleaned up. I'll put him in the big claw tub in my bathroom. He liked that last time he was here. You tend to yourself and don't worry about us. Go straight to bed after you've washed up, if it'll feel good to you. We'll put Donnie down, so you go on now."

"Thanks, Mama. It's good to be home." I hugged her hard. "It's good not to have to worry about the garden club, or a party, or even Geoffrey right now."

"Or go-carts." Mama laughed as she followed me through the screened door.

CHAPTER 5

Withered Things

"Lord, I hope those lilies aren't half-dead and withered by now!" Mama called from the hallway as she passed by my bedroom door on her way to put some clean towels in the linen closet. It was the third time she'd made the statement since leaving the church after we'd spent the morning decorating it for Uncle Prescott's wedding that afternoon.

"They'll be fine, Mama, really," I assured her—again. "I put more water in the vases right before we left. They'll be as fresh as if they were just cut." And just to ensure that they would be, I added in a whisper, "Please, God, even though I know that's really at the bottom of Your to-do list." Mama wanted everything to be perfect for the big event.

Bending down to look into the oval mirror sitting on top of my vanity, I tucked in a few thick strands of hair that had escaped the tight bun at the back of my head. I stood up and smoothed down my light green dress with the cream-colored lace collar. The dress was cinched at the waist with a wide belt that matched the color of the lace, accentuating the fullness of the skirt. The green of the dress made my dark brown hair a rich chestnut color, and brought out the darker green of my eyes. But as I took a last inventory of myself, I noticed that the light circles under my eyes were still there. They'd been darker when I first woke up and I'd hoped they'd fade away during the day, but a shadow of them still remained. I had slept pretty well, but was awakened in the middle of the night with a cough. It had started several days before we left Cabot, but had gotten worse on the train. It had been so dry lately, though, that I was sure it was caused by all the dust. Finally, I'd fallen back to sleep but woke up a little before seven. I was tempted to roll over for another hour of sleep in my old, familiar bed but I knew that the day ahead was a full one, so I'd forced myself to get up.

"Would y'all please come on, now?" Daddy hollered from the bottom of the stairs. "Donnie and I been waiting on you women for nearly thirty minutes. If we don't get a move on, we'll be gathering to celebrate Prescott and Glory's silver anniversary, instead of their wedding!"

Mama laughed. "You have *not* been waiting that long. But we're coming right now."

"I'll grab your corsage, Mama. You left it on the bed." I went into her room and picked up the white orchid that had little wisps of purple running through it. Daddy had bought it for her. It would be perfect on her lavender-colored dress.

"Are we picking up the—" I started to ask about the wedding cake as I hurried down the stairs, but was stopped by a fit of coughing that erupted unexpectedly and violently, causing me to lose my footing and frantically grab the banister. Mama's corsage, however, was in the hand that grabbed the railing and was instantly crushed.

"Kate!" Daddy, still standing at the bottom of the steps, instinctively reached his arms out and took a step up toward us. Mama, hearing me stumble behind her, whirled around and reached an arm out, too, trying to stop me from falling into her.

Pressed against the railing, I'd stopped coughing but was shaking and still trying to catch my breath. "I'm okay," I rasped. "Water . . ."

Mama was holding me firmly against the railing as my father rushed into the kitchen, where I heard glass clinking, immediately followed by the tap running.

"Kate, are you sure you're all right?" She was clearly frightened and continued to hold on to me as I slowly descended the steps; then she guided me to one of the living room chairs. "What got ahold of you?"

"Dust." I took a sip of water. I sounded hoarse, but wasn't coughing. "It's been really dry and the dust has been bad. I'm okay, really. But, Mama, your corsage! It's ruined!" I held it up, showing her the smashed remains.

"Lord, honey, don't worry about some old corsage! I'll pin a lily to my dress as soon as we get to the church—as long as they're not half-dead." She forced a laugh, trying to lighten the mood again.

We took a couple of minutes to collect ourselves, and after I assured everyone again that I was all right, we headed out the door. But the frightening truth was I was beginning to feel like one of those lilies.

CHAPTER 6

A Shivaree

"Jack, would you go on out back and make sure Gerald Parsons isn't passing around any more of that lightning? I swear, more folks are heading out there, walking all straight-like, and then they come back in here zigzagging like they've just come off one of those rides at the fair."

Mama was watching as some of the men, and even a couple of the younger women, went in and out of the back door of the fellowship hall at Howling Cut United Methodist Church. As she had done all through the wedding, and was now doing at the reception, Mama was overseeing every detail. So far, everything had gone off without a hitch and she intended it to stay that way to the end.

I'd been out on the dance floor with Donnie, teaching him how to waltz, but was taking a break while Daddy's sister, Aunt Harriet, whirled him around during a lively square dance. She had come in the night before and was looking forward to a few days reprieve from her hectic work at Asheville's Pelham State Hospital, where she worked as a psychiatric nurse. While she was back in town, she was staying at her childhood home, where her mother, my grandma Lydia, still lived. It was the original house on the orchard's property. It was the one the Harris family moved into when Grandpa Harris bought the orchard, and Daddy and Aunt Harriet were just kids. Grandma Lydia still oversaw the orchard's gift store, and continued to stock it with many of her wonderful handmade items.

Early that morning, I'd gone over to have breakfast with Aunt Harriet and my grandmother before heading over to decorate the church with Mama. It was something I often did while I was growing up. It gave my grandmother and me some time for just the two of us, and since she was a wonderful baker, I often indulged in her luscious cinnamon buns, fresh from the oven, or the most heavenly pecan coffee cake.

Now, with my aunt home, it was nice having a little time to catch up on her life. We rarely got the chance to see each other, but we'd always enjoyed our time together when we did. She was thoroughly engrossed in her work, which gave her little time for a social life, not that she'd been much interested in one, anyway, since her husband, Frank Pierce, passed away from stomach cancer two years before.

I knew the one thing that she'd regretted, however, was not having a child. Frank had been an orthopedic surgeon, and the two of them had thrown themselves into the world of medicine, thinking they'd have a child at some point in the future, but the future came and went, and so did Harriet's chance of bearing children. After Frank's passing, and with no children to come home to, Harriet spent long hours at work, which for the last three years, had been at Pelham.

The hospital was primarily a facility for the mentally ill, but also treated patients with pulmonary and respiratory diseases. For the first half of the century, Pelham had been Pelham Tuberculosis Sanatorium, but with a decline of the vast numbers of people stricken with the disease, the institution had had to reinvent itself as a multipurpose facility and became a psychiatric state hospital, as well. Thanks to government funding, the hospital was alive and well.

As the reception continued into the evening, I sat down in one of the chairs that had been pushed back against the wall to allow more dance room for the more than one hundred guests in attendance, most of whom were from my side of the family. Glory's parents were deceased and she was an only child. However, an aunt, uncle, and some cousins from the Piedmont area had come to witness their kin's nuptials, and from the way several of those cousins were acting, it seemed they'd come to take full advantage of the reception's refreshments.

"Rachel, let's just let 'em be for the time being," Daddy suggested in response to Mama's request that he check on the guests out back. "They're not causing any trouble, at least not so far. If they imbibe too much, we'll just put 'em in the backseat of their cars and take their keys, or lay 'em out in the beds of their wagons, unhitch their horses, and let 'em sleep it off until they're fit to drive."

I was enjoying listening to the exchange between my parents as they stood at the long rectangular table serving punch. I felt like I was eavesdropping, but I stayed where I was anyway, taking a few minutes to cool down beneath one of the ceiling fans. Even though it was spring, the hall was stuffy because of the crowd. I had started to go outside for some air, but there was a soft rain falling, and the only overhang was in the back of the building, where the moonshine was being passed around.

Closing my eyes, I leaned my head back against the wall. It was good to have a few minutes to myself. Since Donnie and I had arrived three days ago, we hadn't stopped. Daddy had happily kept his one and only grandchild busy, while Mama and I had been at it from dawn to dusk, preparing for the wedding. Making the flower arrangements for the tables, as well as for the church, pressing tablecloths and napkins, and doing an endless amount of cooking, the hours had flown, and so had my energy. I was frustrated with myself for feeling so tired these days. My cough hadn't gone away and I'd developed some chest congestion, and I worried I might be coming down with a cold. I was just glad it hadn't become full blown before the wedding. My mother had needed all the help she could get taking over the responsibilities that usually fell to the mother of the bride. In the process, my mother and Glory had grown quite close, and I was glad for everyone's sake, but most especially for Uncle Prescott.

"Well, doggone, if it ain't pretty Kate Harris, as I live and breathe!"

My alone time ended and I opened my eyes to see my brother's old friend Sparky Brody standing over me. The two had gone to school together since the first grade, and they'd had a love-hate relationship for the entire time. They went after the same positions in sports, and the same girls in school, and were too much alike to like each other or to hate each other for too long. The bottom line was that they were great friends, and had remained so, long after the last school bell had rung. "Well hey, Sparky. I saw you across the room with Becky, and was going to come over to say hello. How've y'all been?"

"We're doin' real fine, thanks. How's life in Cabot?"

"Moving faster than ever." I laughed. "How're the young'uns? How many do you have now?"

"Well, three . . . that I know of, anyway." He grinned. "I want to hear all your news, Kate, but your Mama wants me to help corral everyone in here for the cuttin' of the cake."

As if on cue, my mother called me over to help serve cake once Prescott and Glory had made their toasts to each other and cut the first piece, followed, undoubtedly, by the two of them smearing it all over each other's faces. Tradition was tradition. I knew that soon after that the two of them would depart for Prescott's home, which was only several blocks over, and then, about an hour later, the fireworks of the wedding night would start. I laughed to myself, thinking that the shivaree fireworks were most certainly going to interrupt theirs.

After the guests had eaten their fill of cake, Mama asked Daddy and me to box some of it up so that we could take it to Grandma Willa the next day. As we did, Daddy noticed Sparky and beckoned him over. "Did you do what I told you, son? Did you get all the pots and pans pots out of my kitchen?"

"Out of *our* kitchen, Jack? What'd he go and have you do, Sparky?" Mama had walked up behind Daddy, unbeknownst to him. Sparky, looking as guilty as the time he'd been caught by the assistant principal fooling around with Penny Portnoy in the high school auditorium's projector room, stammered around, trying to answer Mama while not getting Daddy into hot water.

"Well, Mrs. Harris, I just borrowed them for a little whi—"

"Rachel, honey," Daddy interrupted, much to the relief of Sparky. "I just had the boy grab a few things to help make the shivaree what it's supposed to be—loud! Can't nothin' much hurt those pots and pans, anyway—or the good cookin' that comes out of 'em." He smiled sweetly.

"Oh, good Lord." Mama rolled her eyes. "Give me patience with this man!" But obviously He had, for my folks had been married for twenty-six years. Beaming at her, Daddy grabbed her hand and pulled her out onto the dance floor. As was their usual style when they danced, Daddy held Mama close. I watched them for a moment, thankful for the love they still felt for each other. Suddenly, I caught the flash of blond hair as my son barreled into me, throwing his arms around my thighs with complete abandon. I immediately picked him up and kissed his overly-warm red cheeks, which reminded me of young pink apples. I laughed. "Oh, Lord, son, I'm feeding you too good! You're gettin' heavy." I'd never struggled picking him up before, but whether I liked it or not, he was growing more each day. I watched his wonderfully expressive face as he excitedly told me about learning how to do-si-do with Aunt Harriet. He had my green eyes, but Geoffrey's light hair and his strong facial structure. There was no doubt that my child would grow into a very handsome man, and while I knew that all mothers thought the same thing about their sons, I had no doubt that my assessment of Donnie was absolutely correct and totally unbiased.

"When're we goin' to that shiva . . . ?" He still couldn't quite get the word.

"The shivaree," I finished for him. "Soon, but remember, not a word to Uncle Prescott or Aunt Glory, okay?"

Just then, the band finished playing its final song and Prescott began tapping a glass to get everyone's attention. We followed people's gazes upward to see both him and Glory standing on the landing of the stairway where they could clearly see everyone. Applause grew louder and louder until Prescott put his hand up to quiet everyone. "Folks," he began, "it's been one of the most . . . no"—he corrected himself—"it's been *the* most wonderful day of my life. First, I have Glory to thank for that. As a matter of fact, I'll thank her in advance for giving me the most wonderful years of my life to come." Everyone clapped again. "Secondly, we have each one of you to thank for helping to make this a day that Glory and I will remember for the rest of our lives. Each of you means the world to us, and we both want you to know how happy we are to have you here today. Unfortunately, though, all good things must come to an end." There was a collective boo in response. Laughing, he continued. "We'll always remember this day, and we'll always be grateful to you. Now, even though this good time has come to an end, I have no doubt that it's only beginning for Glory and me tonight." Everyone cheered loudly, and I laughed seeing the twinkle in my uncle's eye. His double entendre was not lost on Glory, either, for she swatted his arm, and in response he pulled his new bride to him and planted a kiss on her that caused another cheer to shake the rafters. They were a handsome couple. Prescott's blond hair had grown darker over the years and the silver that streaked it gave his baby face a more distinguished look. Glory was actually eight years younger, and at thirty-eight, she was still youthful looking but old enough that her face had interesting character to it. Her light reddish-brown hair was just shoulder length, and she had it in a soft-wave style that reminded me of Elizabeth Taylor's in the movie *Elephant Walk*, which Geoffrey and I had seen just the week before.

We followed them out of the hall, throwing rice and well wishes as they departed in Prescott's truck. Thank God, Mama's pots and pans weren't tied to the bumper, but there were enough tin cans to have fed all of the Allied forces throughout the war, and *Just Hitched!* had been written on the back windshield. We watched them drive off, knowing that the two of them assumed they'd seen the last of us until they returned from their honeymoon in Atlanta, but in another hour, they'd learn that one should never assume anything.

"All right, folks, y'all come on over here so we can get our plans straight." Unsurprisingly, Daddy was the ringleader. "Now, does everyone know how this shivaree thing works?" A couple of people who hadn't been in on it but wanted to be, said they didn't. "Well, a shivaree is the loudest, most obnoxious ruckus that we can make. We're going over to Prescott's in about an hour or so—just long enough for them to get *comfortable*, you might say, and then we're gonna raise Cain. A shivaree is our way of letting the new Mrs. Guinn know that we're mighty pleased she's part of our family now. It's a time-honored tradition to do this, and Glory's gonna be proud as all get-out that we think enough of her to give her a shivaree." Mama muttered under her breath that she wouldn't bet the farm on that.

We finished cleaning and closing up the hall, then everyone piled into as few vehicles as we could, to keep the noise down. The truck-beds were packed full, as were some of the larger cars. There were about forty people in all. Sparky had a hand-painted banner flying off the back of his open-bed truck that read "Presenting Mr. and Mrs. Prescott Guinn." The plan was to park at a church that was about a block down from the house, then, as quietly as possible, walk down to Prescott's, where the shivaree would be kicked off by the lighting of several Roman candle rockets, and the firing of guns. Mama's pots and pans were handed out, and Mama—under the conviction that if you can't beat 'em, join 'em—requested that she be handed her Dutch oven and a wooden spoon to bang it with.

As soon as we neared the church, Daddy killed his truck's lights and engine and coasted into the parking lot. Everyone else followed his lead. Then, grabbing our shivaree gear, Mama directed us to the back of Prescott's house, where we gathered beneath a second-story window that she knew was his bedroom. Everyone waited for the first Roman candle to be set off, and as soon as it was, Daddy fired his shotgun into the air, and everyone else started shooting, banging, and shouting out, "Shivaree! Shivaree!" Almost immediately, a light illuminated the bedroom and a few seconds later the window was pushed up—hard! Framed within it was my very aggravated-looking uncle.

"What in blue blazes are y'all doing? You 'bout gave us both a heart attack!"

"I bet you wouldn't a wanted to be found dead in *that* position!" shouted an enthusiastic reveler, followed by hearty laughter and a few amens.

"It's your and Glory's shivaree, Prescott! We're honoring your union," shouted Daddy.

"Well, didn't you figure you'd done enough honoring at the wedding? And we're just now getting to the 'union' part." A roar of laughter went up. Those standing in front heard Glory's mortified, "*Prescott!*" spoken somewhere in the room behind him. He glanced back toward her, then faced us again, trying hard not to laugh.

"This is tradition," Daddy continued. "Now, where's that pretty bride of yours?"

"Quivering in the corner," Prescott answered. "Let me see if she'll come to the window. Hold on."

"Window nothin'," Sparky hollered. "You bring that woman out here! We're gonna put her in the back of my truck and parade y'all through town!" Obviously the crowd agreed and began shouting poor Glory's name.

"She's gonna kill me," Prescott said, turning away from the window.

"Glory's either frightened or madder'n a hound who can't remember where he buried his bone!" Mama said, followed by guesses from the crowd as to which emotion they'd evoked in her.

Everyone edged closer beneath the window. Packed tightly together, we quietly listened to the heated lowered voices coming from the dimly lit room above. They were obviously arguing, though no one could see them. I couldn't make out what was being said as I was standing toward the back of the crowd, holding Donnie in my arms so he'd have a better view of the goings-on. Those who were closest to the house suddenly snickered, then relayed what they'd heard. Aunt Harriet whispered over her shoulder that Glory had just told Prescott he would be singing five octaves higher if he dared try to take her outside. Then the harsh whispering from the bedroom went completely quiet. The crowd strained to hear, pressing in even closer to the house. Suddenly, a huge bucket of ice-cold water was dumped on them by a laughing Prescott and Glory. Shrieks rang out at the shock of the cold drenching, and everyone ran into each other like bumper cars as they frantically scrambled out of the way in case a second assault was coming.

Fortunately, Donnie and I were spared most of the downpour, but we quickly stepped back from the crowd, more to avoid being trampled than from the threat of another soaking. Glory was no longer assaulting the crowd with water but with a tongue-lashing, telling everyone that they'd about made Prescott a widower before they'd even had one night together as husband and wife. "Y'all scared the pee-wally outta me," she scolded. "And I'm telling you now, I'll find out where all y'all live, and when you least expect it, you can be expectin' me!" Though her words were heated, I could see that it was taking every bit of control for her to not start laughing.

"C'mon, Glory," one of her cousins pleaded. "Let's go for one spin down Main Street, and we'll bring you and Prescott right back. Sparky's gone through the trouble of decorating his truck for y'all. It'd be a shame to let it all be for nothin'."

"Lord'a mercy!" Glory muttered. Then louder, "At least let me grab my coat and put some shoes on!" A great cheer went up and an unspoken but unanimous decision was instantly made that just as much as Prescott belonged to them, Glory now did, too.

CHAPTER 7

One Word

Everyone began to disperse, either pulling their vehicles into line for the impromptu parade down Main Street, or to head on home. Donnie and I were walking back to Daddy's truck after deciding to forego the rest of the shivaree. I didn't know who was more tired; my five-year-old, who walked hand in hand with me, zombielike, or me. Suddenly, I started coughing so hard I had to step out of the way of the others who were also on their way back to the church's parking lot. A couple of friends who passed me asked if I was all right, and I nodded to them that I was. Harriet had been close behind and stepped over to us, then she told Donnie to run on up ahead to his grandma and to tell her that we'd be there in a minute.

"That's a wet cough, Kate. How long have you had it?" We were between the streetlight that lit the church's parking lot and the light emanating from Prescott's place. Caught in the shadows, we stayed out of the way as everyone else passed us. "About three weeks," I whispered, then started coughing again, only this time I was finally able to cough up a good amount of phlegm. My cough had been fairly dry until that morning, and even then, the phlegm I'd been able to bring up had been a very small amount, thick and yellow. Reaching into my purse, I took out a light blue handkerchief and spat into it, but before I could put it back into my purse, my aunt took it from my hand.

"Let me see that," she said, as she walked toward the light. I followed her, objecting to the necessity of her examining it. She stopped as soon as she was able to see and I saw her body tense slightly. As I walked up behind her, she turned, and the look on her face needed no words to frame it; something was wrong. Something was terribly wrong. I grabbed the wrist of her hand that held the handkerchief out to me. This time the yellowish phlegm was mixed with a thick glob of dark clotted blood. "Oh, my God."

"Okay, now, let's not get in a panic," my aunt said, trying to calm me. "How long have you been doing this, Kate?"

I answered with a question of my own. "What does this mean?" I watched her eyes. If she looked away from me, I'd know she wasn't conveying what she was actually thinking. However, her response was noncommittal.

She folded the bloodied handkerchief, then tucked it into her pocket. "Kate, we need to get you tested—"

"You didn't answer me. What are you thinking is wrong with me?" My voice sounded hollow, strange, as if I was hearing it from outside myself.

"I can't diagnose something that—"

I interrupted her again, asking my question a different way. "What is the first thing they'll test me for?"

"Tuberculosis." She said it without hesitating. "They'll take a chest X-ray and a sputum sample." Suddenly, I felt like a ball trying to stay still on a slanted floor. There was a ringing in my ears from the rush of adrenaline, and I took a step back from her as if the word "tuberculosis" could infect me by just hearing it. Seeing my reaction, she grasped my upper arms. "Kate, let's not get more upset by just guessing. We don't know what's going on yet."

"But you see it every day. You know what you're seeing."

"Yes, but . . . Please, let's just get you tested before we get ahead of ourselves here." We were only about a half mile from home, and she suggested that we walk if I felt I was able to. I told her I was, and she hurried over to one of the last stragglers heading to the parking lot and asked him to let my folks know that we were going to walk home.

She slipped her arm around my waist as we walked together in silence. I wondered if she was trying to give me time to collect myself, or if she was just looking for the right words to say. I did know one thing, though: She was keeping me from falling to my shaking knees. Aunt Harriet was shorter than me, but solid and strong. There was no mistaking that she was my father's sister; they'd always looked a lot alike, with the same golden eyes and thick dark hair, but Daddy was much taller. He couldn't have done a better job of supporting me at that moment, though.

"Now, Kate, you listen to me. If, and I do mean *if*, you do have tuberculosis, it's not a death sentence like it used to be. We have antibiotics and different treatments now that are combating this thing like never before."

"I know. But I also know that plenty of people are still dying from it."

"Some are, yes," my aunt had to agree. "But every year, those numbers are dropping. And today, they aren't institutionalizing people for the sole purpose of keeping them from contaminating society. Today, they're able—"

"Institution?" The word finally worked through to my brain. My thinking felt thick and disconnected.

"Kate, I work with some of the best pulmonologists at Pelham, and I know the wonderful work they're doing today."

I was only half listening. "Couldn't I just have an infection that's causing this bloody cough?"

"You could. You most certainly could. The blood you expectorated—you coughed up—could be caused by several things, but TB would be one of—"

"Oh, my God! What about Donnie?" I knew that if I was sick, there was a good likelihood my son was, too. The fear that I felt for myself was nothing compared to the absolute terror that Donnie could be sick as well. Before my aunt could say anything, my soft crying turned into deep sobbing.

"Kate, you've got to pull yourself together! First, we don't know for certain that you have tuberculosis, and even if you do, that doesn't mean Donnie does, too. Most people who are exposed to it never develop the disease. Look at me! I'm a perfect example. I work around people with TB almost every day, and I'm fine. Donnie hasn't shown any signs of being ill, has he? No signs of fatigue, and he's not coughing, right?" I answered that he seemed fine. "Okay." She nodded. "Good. That's good. Now listen, we're going to take this one step at a time, but right now, we need to get home. It's gotten chilly. C'mon, let's go and we'll talk while we're walking.

"Tomorrow, I think we ought to see if the mobile clinic is anywhere near town," she continued. "If the clinic's in town, we'll get you right over there; otherwise, we'll drive down to the hospital in Marion, and have you checked there. Does that sound all right to you?"

I nodded as I started coughing again, and my aunt quickly handed me my handkerchief. I coughed up another sickening glob, but this time I did not have to look to see if the results were bloody or not. The heavy metallic taste told me all I needed to know. As I tucked my handkerchief in my purse, my aunt gently squeezed my shoulder and quietly said, "It'll be okay, Kate. We're going to get you some help." Then neither of us said anything more as we continued to walk.

Finally, we turned onto the long dirt road that led into the orchard and to my parents' home, as well as my grandmother's place. "Look at that!" Harriet softy said, pointing to the huge full moon that hung just above the tops of the apple trees. The face on the moon seemed to be taunting me with its smile. "The rain we had earlier sure left the air good and clear," she said, taking in a deep breath. And as she did, I prayed to God, and to all of His mightiest angels, that before too long, my lungs would be as good and clear as the night air, and that I could smile right back at the moon.

CHAPTER 8

Past Meets Present

It's funny how it seems to take so long getting to a place you want to be, while the trip to someplace you dread going seems so much shorter, even when the distance is the same. My mind was weighing the reason for that as my head rocked gently against the window in rhythm with the moving train. Unlike the trip going to Howling Cut, the sadness and uncertainty about my future made the return trip pass much more quickly than I wanted it to. It had been a sad farewell as my parents and son waved and blew kisses at me from the platform until the train moved away from the depot, blotting out the view of my family with its gray opaque steam. I was glad I'd been able to hold back the tears, but I'd shed so many of them already, it was as though my body was completely dehydrated. I felt as though I hadn't stopped crying since the night of the shivaree.

Aunt Harriet and I had returned home that night to find my parents drinking coffee at the kitchen table, enjoying a recap of the day's wonderful events, and thankfully, Donnie was already in bed upstairs. He'd only been down for several minutes, so we kept our voices low, careful not to wake him. Before entering my house, I had told Aunt Harriet that I wanted to be the one to tell my parents about the bloody phlegm, and the necessity of getting a chest X-ray the next day. Harriet was merely there for moral support and to answer, as best she could, any questions that they or I might have. Needless to say, my parents were stunned and terribly frightened. Not heeding any caution given about the risk of close contact, they kissed me and held me tight, reassuring me, as well as themselves, that I would be just fine.

Harriet had gone home about 11:00 p.m. Daddy walked her home, following the dirt path that connected the two homes, while Mama and I watched from the porch as they made their way along the edge of the orchard. When Daddy returned, we sat down at the kitchen table, and as much as we hated doing it, we discussed the what-ifs, and the must-do's should my diagnosis not go well.

Daddy had bought a newspaper at Taft's Mercantile soon after sunup to check the daily listing of where the mobile clinic would be that day. It was scheduled to be in Flat Top, which was closer than the hospital in Marion, so Daddy drove me over. Aunt Harriet accompanied us because of her medical expertise, while Mama stayed at home with Donnie. It wasn't too hard trying to dissuade him from coming with us as we told him that I thought I might be getting a cold and needed to see the doctor before I got to feeling too poorly. I knew Donnie disliked visiting the doctor or the dentist more than anything else in his young life, so it took very little convincing to keep him home. It pained Mama not to be with me, but we promised to call her from Flat Top as soon as we knew something.

The mobile clinic was a reincarnated school bus that was painted white. The interior looked like a mini version of a doctor's office, complete with check-in desk, one examining room, a compartment for X-rays, and a tiny office. There was only one patient in front of me, and while he was being seen by the doctor, I filled out paperwork. Shortly after I'd completed the forms, I was directed to an examining room by an older-looking nurse, who then took my temperature and blood pressure. Aunt Harriet had accompanied me, and the nurse told us both to have a seat while she let the doctor know I was ready to see him. Several minutes later, a rather young-looking physician, who introduced himself as Stan Black, joined us. We discussed my list of symptoms and I answered his questions, as his nurse took notes. Aunt Harriet went into deeper detail, using medical terminology when she felt it was necessary, and every so often, Dr. Black referred back to my medical history as though he was cross-referencing the past and the present.

"Mrs. Cavanaugh, it says here that you had scarlet fever at age ten. Can you tell me how long you were sick with it, and were any tests run after you'd recovered—to check your lungs or your heart, for instance—to see if there might have been any permanent damage as a result of the fever?"

My aunt looked over at me. "I'd completely forgotten about that. You were sick with it for close to three weeks." She addressed the doctor. "At one point we thought we'd lose her, the fever had gotten so high. She was admitted to Mercy General, in Marion, during the last week and the fever finally broke."

Confused by the questions of an illness that I'd lived through so many years before, I interjected, "What does that have to do with me today?"

Dr. Black's smile had a tad of condescension attached to it. "Mrs. Cavanaugh, past illnesses can leave the door open for other diseases, you might say. You're more vulnerable, more susceptible. We've seen a lot of people who have histories of serious diseases, especially respiratory or pulmonary, coming back years later with new illnesses that were likely contracted due to compromised immune systems. But we're getting ahead of ourselves. At this point, I just need as much information about you—both present and past— as I can get in order to diagnose you correctly, and treat you properly."

Again, he asked me if my heart or lungs had been tested after the scarlet fever, and I told him that I couldn't remember any tests being done, and neither could my aunt. But just to be sure, she quickly checked with my father out in the waiting room, and returned to report that no tests had been run to his recollection. Dr. Black had me open my blouse then, and listened to my heart and lungs with his stethoscope. He listened from both the front and back. Finally, he sat back from me as he hung his stethoscope around his neck. "Let's get a couple of chest X-rays, as well as a sputum smear sample. Whatever bacterial growth occurs within it will help to confirm what we're dealing with. And Ellen"—he turned on his swivel stool to face his nurse—"we'll need a blood sample for a Wassermann test."

"Oh, for heaven's sake, Doctor! Is a Wassermann test *really* necessary?" My aunt sounded more than a little irritated.

"What's a Wassermann test?" I asked, looking from her to the doctor.

"It's a test for syphilis," my aunt disgustedly answered, then, turning back to the doctor, she angrily told him that she could vouch for my high morals and the lack of any promiscuity.

"Dr. Black," I calmly stated, "my parents didn't raise trash. And if there's a question about that, then perhaps I need to see someone else."

"Mrs. Cavanaugh, I'm not insinuating anything of the kind." Dr. Black sighed, as though he was tired of having to explain that he wasn't questioning his patients' moral behavior. "I truly meant no disrespect. The law requires that I administer a Wassermann test. I have no say in the matter. The truth is that many people who've tested positive for tuberculosis have also tested positive for syphilis. Please, let me do my job, and let's get these tests completed so that we can move forward with your treatment, and, hopefully, your recovery."

"Then let's get to it," I said.

CHAPTER 9

Altered Lives

"Next stop, Swannanoa! Arriving in Swannanoa!" The train conductor's voice startled me out of the half sleep that the rhythm of the train had lulled me into. Turning to look out the window that I'd been resting my head against, I squinted from the assault of the midday sun. The long, low hills were dotted with a mixture of newer-looking farms and dilapidated old ones, but no matter the age, they all looked miniscule in comparison to the enormous fields that surrounded them.

"Are we at Swannanoa already?" Aunt Harriet asked as she sat down in the seat diagonally across from me after a visit to the ladies' room. "Then East Asheville is the next stop, and that's ours." she said. "I hope the car from Pelham will already be there. It'll take a while to get you through the admission process, and we don't need to be delayed any longer than we have to be. They don't like the patients to miss or interrupt supper, if it can be helped." She looked around her seat area to make sure she had everything packed away, and found a piece of waxed paper that her roasted chicken sandwich had been wrapped in. Crumpling it up and sticking it inside the small wicker basket we'd carried our noonday dinner in, she glanced over at my wrapped-up, half-eaten sandwich. "Can't you make yourself eat a little more, honey? It's going to be a while before you'll be able to have something else and you have to keep your strength up."

I had forced myself to eat the little I'd consumed. I knew that part of the reason for my lack of appetite was a result of the tuberculosis itself. That was a common symptom. But I also knew that I wasn't hungry because I was emotionally devastated that my life had taken such a horrible turn.

Two days ago, when we returned from the mobile clinic, we found Mama waiting on the porch for us. Hurrying down the steps the moment she saw us turn onto the road to the orchard, she barely allowed the truck to come to a complete stop before she opened the passenger door and pulled me to her. Her words were meant to be comforting and reassuring, but her trembling body gave away her true emotions. She'd been told the news as soon as we'd left the clinic when Daddy called her from a pay phone just down the street. I knew I couldn't talk to her without breaking down, so I'd asked Daddy to call her while Aunt Harriet and I walked across the street to the town square to find a quiet place to sit down.

I had decided to call Geoffrey later. There was no reason to call him as soon as I left the clinic because he didn't know I was there to begin with. There had been no reason to upset him until I knew what was what. Now that I did know, though, I needed time to digest the news before I tried to calmly explain to my husband that the life we had created for ourselves had been completely altered. I would call him after supper, I decided.

The worst part of all, however, would be telling Donnie. I wasn't sure how, but I knew it would have to be right away because my son would quickly realize something was wrong with me. We were connected; connected in a way that continued long after the umbilical cord had been severed. And, though he was so young, he was amazingly sensitive, as well as intuitive.

"I'm not going to ask you if you're all right," my aunt said as soon as we sat down on a bench in the cool shade of an enormous oak tree, "because none of us are at the moment. But, Kate, you're going to be all right. You've got a lot of factors going for you, and you'll get through this."

"What factors do I have going for me? Seems like I had all the right factors to get me to this point!" I was angry, but more than that, I was petrified. "And what if Donnie is sick, too? I gave life to that child! Am I going to be the one to take it away? And what's the likelihood of Geoffrey being sick because of me, and Mama and Daddy, too! And what about you, Aunt Harriet?"

"Kate, the chances are great that none of us will ever get this disease. We've talked about this. Your family is going to be fine, but right now, we need to discuss the best course of action for *you*."

She gently tucked a wayward lock of my hair behind my ear. I'd worn it down and some strands had escaped one of the tortoise shell barrettes that I had clipped above each ear. Her gentle, loving gesture cracked my resolve to hold myself together. Bowing my head, with my chin resting on my chest, I began to softly cry, and a moment later, the sound had another layer added to it. My aunt's façade of professionalism and bravado had finally crumbled and she was crying with me. Reaching over, I grasped her hand, and together our tears washed away all vestiges of hope that I would go home after leaving the doctor's office to live my normal life. Now, I just prayed that I would live.

Aunt Harriet pulled a handkerchief from her purse and offered it to me, but seeing that I had one, she wiped away the wetness on her own face, blew her nose, and cleared her congested throat. "We need to discuss some of these hospitals on the list that Dr. Black gave us. There are several here that I think are excellent. Do you want to wait till we're back home, so your folks can discuss this with us? Or maybe you'd just like to discuss it with Geoffrey. I don't mean to rush you on this, but, well, it's . . ."

"Urgent, like the doctor said," I finished for her.

"Yes, honey, it is. There's no getting around that. I looked the list over, like I said, and there's the Western North Carolina Sanatorium. That's in Black Mountain. That's a good one. And there's Oteen Hospital, in Swannanoa. Both of those are just outside of Asheville. But there's also Pelham State Hospital. Before you look at me like I'm as crazy as some of the patients there, you have to consider the fact that we have some of the best doctors in the state and some that are extremely experienced with treating tuberculosis, because Pelham used to be strictly a tuberculosis sanatorium. It's also a little closer to Cabot.

"The housing for sound-minded TB patients is separate from the other patients' housing. In other words, Kate, you wouldn't be in the same ward with folks who have schizophrenia, for example, even if they have tuberculosis, too. And I work there, honey, so you'll have family around you. I can see you most every day of the week. I know those doctors well, and I know how talented and skilled they are. You'd be in the best of hands . . ."

"Call Pelham, please. See if they'll take me. I don't need to think too long and hard about it. I just want to be as close to my home and family as possible. Geoffrey can bring Donnie to see me. They'll only be about an hour and a half away. And you'll be there. That'd be really good. I want to be able to talk to someone who will be honest about what's happening, and I know you will be. I don't ever want anything withheld from me 'cause folks are worried it'll just upset me. I just want to be told the truth. Every day. And if that means telling me that nothing more can be done, that I won't get well, then I need to know that, too. And I'm going to count on you to do that for me; to always be honest. You will be, all the time, no matter what, right?" I grabbed her hand and held it hard, desperately. I needed to hear her promise me that.

She turned her body toward me and looked me straight in the eyes. "I swear to you that I will always tell you the truth, no matter what. God is my witness."

"Then call for me, please." There needed to be no further discussion. The decision was made.

Mama, like Aunt Harriet, had been amazingly strong and encouraging. Though she was torn up on the inside, on the outside she remained strong. My wonderful glass-half-full mother was supportive of my decision to go to Pelham, even though it was well over two hours away, and promised she'd come see me often. Of monumental importance was the fact that she immediately suggested Donnie stay with them in Howling Cut for a while. He wouldn't be starting first grade until the fall, and with Geoffrey away at work all day, it seemed like the perfect solution for everyone. However, Geoffrey might be more difficult to persuade.

I called him after supper. Mama and Daddy offered to take Donnie into town and buy him ice cream so that I'd have privacy and plenty of time to talk with Geoffrey, and as soon as they disappeared down the road, I dialed my home phone. A straight-back chair sat against the wall by the telephone table, but just as I had done when I was a teenager, I sat on the floor, with my back against the wall and legs stretched out in front of me. After only two rings, Geoffrey picked up. I suspected he'd just walked in the door from work, which made it an early night for him. The busier he got, the later he came in from work, it seemed. I didn't mind that so much, but when it was obvious he'd had quite a bit to drink, I couldn't help but wonder what kind of business was taking place, and I sometimes asked him about it. This was Cabot, he was quick to remind me, where wining and dining clients was all part of cementing a deal and building relationships. Not like Howling Cut, where business was conducted in someone's field, kitchen, or barn, and a deal was finalized with the passing of a mason jar of moonshine. In all honesty, I couldn't argue his point but still, his late nights made me uneasy.

"Are you exhausted from the wedding and all its festivities? I was going to call you in a little bit to see how everything went. What'd Prescott and his new wife think about that shivaree business?" He laughed.

I realized that I'd wound the telephone cord tightly around my finger. It was a habit I'd had ever since I was big enough to use the phone. But I was so on edge that I'd wound it to the point of cutting off my circulation. Unwinding it, I answered Geoffrey's question. "Everything went well. I believe a good time was had by all." I was trying to keep my voice light. "Uncle Prescott and Glory seemed thrilled with it all . . . well, all but the shivaree." I couldn't help but laugh and it felt good. More importantly, though, it was reassuring that a part of the old me was still there, buoying my strength and enabling me to move on to the dire matter at hand. "Geoffrey, something's happened that I need to talk to you about."

"*What?* What's happened?! Are you all right? Is it Donnie?" He sounded scared.

"Donnie's fine. Really. He's fine. It's not him. Geoffrey, I . . . I went to see a doctor in Flat Top this morning. You see, I've had this cough, which hasn't gone away . . . and it's . . ." I just had to say it. "I have tuberculosis, Geoffrey."

There was stunned silence for a moment, followed by an almost inaudible, "Oh, my God." Then more silence.

"I'm sorry, Geoffrey. I . . ." It was taking everything I had not to start crying again. I needed to be strong; for him, for me, but mainly for our son.

"For God's sake, Kathryn, don't apologize! That's ridiculous! It's not like you wanted to get . . . How . . . how is it possible you contracted this? It's not like it used to be, where a lot of people had it. It's not like that anymore. How'd this happen?"

"I don't know. I've been exposed to someone, somewhere, obviously. People still get it, you know. It's just not as prevalent as it used to be. The doctor thinks this had something to do with the fact that I had scarlet fever when I was a young girl. The doctor says my immune system, and certainly my lungs, possibly even my heart, were affected. The fever left me pretty susceptible to anything that's contagious."

"Kathryn, I'll come and get you and Donnie tomorrow. Oh, my God! What about Donnie? He's been exposed . . ."

"It's unlikely he'll become sick. Most healthy people don't actually come down with the disease, even though they've been exposed to it. There's a vaccine that can be given to Donnie, too, just to be sure. We'll have to have him screened, and you'll need to be, as well. Everyone in the family . . ." There was only silence for several seconds. I wondered if it had just hit my husband that he could be infected, too.

"I'll call Ed McNally as soon as we hang up." He was our family doctor, as well as Geoffrey's tennis partner. "I'll talk to him about Donnie and me being screened. And he'll know where we should send you for the best care. You'll go to a private facility, of course, even if it's out of state. I'm sure Ed can get you into any of them. You've got to go where the highest level of care is provided."

"I'm not going out of state, Geoffrey. I want to stay as close to home as possible. I've already decided to go to Pelham. It's close by and Aunt Harri—"

"Pelham! Pelham, as in Pelham State Hospital? Have you lost your mind, Kathryn?"

"No, Geoffrey, I haven't. And I won't be with any of the folks who have." I halfheartedly smiled. "I'll be in a separate housing unit and I'll be able—"

He cut me off again. "I absolutely forbid it. You will *not* go to Pelham. I'll be damned if my wife is going to an insane asylum."

"This is a choice I need to make, Geoffrey." My voice was calm, neutral. "Please, the last thing I need for you to do is fight me on this. I need every bit of strength I've got to fight my illness. Please, let me do what I need to do for myself without there being any arguing involved. I want to go where I have family, and Aunt Harriet's a nurse there. I want to be where it's easy for my family to visit. Please, let me make this decision for myself."

"I'm at a complete loss for words, Kathryn. When you could have the best care, the most comfortable, private care. I just don't understand you. I just don't know what to say other than I'm absolutely against you doing this."

"Then don't say anything other than that you'll be there for me, even if 'there' is not somewhere you'd choose."

But at that moment, Geoffrey couldn't say anything. At first, I could barely make out what it was that I was hearing. It sounded like a cross between choking and gasping for air. But then the sound increased, and I suddenly realized that my husband, whose behavior was always controlled and correct, had reached a breaking point that everyone has, no matter how restrained one's behavior may usually be. For the first time since I'd met the chivalrous, handsome blond-haired man on a winter's night at the Woolworth's five and dime in Durham, I heard something that I never thought I would: I heard my husband crying.

It took a few moments for him to regain his normal composure, and until he did, I talked softy to him, reassuring him that I would—*we* would—get through this terrible time as a family, and be stronger and closer because of it. Though I didn't tell Geoffrey, I'd never felt closer to him than I did at that moment, sitting in the hallway of my childhood home, listening to him cry. He was letting me in, all the way. And though I knew that Geoffrey possessed a deeply hidden sensitivity, it was only on the rarest of occasions that he'd let me, much less anyone else, see that vulnerable side of him. It seemed to scare him to do so, and I wondered if he was afraid that it could be used against him in some way.

I didn't know why, but I had my suspicions that it grew out of his father's great demands and expectations of him; and those included the career path Geoffrey was expected to follow and his comportment as he did. What I did know, though, was that the vulnerable side of him was beautiful in its softness, and it was one of the reasons that I'd fallen in love with him. When Geoffrey was able to talk again, we did so using gentle and supportive words that buoyed both of our spirits. I was grateful we could share some time like that. We both needed reassuring, and we talked on for awhile, even when everyone got back from town. Mama wouldn't let Donnie interrupt me, but immediately took him upstairs for a bath then Daddy read him to sleep. My son didn't mind; he adored his grandparents, and though this was the first time that he'd spent any length of time with them, a deep bond had quickly formed.

I'd often thought it was a shame that my parents weren't the ones who lived in Cabot. Donnie's relationship with Geoffrey's parents was not a close one. They were too formal and prickly for a little boy to cozy up to. With so many hearts breaking in just one day's time, it did my spirits good to see how agreeable Donnie was in allowing Mama and Daddy to do those things for him that I normally did. He felt secure with my parents, and I could certainly understand why. There had not been a day of my childhood, or my adulthood, for that matter, when I did not feel absolutely safe, well cared for, and deeply loved by them. Now, considering the fact that there were many unknowns lying ahead for all of us, I was never more grateful that these two amazing people were my parents, and my son's grandparents.

Fortunately, Geoffrey listened patiently to my feelings and misgivings about taking Donnie back to Cabot at that time, and saw the logic in his staying in Howling Cut through the summer. I hoped and prayed, however, that I would recover long before the summer ended and that we would all be in our respective homes when the autumn winds blew, picking up the pieces of our lives from where they had been so abruptly interrupted in the early spring.

The morning after I was diagnosed, I took Donnie to my favorite swimming hole. The weather was barely warm enough for even the bravest of souls, but I'd learned as a kid that no matter how frigid the water was, if you stretched out on the giant sun-warmed boulder that we jumped off, you could warm up in no time. As a matter of fact, it was quite exhilarating to go from one temperature extreme to the other.

I told Donnie about being sick after we'd been swimming for just a short while. My stamina wouldn't allow for more than a few minutes of splashing around, and I'd stayed in the shallower water, just in case I had trouble catching my breath, or was overcome with another round of rib-breaking coughing. As we sunbathed on the rock, snacking on graham crackers and drinking from a mason jar of lemonade, I watched my son while he crammed a whole cracker in his mouth then started to pull another from the pack in preparation for the next mouthful. "Slow down, darlin'," I said, laughing. "There's no reason to choke 'em down." Then, "Donnie, I need to talk to you about something important." That got his attention, and the cracker he was after was quickly forgotten.

"What?" he inquired, spitting a few cracker crumbs out with the word. His brows knitted together in their usual way when he was looking perplexed or meditative, or angry, but at the moment, he was looking at me real hard, as if he was steeling himself for something big.

"Donnie, honey, I'm not feeling very good these days. I'm pretty sick." There. It was said. I'd lain awake half the night trying to figure out the best way of telling him and had finally come to the conclusion that I trusted myself enough to know how, when the moment came.

"The doctor didn't make your cold go away? I heard you coughing." His brows remained pinched, worried.

"No, it's not a cold, darlin'. It's something else with a real long name that's hard to say. The doctor wants me to see some other doctors who can help me more than he can. I have to go where they are, and stay for a little while. Remember when we went to Asheville to see that play, *The Nutcracker*, at Christmas?" He nodded. "Well, I have to go to a place that's not too far from there."

"Will you see a play?"

I laughed. His five-year-old world was very small, compartmentalized. "No, honey, I'm not going to the theater, just to a hospital that takes care of people who are sick, like I am."

"Oh." He looked away as he digested this and I knew that suddenly the awfulness of my going away was sinking in. The word "hospital" had done it. "How long will you stay?"

"I'm not sure, but I'm hoping it won't be too long. And you'll come to see me." I gave him a moment. Then, "Donnie, how'd you like to stay with Grandma and Papa for a little while, for the summer, until school starts in the fall? Daddy will come to see you, and Grandma and Papa will make sure you're okay and having fun. You know Daddy works all day, honey, and I'd have to get a nanny for you. I think you'd have more fun at Grandma's, don't you?"

"Maybe." He was thinking all of this through. "Daddy'll come here to see me?"

"Of course he will! He's gonna miss you a lot! And in the fall, you'll go home again and start school. Gee, you're getting to be such a big boy and much too fast for my liking!" I tried to shift the conversation away from my illness and all of the changes that it was causing in his little life. "Aren't you excited about starting first grade?" I knew that he was.

"Uh-huh." His answer was soft and distracted. He was confused and frightened, and I needed to acknowledge it.

"Donnie, I know my going away is real scary and sad for you. It is for Daddy and me, too. But I'm going to tell those doctors that they have to fix me up real good so that I can walk you to your class on the first day of school. I bet they have little boys and girls themselves, and will understand how important that is to you and me. And I know they'll do everything they can to make sure I'm as good as new so I can take you to school, just like we planned. In the meantime, though, is it all right with you to stay here for the summer?"

"Yeah, I guess," he said.

"Okay. Good. You're a good boy." I hugged him hard. I didn't want to let him go, ever. Not wanting him to see the tears in my eyes, I turned away from him and started putting away our snacks. "Here, you want another cracker before I put them away?"

"Naw." He shook his head. "Can we go? I'm kinda cold."

"Sure," I said. I could see he was trying his hardest not to cry. Though I knew he didn't understand the magnitude of what was happening, and that he had no real concept of time at his age, he knew I was going away, and he understood enough to make him cry. As he turned to walk away, I caught him by the arm and knelt down in front of him. Not worrying whether he saw the emotion on my own face, I looked directly into his. "I promise you, son, I'm going to be all right. Do you understand?" He nodded his head but his lips were trembling as he fought to be brave. "I'm going to be fine. I promise you! I've never made a promise to you that I haven't kept, right? And I'm not going to start now." But I knew I just had, for there was no way of knowing what the future would hold. I knew I had no business making that promise to him, but he needed hope. We all needed hope. All of a sudden, I was kinda cold, too.

CHAPTER 10

The Threshold

"You ready?" My aunt looked from the window to me as the train came to a stop at the East Asheville station.

"As I'll ever be," I said, forcing a smile as I stood up and ran my hands down the front of my navy suit in an effort to smooth out some of the wrinkles, as well as to wipe some of the moisture off my clammy hands. I was exhausted, petrified, and heartsick, and those emotions had escalated to the point of making me numb.

My aunt took one of my hands firmly in hers. "It's going to be okay, Kate. You'll get the help you need. You'll be in very good hands." She emphasized her statement by squeezing my hand tightly.

"I know I will be, Aunt Harriet. Thanks. Okay," I said, taking a deep breath as I started down the train aisle. The deep inhalation started my coughing again. I sidestepped into an empty row of seats to let other passengers by. Aunt Harriet stepped aside to wait for me, and once the coughing passed, I nodded my head, indicating that we could go.

When we exited the train, my aunt's head swiveled around, looking for the car from Pelham. Any newly arriving patients were picked up at the train station or airport by a car from the hospital. It was just a courtesy that was offered, but the thought crossed my mind that it might also be a way of keeping any would-be patients from deciding at the last minute that they would *not* be patients, and buying a return ticket instead.

"There he is!" Aunt Harriet was waving to a man in a black sedan that was just pulling up to the depot. The man drove over to us and immediately jumped out.

"Nurse Pierce! I didn't realize I was picking you up today, too. I was told your niece was arriving but had no idea that you'd be accompanying her." Turning to me, he bowed slightly. "Good afternoon, Mrs. Cavanaugh. I trust your trip was uneventful."

"It was fine, thank you." He spoke as if he were taking me to meet the lord of the manor.

"Harold, don't they ever let you have a day off?" My aunt smiled. "We appreciate your coming to get us. We have luggage, of course. Kate, let's get you in the car. It's starting to drizzle. We'll get the bags." Harold opened the back door for me, and once I was inside, the two of them walked over to where the porter was unloading the luggage. I laid my head back, closing my eyes. The car smelled of disinfectant. *They must sanitize this car after picking up new arrivals who might be contagious*, I thought. I pitied the next passenger after me. Undoubtedly, his or her nose would be assaulted. I felt the luggage being stowed in the trunk as the car gave a small bounce under the weight of the heavy suitcases. Then the trunk was slammed shut and Aunt Harriet joined me on the backseat.

"You holding up okay?" My aunt looked concerned and I wondered if she was more worried about me physically, or mentally. In truth, I was beginning to wonder if the fact that I was going to a state hospital, where a good percentage of those being treated were psychiatric patients, was most appropriate after all. There were small moments when I wondered if I was going to crack under the pressure. Dying didn't frighten me as much as losing the life I'd planned with those I loved so dearly, and missing so many precious moments—like watching Donnie grow up, or seeing Geoffrey reach his lofty goals, and watching my parents' orchard grow, watching them grow old gracefully with it. I wanted to be witness to it all. I wanted to be with them all.

"Aunt Harriet, is there a phone in my room?" I asked. It would make things so much easier if I could communicate with my family and friends whenever I needed to.

"You'll be in the TB ward, honey. There's no phone in there, but there's one in the hallway in front of the nurses' station, which is just outside your ward. They want the patients to stay as quiet as possible, especially those who are extremely ill. The staff tries to keep the noise level down and by having fewer phones, there's less noise. So, to answer your question, there's just the one phone for the two wards to share.

"Who is housed in each of the wards?"

"The tubercular patients are on the second floor, but they're separated by gender; women on one side and men on the other. The first floor houses a few of the administration offices. The third floor of the building you'll be in, which is building three, by the way, is restricted to psychiatric TB patients. But you're rarely around each other, with the exception of the outdoor areas, and then there are always staff members in attendance. It goes without saying, our psychiatric patients are kept under lock and key most of the time. Everyone else has the freedom to move around, with the doctors' approval, of course. Tubercular patients, however, are required to remain separate from non-tubercular patients inside the buildings, but they're free to be in the company of each other outdoors, as long as they remain a safe distance apart to prevent spreading the disease. I know all of this probably makes you feel you'll be treated like some common criminal for having tuberculosis, but it's really not like that. You'll learn the rules in no time and understand the reasons for them. I promise you, Kate, it'll be okay. It isn't a dreadful place." But I knew she was looking at it through the eyes of someone who could come and go as she pleased, and I wondered if she'd feel the same way if she saw the place through the eyes of a patient.

"I'm sure it'll be fine, Aunt Harriet," I said, laying my head back against the seat again and closing my eyes to shut out the world. I was beginning to understand what lepers had been dealing with for centuries. The isolation and the stigma were shared by those suffering from tuberculosis. Quickly brushing a tear away with my beige-gloved hand before my aunt could see, I turned to look out the window and saw the raindrops leaving trails as they slid down the frosted glass, as if mocking me.

"About twenty minutes to go," she said. "It's quite a ways out of town. The hospital sits in the middle of sixty-two acres. There are wonderful open spaces, flower and vegetable gardens, even a greenhouse. Patients are encouraged to spend time outdoors. It's believed to be a curative thing, especially for TB patients. Fresh air, especially cold fresh air, is good for tubercular lungs. The doctors say it inhibits the progress of more cavities and lesions from forming, and it helps to heal the ones that are there."

"It'd be nice to work in the gardens and greenhouse. Do y'all grow the food you're eating?"

"Most all of it. Let's get you halfway back on your feet, then see if we can't get you out growing vegetables, all right?"

"Yes, that'd be good." It was one of the only things that had sounded good in the last few days.

"I'm sure your activity will be restricted for a time," she continued, "but before too long, I bet you'll be out digging in the dirt."

"How 'restricted'?" The word struck a chord deep within me; I had grown up freely roaming the mountains.

"Kate, you've got to understand that you're dealing with a progressive, deadly disease. If you don't get plenty of bed rest and confine your daily activities for a while, you'll never get better. You're going to be told over and over again to be patient with your recovery. But, honey, Pelham is a good place with excellent doctors. They're not there to make your life miserable. They're there to save it. Let's just wait and see what they prescribe for you, okay? Just rest a little bit now. It won't be much longer till we're there." She patted my hand as a sign of support and comfort, but I was beginning to feel like a child about the same age as my son.

I realized that for the first time since I'd become a woman, doing exactly what I wanted to do, in a life of my own choosing, I was faced with the unpleasant fact that many choices would be made for me by others, others who didn't know a thing about me. They wouldn't know my likes and dislikes, my fears, passions, or the many things that brought me joy or sadness. To them, I would just be another patient with an ID number, and yet, they'd be orchestrating all of my days and nights—my life—at least for a time. And because I wanted to get well and pick up the pieces of my life again, I knew I would go along with those choices, like them or not.

Suddenly, we turned off the highway onto a private drive. Leaning forward in my seat so that I could see exactly where we were going, I realized we'd arrived at Pelham. The entrance was fronted by two large brick pillars that were connected by an iron arch with the words "Pelham State Hospital" welded in place across the archway. The entire complex was fenced, though just the main entryway had the dramatic brick and iron façade. Though the high brick wall continued off to the right and left for a short distance, beyond that, a simple wire fence enclosed the entire property. Topping the wire fencing was barbed wire which would deter even the most ambitious would-be escapees from attempting to climb it.

Just before the gated entrance was a small brick guard house with windows on all sides of it. As we pulled up, a man in a security uniform stepped out. "Back already?" he asked Harold, then turning to look at the passengers in the back and recognizing my aunt, he continued, "Oh, hey, Nurse Pierce! I didn't know you'd be back today. How was your trip?"

"Real good, Leo, thanks. Leo, this is my niece, Kathryn Cavanaugh." Then, "Kathryn, this is Leo Sacks. He keeps a good eye on this place."

"Good to meet you, Miz Cavanaugh," he said, tipping his police officer–style cap. "Welcome to Pelham." Then, reaching inside the gatehouse, he maneuvered something that caused the massive right half of the gate to swing open, allowing us through.

The driveway was long and curved in places, and evenly lined with tall white pines. In the distance, I could make out a large, imposing brick building that was gothic in style and several stories high, with wings that jutted off to each side of it. Behind the building was some kind of giant tower. My aunt told me that it was the complex's power house and laundry building. The facility generated its own electricity, so even in the event that the rest of the world was plunged into total darkness, Pelham State Hospital would remain up and running, with staff and patients alike going about their business in clean clothing, all while lights burned brightly and machinery continued its mechanical humming.

As we pulled into the circular driveway in front of the main building, Harold put the car in park and his chauffeur's cap back on. "Here we are, ladies," he announced, opening my door and holding an umbrella over me as I got out. Aunt Harriet scooted out the opposite door and hurried up the steps to the deep covered porch. The drizzle hadn't let up since we'd left the train station. If anything, it was coming down a bit harder. Making small talk about the weather not being very cooperative, he walked me up the steps and joined my aunt.

"Harold, would you please bring Kathryn's luggage in and leave mine in the trunk. If you don't mind, I'll have you drop me off at home when I'm done getting Kathryn settled in. It shouldn't be too long. They'll want to take her right from admittance to the shower and then to her room. I'd say maybe an hour. If you have somewhere else you need to go, though, just leave my—"

"No, no." Harold interrupted her. "I'll stay right here and wait for you. If another driver is needed, Carl is around today. I saw him pulling in as I was going out to pick you up. You go ahead and get Mrs. Cavanaugh taken care of."

As they spoke, I looked around, taking in my surroundings. I noticed that there were many chaise lounge–style chairs neatly lined up to either side of us. I assumed they were there for the patients so that they could be out in the fresh air even when the weather was bad. The imposing column that Harold stood next to dwarfed him in both height and width, and the front porch was lined with six of them. The roof that the columns supported came to an apex, and following the angle of the roofline were beautifully painted tiles and medallions, some with religious symbols and some that were purely decorative.

"Ready, honey? Kathryn?" My aunt gently touched my arm to get my attention.

"What? Oh, yes." She'd startled me. "I'm sorry. I was a million miles away." *And wouldn't I give anything to be exactly that*, I thought.

"C'mon. Let's get admissions behind you so that you can settle in. I know you're worn out."

She was correct. I *was* worn out—well beyond it. Physically, I felt my body wasting away. In just the last two days I'd dropped more weight, so that the traveling suit I'd worn on the train to Howling Cut was a size too big now. It seemed as though my body was being eaten away. And my coughing had gotten much worse in just a short time, too. I felt like I was coughing up my insides and breaking ribs as I did so. The amount of blood that I'd been expectorating had increased as my weight had decreased. It seemed as though the weight I'd lost had been in blood alone. I was awake coughing for the better part of the night, and I was running a fever. I had dark circles under my eyes, and my skin had grown paler. I was looking more and more like the perfect model for a Christmas Seals poster. The sale of the seals had come about in order to fund yearly examinations to detect the early onset of tuberculosis in school children. If the posters were intended to scare them into getting their X-rays taken, then I would soon be the perfect candidate. I was a tubercular, both inside and out now. I looked like one, and felt like one.

As Aunt Harriet held the door to the admissions office open for me, I stood frozen in place, unable to move. I literally stood at the threshold of a strange and frightening new life, in a strange and frightening new place. But in order to return to the life that was so familiar and so loved, I had to experience this. As terrifying as it was, I realized that this, too, was a chapter of my story, and I could choose to live it with dignity and determination, or bemoan my lot in life by cowering in bed and doing nothing to help advance my recovery. And with that clear understanding, along with exhausted resignation, I stepped over the threshold and through the door, unsure if I would ever cross back over again.

PART TWO

CHAPTER 11

Rules and Rebels

The high ceilings and long hallway gave the room a cold, sterile feeling. Gone were the warm bricks that made up the building's façade, and in their place were stark white walls that were interrupted by heavy dark oak doors spaced several yards apart. I realized that there wasn't one admission office, but many. At some point, there must have been an enormous influx of people to have needed so many offices to check people in and, I hoped, check them out, as well.

Aunt Harriet told me to wait where I was, then she walked into an open office door several yards down the hallway on our left. After a moment of muffled conversation, she stepped back into the hallway and waved me in. I was quickly introduced to the admissions nurse, who immediately handed me a rule book that was nearly as thick as an encyclopedia, along with a form to sign stating that I'd read the book. When I was shown where to put my signature, I looked up at the nurse with a look of confusion. Laughingly, she told me that the first rule was that the patient must sign the form. No one actually reads the book, not at first anyway, she'd explained.

"Then why have it?" I asked, incredulous.

"Dunno," she'd flippantly answered. "We just do, and everyone does—sign the form, I mean." When I told her that I wanted to read about what would be expected of me, she said she hoped I'd brought food along to keep me going because only after I signed the form could the hospital legally feed me.

Aunt Harriet rolled her eyes at me and whispered, "Just sign the damn thing. No one follows what's in that stupid book anyway. It's just protocol." And so I signed it.

After filling out more paperwork and saying a quick good-bye to my aunt, assuring her I'd be fine, I was escorted to the shower deep in the interior of the building. Every new arrival was required to take a shower, "Because," the nurse's aide informed me, "we can never be sure what's carried in off the streets." I objected because I'd just taken a shower that morning before getting on the train. My objection fell on deaf ears, however. The washing started out uncomfortably because it was overseen by an aide who stood sentinel outside of the shower, which had no curtain. But it became downright humiliating when she took the liberty of helping me wash those harder-to-reach areas, and quite invasively and roughly so.

As I was being scrubbed raw, I told the aide that if she rubbed any harder, I was sure she'd draw blood, to which she laughingly replied that it wouldn't be the first time. With that, I firmly stripped the bar of harsh soap from her hand, not saying a word as I did so, but pinning her with a look which promised that should she try to continue to wash me, I might not be the only bloodied one by the time the shower was over. She not only allowed me to finish washing myself, but silently handed me the shampoo bottle when I handed the offensive lye-smelling soap back to her. Once I was done, she gave me a towel, which I used to dry myself without her assistance. I was not allowed to put my street clothes back on; they would be thoroughly laundered and returned to me later. Instead, I was given a hospital gown, robe, and slippers to put on, then reminded to grab my purse and packet of paperwork, which I'd set on a chair, and told to follow her.

We exited the building through a tunnel system that connected every building of the facility. The tunnels were not only a convenient way of moving from place to place while staying out of the elements, but also provided the facility's heating system. Large pipes snaked their way through the tunnels' ceilings, piping hot air into each building on the property. I noticed that there was also a steel cable strung along close to the top of the tunnel, and running the length of it. The cable seemed to be some kind of pulley system, with large hooks hanging down and spaced a couple of feet apart from each other. "What are those used for?" I asked.

"To move stuff," she answered.

"What kind of stuff?"

"Just stuff. Equipment, giant bags of food, bodies . . ."

"Bodies!" I slowed down.

The aide turned to look at me. "Miss, this ain't the Ritz. Folks are here 'cause they's sick. Some are lucky enough to make it out on their own two feet, while others need a little help. So"—she pointed toward the pulley system—"we help 'em get out." She laughed at her dark humor. "It ain't good for the other patients to see folks they know being pulled out of here on a stretcher and shoved into a hearse. We try to be thoughtful and do it so's they can't see 'em go.

"Now, let's talk about the livin' part instead of the dyin'." As we continued on toward the building where I would be housed, she proceeded to explain the daily regimen of meal times, rest times, social time (if permitted), and bedtime. She told me there was a schedule in the packet of information that I'd been given at the administration building, so there was no need to worry about forgetting it. That was a good thing since I heard only half of what she was saying. My eyes and mind were still stuck on the hooks and pulley system above us.

When we finally reached the TB ward, I was introduced to the nurse there, Dana Montane. The first thing she said after greeting me was that I was to call her Dana. "I only know my mother-in-law as Mrs. Montane. Anyone calls me that, I take it as an insult!" She laughed warmly. Dana was quite tall and reminded me a little bit of Jane Russell. She had thick, dark, wavy hair, much like mine, actually, but shorter. Her eyes were a soft brown, and her smile was genuine and comforting. She turned to the aide, thanked her for her help, and told her that she'd take it from there. Dana asked me a few basic questions, then suggested that I meet the other "girls" in my ward.

There were three patients in the ward at that time, the fewest, Dana explained, in the nearly twelve years she'd been there. The other patients were Roberta Truman, Annabelle Ryetower, and Peggy Porter. All three women stopped what they were doing when we walked in. Almost in unison, they greeted Dana, while looking me over with great interest. When Dana introduced me, Roberta and Peggy remained in bed, but Annabelle came over and shook my hand. She was a large woman, not fat but solid, and she looked about as strong as she was tall. Her hair was medium length, parted in the middle and jet black. Her eyes were a perfect match. To some, her gaze might have seemed hard, but she reminded me of an eagle, ever alert and ready to react. She looked both intelligent and energetic. In looks and temperament, she reminded me of an exotic gypsy.

Dana pointed out my bed by the window, and the nurse call-button attached to my headboard, which would ring at the nurses' station should I ever need assistance, day or night. Then, she walked me over to the lockers at the far end of the ward, showed me which one was mine, and told me that I'd be given the combination number for the lock on it. With relief, I saw that my suitcase had been placed in it. It had obviously been brought up by an aide while I was showering. There were hangers for my clothing, cubby holes for incidentals, a fresh bar of soap, toothpaste, and shampoo.

"So," Dana continued, "that's all of the grand tour for now." She smiled at me, gauging, no doubt, how I was handling my orientation to this new place, to this new life. "You okay?" She placed her hand on my shoulder and looked at me closely. There was genuine concern in her voice and eyes.

"Supper will be served shortly," she said after glancing up at the clock on the wall. There were two in the ward, one at each end. "I hope you're hungry, kiddo. 'Cause if you're not, they'll give you something to make sure you are. We like our patients to be as plump as little piggies." She laughed, and I knew there was no sarcasm or condescension in her remark. I could tell in just the short time that I'd been with her that she truly cared about her patients, or "her girls," as she often called the women on her ward. "From just looking at you, I think you're strong enough to go to the dining room tonight, rather than having a tray brought to you. If Dr. Ludlow wants you on complete bed rest, then he can order that tomorrow, but tonight you'll go with Roberta and Annabelle to the dining room." Then, turning to Peggy, she asked if she knew how long Dr. McCann had ordered total bed rest for her. Indefinitely, Peggy answered. "Well, hopefully that'll change before too long. Just keep doing what he wants you to do, Peg, and you'll be right as rain." Her words said one thing, while her eyes said another. Dana wished us all a good night then, and left the room.

I put my pocketbook and paperwork in my locker, but brought the rule book back to bed with me. I saw the women taking glances at me as I moved about, but they said nothing. When they did speak, it was only to each other and quietly so. They later explained to me that they tried to be respectful of new patients because not everyone was in a chatty mood when they first arrived, and they understood that. They'd learned to give the newcomers a little space in which to settle themselves or, perhaps, resign themselves to their new situation.

I sat down in the chair next to my bed, with the rule book in my lap, conscious of the quiet conversation taking place around me. I didn't think they were talking about me, but it made me uneasy that no one had addressed me other than to say hello. This first night would be even longer if I didn't try to break the ice. "Have any of you actually read this thing?" I asked, holding up the rule book.

"I got to chapter three." Annabelle jumped right in, as though she'd been hoping I'd speak up. "After that, I only used it as a sedative to put me to sleep." They all laughingly agreed.

"That's the truth," Peggy piped in. She was sitting up in bed, but remained under her covers. She had not gotten up since I'd come in. She looked all of eighteen but was actually twenty-five, as was Annabelle. The two of them had gone through grammar and high school together. Then, after having gone their separate ways after graduation, with Peggy marrying her high school boyfriend and settling down to raise a family in Asheville, and Annabelle moving on to the University of Georgia to earn a degree in art history, the two had had a bittersweet reunion at Pelham. They had been admitted within weeks of each other, three months ago.

Peggy Porter looked like a living porcelain doll with her long, flaming red hair, fair skin, and pale blue eyes. Her husband, Joseph, I learned, was a foreman at one of the quartz mining companies outside of Fork Mountain, and was doing an admirable job working his way up the ladder despite his young age. Peggy had worked part-time at the library but otherwise stayed at home, contentedly playing the part of housewife and hoping to start a family right away. After a couple of frustrating years of trying, she'd gotten pregnant and it seemed as though they were finally on their way to starting the large family they'd dreamed of having. But tragedy struck when Peggy tested positive for TB. She had been showing signs of the illness for quite some time before it was finally confirmed, but she had waited to be tested for it because she'd thought her increasing fatigue was due to the pregnancy and her weight loss to a lengthy case of morning sickness. But her suspicion that it might be something other than the symptoms of early pregnancy were verified with the onset of the first bloody phlegm. By the time she saw the doctor about it, both lungs were infected with tuberculosis, and the disease was rapidly progressing. She had multiple lesions and three cavities, two of which were quite large. Rounds of antibiotics were immediately started and she was admitted to Pelham within a week. Six days later, Peggy lost the baby. She was devastated, which didn't help her recovery process, and everyone wondered if the heaviness of her despair over the miscarriage was taking more of a toll on her than the tuberculosis was. From what Annabelle would later tell me, Peggy had always been the soft-spoken, shy girl in class, but never so withdrawn. However, along with the loss of her child came the loss of her interest in life, for the doctors had told her that it was unlikely that she could, or should, conceive again. Overnight, it seemed her once bright blue eyes had dimmed to a pale shade.

Roberta Truman, whose bed was just two over from mine, had gone to the bathroom, which was at the far end of the room. As she was making her way slowly back down the aisle between the ward's two rows of beds, she was obviously listening. "Listen," she said, crawling back beneath her covers, "if you need something to read, we have stacks of books. All the rules you'll need to know are in one of those little pamphlets in that packet of paperwork they gave to you on intake. That's pretty much the ABCs of what you can and cannot do."

Roberta was middle-aged, rounder and shorter than the rest of us. Her hair was thick, rather short, and light brown. Her eyes were almost identical in color. At first impression, she seemed upbeat and friendly, but I was later warned that one of the things that kept her energy level up was gossip. It wasn't just limited to the women in our ward; every patient was fair game for her wagging tongue.

Later that evening, when Roberta was in the bathroom brushing her teeth, Annabelle advised me to keep letters, diaries, anything personal that I wanted to keep private, out of sight or locked up. Otherwise, there was a pretty good likelihood that Roberta Truman would find them.

"Tell you what," Roberta continued. "Let's save Kathryn the aggravation of having to read the rule book or any of that other baloney! Ladies, how 'bout we recite a few of those rules we know all too well. Rule number one: 'No whining. There is never a valid excuse for a patient to whine. It benefits no one.' And most especially the staff," she sarcastically added.

Annabelle spoke up. "And rule number two, 'No crying in front of the other patients.' For God's sake, never do that," Annabelle dramatically amended. "'And do NOT, under any circumstances, discuss your illness. It only depresses the other patients.' Or so says rule number three in the book." Peggy started laughing at Annabelle's animated recitation, which led to a serious coughing fit, though no one paid much attention.

"Is she all right?" I quietly asked Roberta.

"Good heavens, no!" she answered, which struck all of them as extremely funny, all but me. It seemed insensitive and callous. I couldn't know at the time, however, that their so-called callousness and insensitivity were small pieces of armor in their constant battle to survive, both emotionally and physically. The rules about no whining and no crying were supposed to help the patient maintain a positive attitude. But what had been forgotten was that these rules applied to human beings, and human beings had emotions that required expression, in one way or another. And if the rule-makers vetoed the right to cry and complain, then the patients found other ways to purge their feelings, through humor, sarcasm, and at times, downright defiance.

"Rule number four," Annabelle continued. "This one's my favorite. 'Interaction with patients of the opposite sex should be kept to a minimum, and should only take place at appropriate times and in appropriate situations; such as during social events, activity time, or in classes. Under no circumstance will sexual behavior of any sort be tolerated. Any violation will be cause for immediate discharge, and denial of future admission to the institution.'" She wagged her finger at us. "So forget cousining, y'all."

"What's 'cousining'?" I'd never heard the expression before.

"That's what the san—the sanatorium—calls a little tryst," Annabelle continued. "You know, a little one-on-one time—literally and figuratively speaking." Everyone laughed, including me. "It's not really cousins having fun together," she explained. "That's just the name someone at the san gave it." Suddenly, she grew quite serious. "Look, sugar, people get lonely in this place. The average age of people with TB is between fifteen and forty-five. Now, I don't know how old you are, but I feel fairly certain that it's somewhere between those ages. Hormones are bouncing around, and in all honesty, folks are bouncing off the walls 'cause they're sexually frustrated and seriously bored. They're missing home, their children, and their spouses. And, most especially, their spouses' big—"

"Rule number five," Peggy quickly interrupted, giving her close friend a reprimanding look. She'd finally stopped coughing but was hoarse and still winded. She wanted to take part in the camaraderie, though, which earned my respect early on, and she never once caused it to falter. "'The consumption of alcohol is strictly forbidden. Possess—'" She began to cough again so Annabelle finished for her.

"'Possession of it will result in an immediate discharge.' Well, hell, ladies, I don't know about y'all, but a highball would sure do me good about now. How 'bout it!" And with that, Miss Annabelle Ryetower, once the lovely dark-haired, dark-eyed belle of the ball from the upper crust of Asheville, whipped out a half-empty bottle of Old Crow whiskey from beneath some clothing in her nightstand drawer.

It seemed each rule, or deviation from it, was more surprising than the last. "How'd you get that in . . . ?"

"She's got rich beaus," Peggy quickly explained. "They'd do anything for her." Peggy looked downright proud of Annabelle for having that kind of sway with men.

Holding it high for all of us to see, as if it were a fresh scalp, Annabelle practically did a pirouette across the floor to the pitcher of ice water that Dana had filled and set on my nightstand.

"Everyone hand me your glass," she said, going from bed to bed with both bottle and pitcher before returning to her own.

"Only a tad for me, but straight up," I said, laughing as I held my cup while she poured.

"Just a smidge for me, too." Peggy looked like a naughty child at a slumber party.

Roberta said she'd take what we didn't want, and after pouring herself a hefty amount as well, Annabelle held her glass high. "To the bugs!" She tossed her whiskey back.

"Bugs?" I didn't much like them and definitely not enough to toast them.

"*We're* the bugs." Peggy laughed, looking flushed after having her "smidge." "That's what they call us, 'cause we have the bug—the crude, the virus, the disease, whatever you want to call it. We're known as bugs."

That unsettled me badly. I didn't know what to say. So, that was how society saw us—no better than *bugs*? I tossed my shot back, then held out my glass for a refill. Annabelle kindly obliged.

CHAPTER 12

Patients and Patience

Annabelle and Roberta drank two full drinks, while I, apologetically, couldn't finish my second one, nor Peggy her first. Whether by coincidence or not, her coughing subsided, and I was glad for the poor little thing. Just in the short time I'd been around her, I'd seen her tire, which wasn't surprising given the violent nature of her hacking cough.

"Well, ladies, that wraps up cocktail hour for this evening. Shall we get ready to dine?" Annabelle had stored away her bottle and was in the midst of a vigorous stretch. She was already dressed, but Roberta, Peggy, and I were in our pajamas.

"Give me a sec," Roberta said as she headed for her locker, which spurred me in that direction, too.

"Peggy, you aren't able to come?" I asked her as I was attempting to zip up the back of my dress. Watching how the other women were dressing, I'd chosen a simple, long-sleeved brown dress with white piping along the hem and rounded collars. It was plain and conservative, but the last thing I wanted to do was stand out, and most especially on my first night there.

"Here, turn around," Annabelle said when she saw me struggling. "Peggy's on FBR—full bed rest. She can't leave the room except for tests. If her doctor knew she was drinking and gettin' all excited this afternoon, he'd shoot us all. They'll bring a tray in for her any minute."

"I'm sorry," I said to Peggy, though I wasn't sure why. But I *felt* sorry—sorry she was so ill, sorry she had to be left alone to eat, sorry her eyes had lost their brightness, sorry she was classified as a bug. Sorry, sorry, sorry! Unexpectedly, I felt my eyes welling up. "You need the bathroom right now?" I asked Roberta, who was standing just outside of it.

"Naw, s'all yours," she slurred.

Hurrying past her, I quickly closed the door, turned the faucet on as hard as it would go, then sat down on the toilet and cried. I cried for all of the sorries that this sorry world owed to every person who was ripped from their homes, their lives and families, and made to endure the torture of this disease; and the separation and degradation that was a result of it. I cried many of the tears that I'd held in all afternoon.

After five minutes or so, I heard Annabelle softly call to me through the door. "Kathryn, should we have a tray sent up for you?" I told her that it wasn't necessary, that I'd be ready in a minute. "You take your time, sugar. You take all the time you need. We're not going anywhere." And that was my greatest fear of all; that none of us were, unless it was by that pulley system in the tunnels.

I pulled myself together, washed my face, brushed my teeth, and taking a steadying breath, opened the door to the expectant faces of the women who were surely wondering if I was doing myself in, or making myself up. There was almost a collective sigh when they saw me emerge, relatively unscathed except for my red eyes and nose.

"All righty, then. Let's see what poison they're serving up tonight." Annabelle's joviality sounded forced. I knew that the women understood exactly what I was feeling, but were being tactful and trying not to embarrass me by making a fuss over me. Instead, Roberta walked up to me and gave me a reassuring hug but said nothing, while Annabelle told Peggy we'd be back shortly and asked her if there was anything from the dining hall she wanted. Then the two women ushered me out of the room to the same elevator I'd ridden up in on my arrival.

"Where's the dining room?" I asked, still sounding congested from crying.

"In an adjoining building connected to the first floor. Just follow the smell—or run from it, which sometimes we're tempted to do." Annabelle smiled.

"Oh, stop it, Annabelle! You'll have the poor girl gagging before she's had a chance to take one bite. It's really not bad, Kathryn. It just gets tiring eating the same old things, in the same old place, with the same old people. No offense."

"None taken." I smiled. "How many patients eat together? Are there different shifts? Are we totally isolated from non-tubercular patients?"

"Patience, patience, new patient. All will be revealed."

We were just coming to the end of the hall, and reached a set of double doors with a brass plaque that read, "Women's Dining Hall." Without slowing down, Annabelle and Roberta each pushed open a side of the double doors and we walked down an enclosed corridor to an attached building.

The room was larger than I'd thought it would be, big enough to hold about 150 people. However, there were both men and women eating there, though they did not sit together. As we made our way toward a cafeteria-style line, I realized that many sets of eyes were upon me. I was the new kid on the block, and it wasn't too hard to figure out that in a place where not much changed except for the people and their prognoses, any newcomers were of interest to those who had been there for a while.

"I thought this was the women's dining room."

"It was," Roberta clarified, "until about ten years ago. A lot's changed here in the last decade. Used to be that not only were men and women separated at all times, but they weren't allowed to say so much as hello if they passed each other in the hallway. Shoot, you could be disciplined pretty severely. They'd put restrictions on visitors, or social activities like movie night, or going to the san's beauty parlor—that kind of thing."

"There's a beauty parlor here?"

"Not anymore," Annabelle said. "No money for it now that it's a state-run hospital. The good thing, though, is that they're not as strict as they used to be—either that or they don't really care. I haven't figured out which one yet. But I guess the powers that be realized that if folks are determined to have a little roll in the hay, they'll figure out a way to do it, and that telling them they can't say hi to each other on a walkway wasn't helping to prevent it." She laughed, shaking her head as she handed me a tray. We moved down the line. "But old habits die hard, I guess, and men have always been told to eat on one side, and women on the other."

"Whatcha havin' tonight, honey?" A pencil-thin, dark-as-night woman was standing before me, serving spoon in hand and vats of food between us.

"Evenin', Abilene," Annabelle interjected before I could answer the woman. "This is Kathryn, and it's her first night here at the Ritz. Kathryn, this is the grande dame of the Ritz, Mrs. Abilene Greene, from—where else?—Abilene, Texas!"

"Happy to meet you." I smiled.

"No, you ain't. If'n this is your first night here, you ain't pleased at meetin' nobody! Matter of fact, I'd be willing to bet that you hate just about everybody in the world right now, but you'll be okay. And I gotta tell ya, good food's gonna help you. Now, what can I get for ya? You have a choice of two of everything. I serve ya the meats. Tonight, we got pork chops, meatloaf, fried catfish, short ribs, and roasted chicken. So, what'll it be?"

"I'll have a pork chop, I guess."

"All righty." She put one on a plate but didn't hand it to me. "Now, what else?"

"Oh, no, I only need one meat. Thanks, though." I started to reach for the plate, but Abilene actually pulled it farther away from me.

"Miz Kathryn, you got to have two. It's the rules. Didn't they tell you they're gonna fatten you up or kill ya tryin'?" She laughed at her own joke; either that, or she was laughing at the absurdity of it.

"Oh, Lord. Well . . . okay." I looked over the selections. "All right, let me have a little chicken, please." Just the amount of food on my plate was starting to make me nauseous, and we hadn't even gotten to the vegetables, starches, breads, or desserts. "Thank you, Mrs. Greene," I said as she handed me my plate.

"It's Abilene, and you're welcome, darlin'. You need anything in the area of food, you jus' let me know."

"Thanks." I smiled at her and moved on to the vegetables. Then, after working my way through the line, I pushed my heavy tray of collard greens, fried squash, macaroni and cheese, cornbread, and fruit salad (we were required to take two meats, two vegetables and one each of a starch, bread, and dessert), down to the end of the line, where I was given a bundle of silverware wrapped in a cotton dinner napkin and offered my choice of sweet or unsweetened iced tea, or lemonade. Pitchers of coffee and ice water were already on each table. I followed Roberta as she selected an empty table toward the middle of the room, away from the chilly draft coming through the many huge windows lining each wall. I was sure that I'd never get used to open windows during every season of the year, and I prayed I wouldn't be experiencing all four of them. *Don't think about it,* I told myself. *Thoughts like that'll weigh me down more than this food.*

I was anxious to meet with Dr. Ludlow first thing in the morning to discuss his views on my X-rays and sputum test, both of which had been sent to him from the clinic at Flat Top. The test results weren't even a week old, but I wondered if I'd have to repeat them immediately.

One of the first things I wanted to ask him was how often I could have visitors, most especially my husband and son. I ached for them. I'd been apart from Geoffrey for less than three weeks, but it felt more like three years. And I'd been away from Donnie for less than twelve hours, but it felt like a lifetime. I was anxious to know how long Dr. Ludlow thought I might be at Pelham. One thing I knew, though, was that I wanted this damned disease to be treated as aggressively as possible so that I could get out of here and back home to my little boy, my husband, my work at the Children's Home, and just back to living life in general.

Roberta interrupted my thoughts. "Think you'll have enough to eat?" It was a running joke in the san that none of us would die from whatever disease had brought us there, but from obesity instead. However, the truth of the matter was that tuberculosis patients rapidly lost weight and one of the main reasons was our lack of appetite. I hadn't had much of one for a few weeks. I took a bite of the greens. That was the easiest thing to eat. It was comfort food. It reminded me of home, of Mama putting a slab of salt pork, or what some called "white bacon," into a pot of them. She'd simmer the greens for hours, and every hour or so I'd lift the lid, take a peek, and have a forkful, *Just to make sure they're comin' along okay.*

They all right? Mama would ask. I would confirm that they surely were, and, hour after hour, the amount decreased by several forkfuls. The other comfort food was cornbread. Lord, how I loved it! I loved it most especially with home-churned rich butter slathered all over it, or with maple syrup poured over the top and dripping down the sides. I loved it broken up into my bowl of greens, floating around in the greasy pot liquor. And I loved cornbread just plain. I had once declared that if God didn't provide us with cornbread and greens upon our arrival at the pearly gates, he was obviously a Yankee, which would force me to check out what my other options might be as far as where I'd be spending eternity. Cornbread and greens were Heaven to me, so it went without saying that I expected the good Lord to have plenty of them on the menu.

"Do they really expect us to eat all this?"

"Of course not." Annabelle laughed, reaching for the sugar bowl. "But they know that if we only take a tiny amount of food, we'll only eat part of that. So I guess their strategy is if we take more, chances are we'll eat more. But it's nauseating, I know. There's enough there to make a lumberjack gag. So, Kathryn, you doin' all right?" she asked, diving right in. Her dark eyes scrutinized mine carefully. "You don't have to be polite with us, you know."

"Oh, I won't be—I mean, I'll be honest with you. Well, it's all a little overwhelming at first. It's just too . . ." My voice cracked and I didn't finish. If I said another word I'd start crying again.

Roberta, who was sitting on my left, gently took my hand. "It's all right, Kathryn. Everyone here felt the same way you did on their first day. You'd be an odd one if you didn't feel the way you do. But we're here to tell you, you'll adjust. You'll start to feel comfortable and then you'll be—"

"I don't want to feel comfortable." I softly blew my nose, then started coughing again. I'd been coughing more in the last hour, and I wondered if being tired and upset could actually aggravate my symptoms. Roberta and Annabelle sat patiently, waiting for the coughing to subside. When it did, I continued. "I don't want this place to start feeling like it's home. I don't want to . . ." I realized how pitiful I sounded. I was already breaking one of the rules: no whining. "Oh, Lord, I'm sorry. I sound like . . ." I didn't finish my sentence. I could feel the sob waiting to escape, but this time I felt like crying over my shameful behavior. It helped no one. I took a sip of tea to stifle any other sounds and stared down at my fruit salad.

"Don't you apologize, honey." Roberta's eyes were warm, the color of honey. "You just eat what you want and head back to the ward anytime. This isn't a jail, you know, though I bet it feels that way right now. You want me to walk you back?" I looked up and realized she was on the verge of tears herself. The last thing I wanted to do was upset anyone. I'd already done enough of that to my family over the last several days.

"No, no," I assured her, giving her a weak smile. It was all I could muster at the moment. "I'm fine, really. I'm so sorry, y'all. I hate that I'm being this way. Maybe after a good night's sleep, I'll feel better."

"Then you'll be the first one to feel that way on their second day here. C'mon, see if you can eat just a little more," Annabelle encouraged me. "Then, if you want to, we'll go for a short walk around the grounds."

"Yes . . . yes, I'd like that." I made myself finish most of the cornbread and greens, and a bite or two of the fruit salad. The meat was left untouched. I just couldn't force any of it down. We put away our trays, then left the dining room, with many sets of eyes following our exit. Out in the corridor, we walked about halfway down, then, instead of taking the elevator on our left, we exited through a door on our right that led us outside. The administration building stood like a sentinel at the end of the long drive, which I'd driven down earlier that day. It seemed like a lifetime ago.

"C'mon." Annabelle directed us down the right fork of a walkway. "We'll take you over to the koi pond."

"The what pond?"

"The koi pond. Koi are a Japanese fish; pretty to look at but not good to eat. The pond is part of a water garden. When this place used to be only a tuberculosis sanatorium, they wanted the patients to spend a lot of time outside, just as we're supposed to do now. And to get people to go out when all they wanted to do was stay in—sleeping, coughing, spitting—they decided to make the outside a better place to be than the inside. So they built different things, like the koi pond, and put in gardens, both flower and vegetable, and a greenhouse. They also put in gazebos, a small band shelter—the list goes on and on. Some of those things have been neglected over the years, or even torn down since this place became more of a psychiatric hospital. Nowadays they try to keep most of the patients *inside*. There's less opportunity to make a run for it, or get into some other crazy kind of trouble."

"So they're pretty much under lock and key, day and night?" I asked.

"Some yes and some no. The criminally insane, of course, are kept locked up, and so are the ones who have the potential to be dangerous to themselves or others. But others, who may be loopy but harmless, are allowed to be outside more. Speak of the devil!"

Annabelle stopped, so Roberta and I did, too, and looked around to see what she was looking at.

A group of patients was gathered around a man who was talking to someone or something up in an oak tree. Most of the patients were wearing hospital-issued clothing, the men in lightweight pants and scrub-style tops, the women in shift-style dresses. Some were still wearing their pajamas. All of their clothing was light green, whereas the pajamas I had been given were light blue. Non-psych patients were allowed to wear street clothing and pajamas of their choice, but all psych patients were required to wear the institution-issued clothing. It was easier for the staff to identify them that way.

The man who was looking up into the tree was wearing street clothes, however. He seemed to be in his early thirties, with wavy brown hair the color of coffee with a lot of cream in it, longer than most men wore it. He wasn't dressed like one of the doctors, but he seemed to be directing things; perhaps he was a therapist, or even a visitor? But visiting hours were between 7:00 and 8:00 p.m., and I knew it was only 6:50 because I'd checked the clock in the dining room as we were leaving, knowing that I had a schedule to follow now, and I didn't want to be reprimanded like a tardy schoolgirl, especially not on my first day there.

"What's Philip doin' now?" Roberta stood there with her hands on her ample hips.

"Probably trying to talk Captain Crow down." Annabelle laughed. "Case in point," she said, turning to me. "Here you have a nutty buddy up in a tree who we call Captain Crow 'cause he thinks he's a bird. He's harmless though, so they let him have some outside time. But someone has to keep an eye on him, or he shimmies up a tree. He's been known to sit on a nest, 'to relieve the mother bird so she can get some rest,' and he'll swear on a stack of Bibles that he can communicate with birds—that they understand him as well as he understands them. He'll also swear on that same stack of Bibles that he was a bird in a previous life—a crow, and that he was killed by a cat. Lord God, help us all. I swear, I've seen that man eat worms an—" Annabelle started coughing hard. Reaching into her pocket, she pulled out a handkerchief and spat into it. "Good, not as much as yesterday."

"Here, let's take a breather on this bench," Roberta suggested. "We can watch the spectacle from here." Annabelle sat down hard, breathing heavily. Of the three women in the ward, Roberta seemed the least sick. Annabelle didn't seem nearly as bad off as Peggy, but she coughed more than Roberta, and from my limited observations, I seemed to be closest to Annabelle in frequency of coughing.

"How long have y'all been here?" I asked.

"Too long," Annabelle answered immediately. "I've been here almost three months, and Roberta's been here about, what"—she turned to her—"four months now, Berta?"

"Five, but who's counting? Hope it won't be like last time, though. That was a thirteen-month stay. Too long for my liking."

"You've been here before, Roberta?" Now I remembered her saying during supper that a lot had changed over the last ten years. It never occurred to me that some of these folks might have come back. *Lord God, please don't let me be one of them.*

"In '44," Roberta said in answer to my question. "I was here for over a year. Lordy, I was bad off! I know everyone wondered if I was gonna come out feet first." She grimaced. "Poor Bob. He *did* come out feet first. He was my husband," she explained. "Both of us were working in a factory that made bicycle parts, down in Franklin. There was an outbreak of TB, and we both got it. We came here together. I made it out but he didn't. Now, here I am again!"

"I'm sorry, Roberta. I didn't know. Do you have children?"

"One son, grown and gone. He's making the military his career. He's stationed in Fort Bragg, and still single. And I remarried two years ago—a fella from my church, Jim Truman."

"That's good, Roberta," I responded, but was only half listening. I was still trying to digest the fact that recurrences of TB were quite common. "What's the likelihood of getting TB more than once?"

"Oh, now, sugar, don't go worryin' about that," Annabelle said to reassure me. "Some people just have weak constitutions, and they get sick more than others. Those are the ones who come back. Then there're the ones who don't follow the doctors' orders and they do too much, or too little, and they have to come back, but then it's their own fault. And with some, it's just plain bad luck. Anyway, don't think about that."

"I didn't think about that either," Roberta joined in. "And look where it got me!"

"Try to keep that glass half full, Roberta." Annabelle smiled but sounded slightly annoyed. I thought of my glass-half-full, positive-thinking mother. Oh, Lord, how I missed her!

"I am, Annabelle. I am," Roberta countered. "Oh, mercy! Would you look at that!"

Annabelle and I were already looking toward the noise coming from the crowd at the tree. The man in street clothes, Philip, had hoisted himself up into the oak tree and was crawling across a massive limb toward Captain Crow, who was sitting at the end of it. No one said a word as we waited to see what would happen, and because the bench we sat on was perched on a small rise directly across from the oak, we had a bird's-eye view. We could also make out some of what they were saying.

". . . Okay, I understand that, but you have to come down, or they'll bring you down with a net, Captain. You want to be treated like the dignified bird you are and not a lowly butterfly, right?"

"Oh, hell no!" objected the Captain. "I ain't no butterfly! No way! They's all delicate-like, even the males. No, sir! I ain't no butterfly!"

"Well, then," Philip continued, "don't give 'em any reason to treat you like one. C'mon, man, don't shame yourself. Let's get on down now, okay?" He started backing up, obviously in the hope that he'd draw the Captain with him. And he did. Slowly the two made their way down through the branches to the lowest one, then, hanging off it, gently dropped down. Everyone clapped, including two nurses and a couple of aides.

"Is he a therapist?"

"Philip McAllister? No, he's a TB patient, that's why he's in street clothes," Annabelle explained. "He was eating in the dining room when we got there, but left before we did. Those guys standing around the tree in street clothes are also TB patients, but the nutty buddies are wearing their pajamas. The psych ward tuberculars eat supper early, on the shift right before us. Afterwards, they get a little outdoor time, but they really have to be watched." More and more people had gathered to watch Philip and the birdman.

"Has he ever actually tried to fly?" I asked as the two men stood talking to the nurses.

"Who, Philip or the Captain?" Annabelle asked, laughing.

"The Captain." I laughed. It felt good.

"Yeah, don't you remember, Annabelle?" Roberta interjected. "I told you about the time he jumped from that old maple." Turning to me, she said, "It's not there anymore because it got struck by lightning." Then, turning back to Annabelle, she added, "Remember, I told you he broke one of his legs and a wrist. After he woke up from surgery, the doctors told him they had clipped his wings. Poor ol' thing cried like a baby. They reassured him that he'd be good as new when he was released."

"They're not, though—releasing him?" I asked incredulously.

"Honey! The man sits on nests trying to hatch eggs, and flies out of trees. What do you think?" Roberta chuckled.

"Thank the good Lord." I laughed, too. Then we all started coughing, which made us laugh and cough even harder, and pull out our handkerchiefs. "Having you two as roommates is going to kill me," I croaked, tucking my hanky back in my pocket.

"And here you thought you were coming to a place that would heal you," Annabelle said. "C'mon. Now that we know Captain Crow shall live to see another day, let's go look at the koi pond." As we headed down the pathway, I couldn't stop thinking about the Captain. I wondered if he had always had the compulsion to fly, and always thought he was a reincarnated bird. I felt sympathy for him. And then the thought struck me that the Captain probably felt like a bird in a cage, being locked away in this place. Suddenly, his behavior didn't seem quite as crazy as before, and my sympathy turned to empathy.

CHAPTER 13

On the Front Lines

"Kathryn, you have a visitor, and she comes bearing gifts," I heard Roberta say from outside the bathroom door. We'd been back from the koi pond for about half an hour and I was in the middle of brushing my teeth. I rinsed my mouth quickly and opened the door to find Aunt Harriet standing there. She'd brought up our evening snack after intercepting the aide who was pushing a cart from room to room with the trays. Without saying much of anything, I hurried to her, hugging her tightly.

"You're a sight for sore eyes!" I breathed in that familiar family scent. I was so relieved to see her that I was on the verge of tears. I held them back, though. I refused to keep crying. I'd done enough of that to last the entire time I was here, and I was determined to not only be strong for myself, but for my roommates, the medical staff, and most especially, for my family. Taking several steps back from her so that I didn't breathe in her face, I asked what she was doing there. It was a Thursday night. As a rule, she only worked weekdays, unless the hospital was short-staffed, and her duty did not include any of the TB wards. Primarily, she worked with the most severe cases of mental psychosis; especially male schizophrenics and men with multiple-personality disorders.

"Did you really think I'd let the day end without checking on you? How are ya, darlin'?"

Her voice was home. It was all that I was familiar and comfortable with.

"I'm doin' okay. Really. Did you-all meet?" I turned toward Roberta and Annabelle.

"Roberta and I go way back, don't we, Berta?"

"Your aunt was my nurse when I was here ten years ago. She was on the TB ward at the time." Roberta smiled warmly at her. "And I introduced her to Annabelle and Peggy while you were in the bathroom. Harriet was kind enough to bring us our evening snack."

"Lord, more food? Dana wasn't kidding when she said they'd fatten us up."

"Never mind that," my aunt said, passing each of us a small plate that had a biscuit with pats of butter beside it, and a small bowl of strawberries with cream. "Eat up! I even snatched one for myself." She sat in a chair next to a tray table where she'd set the food down, and buttered her biscuit. I knew she was eating just to encourage me to do the same. Knowing my aunt, she'd had a decent-sized supper and was no more interested in biscuits and strawberries than I was. Each of us, however, joined her.

"I thought Harold was taking you home." I remembered her asking him to do so.

"He did, then after I unpacked and got some dinner, I drove back over. I knew I wasn't going to get any sleep if I didn't check on you—being that it's your first night here." She ate a strawberry.

"You could have called, Aunt Harriet. You didn't need to come back out again. Honestly, I'm okay, just tired more than anything."

"Honey, you need to get a lot of rest," she said. "Lord, I wish someone would tell me to rest awhile." She laughed, trying to keep things light. "You'll be seeing Dr. Ludlow tomorrow. I checked your chart at the nurses' desk and saw he's your primary doctor."

"Yes. I was told I'd see him first thing in the morning. I guess I'll skip breakfast. I don't want to miss him. Lord, here we are eating again and already talking about the next meal!"

"You're not going to miss breakfast, m'dear." There was nothing light in Aunt Harriet's tone. "They'll bring a tray up to you. Just call down to the nurses' station and let them know you're waiting for Dr. Ludlow. He's wonderful, by the way, with a nice bedside manner. He's straightforward, too, which I like, and I know you do, too. He'll tell you what's what without candy-coating anything."

"Good." I was relieved to hear that. "He'll go over my schedule, and any restrictions he wants for me?" I asked. She confirmed that he would. I asked her about visitors. I couldn't stop thinking about Donnie. I wanted to see him so badly.

"Dr. Ludlow will tell you if and when you can have visitors. I would think he'll let you have them right away, but only short visits and just a couple of times a week, for now. Depending on how you're doing, he can always adjust that. He'll let you know all of this tomorrow, though. Now, not to change the subject, but have you got everything you need? Have you forgotten anything that you'll be wanting?"

"No. I think I've got everything, but thanks. You go on home now. I love seeing you, but I hate that you had to come back tonight. Honestly, I'm doing all right. I would tell you if I wasn't."

We both stood up, and she walked over to me. "No, you wouldn't." She cupped the side of my face with her hand and looked me in the eyes. "I wanted to see for myself that you were okay. And now that I see you are, I'll bid you gals a good night."

I walked her as far as the elevator. She hugged me, then held me at arm's length. "This won't be forever, Kate. You're gonna get through this."

"One way or another." I smiled. We both knew the gravity of the situation, though, and beneath our bravado was unspoken fear.

"I'll see you tomorrow." She pushed the elevator button. "I'll want to hear what Ludlow said, and what you thought of him. I love you, Katie." The door to the elevator slid open. There was no one in it. She stepped inside but kept the door from sliding closed.

"I love you, too, Aunt Harriet. Now, you go on home. I know it's been a long day for you, too."

"Oh, heck, I'm fine," she said, waving my concern away. But while her mouth said one thing, the dark circles under her eyes said another. "Night, honey." She let the door close.

I was restless throughout the night. Everyone's coughing—including my own—bothered me. Still worse, I kept thinking about all the what-if's: *What if I never get better? What if I do get better but have a reoccurrence? What if I infect someone? What if Donnie gets sick, or anyone else I love? What if, what if, what if!* I nearly drove myself crazy worrying about it all.

* * *

Just after eight the next morning, Roberta and Annabelle headed down for breakfast. We'd already notified a nurse that I was waiting for Dr. Ludlow, so trays for both Peggy and me were being brought up. Not long afterward, the food arrived. The amount of food was overwhelming and I was no hungrier than I'd been the day before, but I was more exhausted. The nervous energy that had kept me going had faded, and I was feeling the weight of my fatigue full force. After drinking my coffee and forcing down one slice of toast, I'd gone into the bathroom to get dressed when I heard a series of sharp raps on the ward's door. "Get decent if you're not already," a man's voice called through the door. I smoothed down my navy-and-green plaid dress, but I couldn't reach the buttons on the back. Not wanting to meet the doctor that way, I quickly pulled it off, making a mental note that I'd need more functional clothing, pieces that were easier to get in and out of by myself, as well as warmer. The chill from the open windows remained in the ward well into the morning. Just thinking about what the room would feel like in the winter made me cold. I needed to switch my dress for something else in the closet, but with the doctor waiting for me, I just threw my robe back on.

"Good morning, Doctor." I was embarrassed to be coming from the bathroom on my initial meeting with him, and still wearing my robe, to boot. His back was to me and he was reading some paperwork attached to a clipboard. I assumed it was my chart. He turned around and I guessed him to be in his later-forties, of medium build and height, with salt-and-pepper hair that was combed straight back.

"Mrs. Cavanaugh, I presume." I nodded and he stepped toward me and shook my hand. "I'm Martin Ludlow, and I'll be in charge of your care while you're here. Have a seat." Pointing with his pen, he indicated the chair closest to him. Every bed had a chair next to it, and this one happened to be by Annabelle's bed, and not far from Peggy's, where she quietly watched us.

"I'll go on down to the sunroom, so you two can—" She started to get out of bed, but I interrupted her.

"Don't, Peggy. That's not necessary. Just stay where you are. I'm fine with you being here, as long as Dr. Ludlow doesn't mind." I turned to look at him.

"You're on FBR, aren't you, Mrs. Porter?" She confirmed that she was. "Then stay put. If Mrs. Cavanaugh is fine with your being here, I'm fine with it, too." Grabbing a chair from beside the next bed, he sat down across from me and pulled a stethoscope out of the breast pocket of his white lab coat. Putting the ends of it into his ears, he listened to my chest, then leaned back in his chair, looped his stethoscope back around his neck and made a notation on my chart.

"Mrs. Cavanaugh," he began, "you've got a lot of phlegm in your lungs, but especially in your left lung. Your recent X-rays from the mobile clinic show you have a good-sized cavity in the left bottom lobe of your left lung. You also have multiple lesions in both. An antibiotic regimen should stem the growth of more lesions, provided we get the right antibiotic mixture for you. Effective medication combinations vary from person to person, you understand. However, that cavity is another problem altogether and what concerns me the most.

"I do know that at this point, we must start you on the antibiotics immediately. We'll see how well you respond to them. I want to see if that cavity will at least shrink some, if not heal altogether from them. Once we see your response to the drugs, we'll decide our next course of action; it could be anything from trying a different antibiotic regimen to having a pneumoperitoneum or possibly a pneumothorax for that cavity, or a combination of those treatments. We'll just have to wait and see.

"The good news is that we have options to help you, but the bad news is your lungs have been greatly compromised by the scarlet fever you had as a child. Though you may never have felt as though there was any impairment, you will now, because your lungs are being asked to work that much harder to keep doing their job. Has your hemoptysis—coughing up blood—changed in the last week?" I answered that it had gotten heavier.

"That's par for the course, I'm afraid." The doctor was writing as he listened. Suddenly, he stood up.

"All right, Mrs. Cavanaugh. I want to get another X-ray immediately, as well as another sputum smear. Though we usually do it once a month, your symptoms and the presentation of them have changed quite a bit in less than a week's time, from what you're telling me. I want to make sure we're not dealing with the onset of rapid-growing cavities, and a greater number of lesions. Do you know how to get to the lab building—where the testing and X-rays are done?" When I told him I didn't, we walked over to the bank of windows on the opposite side of the room and he pointed out the building.

"I have other rounds to make, otherwise I'd walk you over myself. Here, give this to the technician or nurse on duty." He handed me a piece of paper. "It's a prescription for the tests. I'll call them to let them know you're coming down. I'll get back to you this afternoon with the results and we'll decide how to proceed from there. In the meantime, do you have any questions?"

"Without seeing the test results first, could you venture a guess as to the length of time I'll be in here? Also, can I have visitors?"

"I really can't give you an accurate guess before seeing your newest test results, or how responsive you are to treatments, but I wouldn't think it would be any longer than a year. By a year's time, patients are usually cured entirely, or have progressed to the point that they can continue drug treatments at home." I noticed his tact in avoiding discussing the possibility that I might not get well, so I asked him point blank.

"What percentage of folks don't make it out of here alive, Doctor?"

"Those who decide it's likely they won't. Mrs. Cavanaugh, we know from a great deal of experience that the majority of people who overcome this disease are those who stubbornly set their minds to doing so. We've found that patients with the strongest mental constitution and will to survive usually do, as long as they follow their prescribed forms of treatment; whereas those who give in to their fear and self-pity, or don't follow their doctor's orders, don't." Almost as if he'd just remembered that Peggy was in the room with us, he looked over at her, but she was either sleeping or just resting with her eyes closed. The doctor turned back to me and continued in a softer voice. "Unfortunately, though, that's not always the case. Some of our patients give it everything they've got in trying to beat this disease, but, still, it's just not . . ." He didn't finish. We both knew he was talking about Peggy, and it hurt. I hoped to God she was really sleeping. He took a deep breath. "Help us to help you, Mrs. Cavanaugh, and if you do, there's a good chance you'll survive. To help bolster your motivation, I'm granting you visitations—for now, anyway. But do know that if you should worsen at all, I will order full bed rest and very limited visits until you show improvement. Does that sound fair?" I answered yes. "I want your activities limited for the time being, so I want you back in bed following your tests until lunchtime, or dinnertime, rather." He smiled. "I'm from Pennsylvania and will never get used to calling lunch 'dinner,' and dinner 'supper.'" He shook his head as if to say, *Now, why do you Southerners feel the necessity to reverse the names of meals?*

I smiled, too. "How 'bout we just call it the noonday meal?" He chuckled and I continued. "Thank you, Doctor Ludlow." I shook his hand again.

"You can thank me by following the regimen of care I lay out for you, Mrs. Cavanaugh. I'll see you later this afternoon." Almost as an afterthought, he added, "I have a feeling that you're one of those strong-willed patients."

I smiled. "I have Scotch-Irish blood in me, and some Native American, too."

"Well, I'd want you on the front lines with me in a battle, then."

"Aren't I already, Dr. Ludlow?"

He laughed. "Indeed you are, Mrs. Cavanaugh, indeed you are. And we're going to win this war together."

CHAPTER 14

Crossing Paths

The walkway leading to the lab would have flowers lining it come late spring, but for now, the beds lay empty. I wondered how many people it took to maintain the enormous grounds. Thinking about my conversation with Dr. Ludlow just moments before, the idea of getting my hands in the rich-looking soil of this place was motivation enough to make me a stellar patient. I was born of the earth, and raised in the deep belief that through the careful tending of it, the earth would take care of me, as well. I needed to physically connect with it again. As far as I was concerned, working with the earth was as vital to the health and well-being of the soul as food and water were for the body. As I passed the janitorial building, I was able to look out at one of the huge vegetable gardens. The garden was actually a field. I realized that I needed to get to the lab, but the weather was beautiful, and an empty bench just ahead of me was too tempting to walk by. Sitting down on the cold granite, I closed my eyes and tilted my face up toward the morning sun. The familiar warmth was like an old friend. It eased away all remnants of chill from the night before, and I was able to take my sweater off. Suddenly, I was hit hard by a coughing fit that felt as though I was breaking every bone in my torso. I was glad that I was sitting down, for the intensity of my coughing was worse than any I had suffered up to that point. I gripped the edge of the bench for support, praying it would pass. When it finally did subside, it left me completely winded, so I stayed on the bench and tried to focus on something other than the terrifying fact that I was slowly suffocating to death.

Out in the field, several men and women were working the rows with hoes and rakes. They were obviously preparing the ground for the spring planting, which would likely happen in the next week or so. In Howling Cut, however, planting would have to wait until after Mother's Day, for the ground was still much too cold to trust the vulnerable little seeds to it. *Ah, home.* My thoughts turned to what each member of my family would be doing at that moment. Donnie would be tagging along with Mama or Daddy; maybe working in the orchard or the kitchen, or even helping to prepare the garden. In Cabot, Geoffrey would be at his office by now, and thoroughly engrossed in some legal protocol. I was anxious to talk with them all, and not simply because I wanted to hear the voices of those I loved most in this world, but because I wanted to know if they'd all been tested for TB, and what the results had showed.

Focusing back on the field, I noticed that there were mainly men working it, but there were a couple of women, too. All of them were in coveralls, some dark blue ones, while others were brown. Even from that distance, I could see block lettering across the fronts and backs of them. Obviously, they were institution-issued, and these were patients. I suspected that the colors differentiated the psych patients from the non-psych ones. One of the workers particularly caught my attention—a woman wearing blue overalls, and while all the others were involved in working their particular rows, this woman seemed to be frozen in place. She stood completely still, staring out at something only she seemed interested in, or, perhaps, was able to see. She craned her head as if trying to see it more clearly.

She was small and frail looking, her back slightly bent, as if the world's weight had been far too heavy a burden for her to carry. She didn't strike me as being old, though, for her hair was very dark, perhaps even black. It was rather long and in the morning's stiff breeze, it blew about her head like wild, long fingers, twisting and twirling through the air. Several times, she swiped the restless strands back from her face to keep them from interfering with whatever she was trying to see. Finally, she held her hair back with her right hand, which gave me a clear view of her profile. She was femininely delicate looking, but her chin jutted out as if in defiance, giving the impression that there was determination in her character, perhaps stubbornness, too. As though I'd called her name, she turned slightly to look at me. She kept her hair swept out of her face and leaned on the hoe with her left hand, like a makeshift cane. She stood that way, unmoving, staring at me, and it made me very uncomfortable. It was more than just the fact that she wouldn't take her eyes off of me; it was the intensity of her gaze. I could see that she was middle-aged, but that her weathered face had probably been beautiful at one time. There was a hardness to it now, though, and a wildness. Just like her hair. I looked down to break eye contact.

"C'mon, now, Mary." Hearing a voice, I looked up and saw Philip McAllister, the rescuer of Captain Crow, talking to the strange woman. The breeze was blowing toward me, so it carried his voice. "You've got to get back to work or they're gonna make you go inside. You don't want to do that, do you? It's a beautiful day. C'mon, I'll give you a hand."

The woman, Mary, did not answer him but began to hoe. As she did, he walked behind her, further working the ground. "How you feeling today?" he asked her. I didn't think he really expected an answer; he was simply trying to put her at ease. Rather than ask another question, he began to softly sing: "I've been working on the railroad, all the livelong day. I've been working on the railroad, just to pass the time away." When Philip got to the chorus, Mary stopped hoeing, turned around to face him, and with absolutely no expression on her face, began to sing, too. "Someone's in the kitchen with Dinah. Someone's in the kitchen I know oh-oh-oh. Someone's in the kitchen with Dinah, strumming on the old banjo!" Mary sang each word in the last sentence of the chorus louder than the one before it, with Philip following her lead. When the last note of the last word died down, her deadpan expression finally broke and they laughed together like two small children.

"Mrs. Cavanaugh?" I was startled out of my fascinated observation by a young man in a white lab coat. "Are you Kathryn Cavanaugh?" I told him that I was. "I'm one of the lab techs, Ernie Glass. Dr. Ludlow called down to let us know to be expecting you. Said you were coming in right away. That was nearly thirty minutes ago. I'm sorry, I don't mean to hurry you, but we've got a full load of patients coming in this afternoon, so we need to get started with you."

"Oh, Mr. Glass, I'm so sorry! I was just gonna rest for a minute, but the day is so nice . . . I got sidetracked watchin' everything going on around me."

"No problem, Mrs. Cavanaugh. It *is* a nice day." He looked up at the sky, then across the field. "Spring has sprung." The sun shining down on the land illuminated all of the new growth in a golden haze, making the grounds a lemon-lime color. "Let's get your tests done and then you can come right back here—as long as you're not on FBR."

"As of now, I'm not, but Dr. Ludlow is limiting my activities." I stood up, grabbed my sweater, and we started down the walkway. "But I guess depending on what my tests show, that may change. I do need to get a move on, though. I told my family I'd try to call them sometime this morning."

We walked for several yards then the walkway curved and immediately ended at a one-story brick building with an A-frame roof. It looked more like someone's summer cottage than a laboratory at a state hospital. "Here we are," Ernie said, as he quickly stepped ahead of me and opened the lab's front door. Inside, he spoke to the receptionist behind a sliding glass window, and she jotted something down in her logbook. Then he led me down a short hallway to a dressing room, where he handed me a hospital gown and instructed me to meet him in the X-ray room, two doors down from the dressing room. From there, it was nearly a carbon copy of my visit to the mobile clinic, except that my test results would not be reviewed while I waited in the waiting area, but instead would be sent to Dr. Ludlow's office in the main administration building.

I wasn't there for more than fifteen minutes before I headed back toward my building, following the same walkway back. I passed the field where people had been working less than half an hour earlier, but it was empty. The clock on the outside of the huge administration building read ten forty-five. I wondered if Mama would be in the house to answer my call.

"Hey." The voice came from just behind me. Startled, I turned around and saw Philip McAllister step onto the walkway. He was lugging a heavy sack from which protruded the handles of the farm tools the workers had been using. "Sorry, didn't mean to startle you." His smile was a little mischievous, which made me smile, too.

"Do you always pop out at people? Isn't that a bit risky around here?"

"Well, I guess if it causes someone to have a heart attack, they're in the right place, wouldn't you say?"

I laughed. "Lord, that's some way of looking at it."

"Where're you headed?" He shifted the awkward weight of the sack. I could see he was breathing a little heavily.

"Here, do you want me to carry something, Mr...?" I didn't want to let on that I already knew his name.

He set the sack down. "I'm sorry. I'm Philip McAllister, and you're Kathryn Cavanaugh." He didn't mind letting me know that he knew mine.

"Uh, yes. I am." We shook hands. "How'd you know that?"

"I read the papers. I've seen you in the *Asheville Citizen Times*, and the *Cabot Tribune* a few times. You're a busy lady."

"*Was* a busy lady." I smiled, then started to walk again. I needed to make my phone calls. "Where're you from, Mr. McAllister?" He had no Southern drawl, so I knew he wasn't from these parts.

"Illinois. Outside of Chicago for much of my childhood, then in the city later on."

"Are you a White Sox fan?"

"Ahhh, now, Mrs. Cavanaugh, you've gone and insulted me, and I've known you for all of two minutes. Tell me, do I look like a degenerate White Sox fan?"

"Oh, you're one of *those*." I laughed, nodding my head. "You're one of those faithful but pitiful souls who believe the Cubs will win the World Series someday. Surely you've heard about the curse?"

"I believe in the curse about as much as I believe in Santa and the Tooth Fairy."

"Oh, *really*? Well, if that's so, then how come I send a letter to Santa each year—I personally pop it right in the mailbox—and I always get what I ask for."

"I bet you do." He chuckled, nodding. "Yes, ma'am, I bet you do. Well, I bet there's one thing you didn't ask for that you got, though."

"And what's that?" I was enjoying this repartee.

"To be stuck here, on this most glorious spring day. I bet that wasn't on your list."

"You'd win that bet, Mr. McAllister," I said with a fading smile. We looked at each other with a certain kind of understanding that only two people navigating a leaking boat in rough seas could share.

"I'm sorry, Mrs. Cavanaugh. That wasn't a very nice thing to say in our first conversation together."

"Maybe not, but it's the truth."

"Yeah," he said softly. "That it is." We continued to walk, comfortably quiet, until we came to a fork in the walkway; then Philip stopped. "Well, this is where I leave you," he said, shifting the weight of the bag again. "I have to check these back in. I'm sure this is not the most appropriate thing to say, but welcome."

"If the shoe fits . . . Thanks." I started to turn away, then thought of something. "Mr. McAllister? Can I ask you something?" He turned around. "That woman you were helping in the garden a little bit ago, the one with the long dark hair." I was embarrassed to let him know I'd been watching them that closely, but my curiosity was greater than my pride. "If you don't mind my asking, who is she?"

"You mean Mary Boone? The one singing with me?"

"Yes, that's her. I don't mean to be nosy, but is she from around these parts?"

"I think she might have been originally, but from what I've been told, she lived out West—California, I think, for a good while. Why, you think you might know her?"

"No, no, nothing like that. I was just curious, that's all. She's very . . . striking." For some reason, I didn't want to use the word 'strange,' but apparently, it was the word that best described her.

"She's a strange one, that's for sure—intense, too. Doesn't say much but when she does, it can be really out there. She's got a short circuit somewhere, that's for sure."

"Can you tell me, is she a TB patient? I know it's none of my business, and you certainly don't need to tell me."

"Oh, you'll know everyone here before too long, Mrs. Cavanaugh. It might seem like a big place when you first check in, but really, it's not. This 'big place' is really a very small world. She's a psych patient. Sometimes she's way, way up. And sometimes she's way, way down. But when she's 'way, way' anything, it's best to just leave her alone. She can be pretty damn scary then, to be honest about it."

"Okay. Thanks for telling me."

"You take care of yourself, Mrs. Cavanaugh," he said. I told him to do the same, then continued down the walkway toward my building, while Philip headed off toward the tool shed. I was lost in my thoughts, and without even realizing it, began to softly sing, "I've been working on the railroad . . ."

CHAPTER 15

News from Home

"The doctor didn't want to take any chances on Donnie getting full-blown TB, so he gave him that BCG vaccine," Mama explained on the phone as she filled me in on the family's test results. "Lord bless that baby! He hollered at the top of his lungs when the doctor put that shot into him. Finally, your daddy got him to calm down by telling him he'd take him to the mercantile afterwards and get him a baseball glove he'd been eyeing. That child played it for everything it was worth, too. He stopped hollerin', and with lips still tremblin' says, 'An' a baseball, too?' And your daddy tells him okay, and the floodgates were immediately shut off. Lord, Kathryn, that child ought to run for president, seeing as how he can sway people into giving him what he wants!" Mama laughed. I laughed, too, but felt more like crying. *It should be me there consoling him.*

Mama told me that both she and Daddy had tested negative, and even though Donnie's skin test had been positive, the doctor emphasized that the results did not mean he'd have the disease, it simply showed that he'd been exposed to it. But knowing that Donnie had been exposed to TB—to me—for some time, the doctor did not want to play the "wait and see game," so, erring on the side of caution, he gave Donnie the Bacillus Calmette-Guérin, or BCG, vaccine to ensure that he wouldn't get it. It would be a day or so before we would know if he had any reactions to the injection, but I knew that any reaction would be better than falling victim to the disease. He was too young and too small to fight off a monster of this size and ferocity. I said a silent prayer and thanked God for Calmette and Guérin, who'd developed the inoculation.

"How's Donnie eating and sleeping—just doing in general, Mama?"

"Oh, he misses you, that's for sure. He's been real quiet since you left, but that baseball glove cheered him a little, and so did the home-made butter pecan ice cream we churned up last night. Honestly, honey, he's doin' okay. I wish he was here to talk to you, but he's gone to town with your daddy for some fertilizer. I'm sorry. I guess I should have made him stick around here so you could talk to him, but I just wasn't sure when you'd call."

"No, Mama. I'm glad y'all are keeping him busy. I'm glad y'all are just plain *keeping* him. He'd be miserable back home, stuck with a nanny all day. God forbid that Charlotte would want to spend any time with her one and only grandson. I swear, as much as that family cares about their heritage and the family bloodline, you'd think she'd be all over Donnie, spoiling him rotten or, at the very least, trying to mold him into a miniature version of Geoffrey. I always knew she was disappointed that Geoffrey didn't marry someone from his own side of the tracks, but not to the point that it would keep her from enjoying her own grandson. But that fifty percent of Donnie that's Harris blood keeps that woman away better than kerosene does mosquitoes. Besides, spending time with him would interfere with her bridge club and hair appointments. Lord, listen to me. I'm carrying on like an ol' crabapple. I'm sorry. It's just that—"

Mama jumped in. "You've got nothin' to be sorry about. That woman ought to be ashamed of herself for having so little to do with her own flesh and blood. Guess our lineage can't measure up to hers, but if you ask me, we're pretty good folk! Listen, enough about that ol' fool. Tell me how you're doing, honey, and what the doctors are sayin'."

"I'm doin' okay, Mama, really. It's a good place, with good folks, at least the ones I've met so far. I have three nice roommates. And I like my doctor, very much. Oh, I saw Aunt Harriet last night! Bless her. She went all the way home and then came back. She brought up our evening snack. She was worried about me, she said. It's really good knowing she's around.

"I had more tests run this morning, right before I called you, and I should know something this afternoon. The nurse told me Dr. Ludlow would be in around two o'clock. Then I'll know if this thing has progressed any, and what treatments they'll have me on. I'll also find out if the doctor wants to put me on full bed rest and restricted visitations. I don't think he will, though, from what he said earlier. Let's just hope and pray my test results won't change his mind."

"Well, if the doctor says it's all right, how 'bout if we come to see you on Wednesday? Geoffrey might want to come on the weekend since he has to work during the week, and that way it'll spread out your visitors a little."

"Oh, Mama, I know it's a long drive for y'all. It's about two-and-a-half hours each way. Why don't y'all wait and come week after next? Maybe it'll give my medications a chance to start working and I'll look a little better by then. I'd hate for y'all to see me looking any worse than I did when I left. It would really scare Donnie."

"Are you feelin' that much worse, honey?" I could hear the worry in her voice. I assured her that I wasn't. It would do no good to tell her the truth. "Well, all right, I guess," she acquiesced. "We'll wait till a week from Wednesday to come, but only because I understand your concerns about Donnie. Don't worry about the drive, though, honey. We'll make it a nice outing. I'll pack us a picnic lunch or we'll stop and get somethin' along the way. You just let me know if we can come, and what times y'all are allowed visitors."

"I already know that visiting hours are from ten to one, then three thirty to five in the afternoon, and seven to eight in the evening. Could y'all come around eleven, then head back after one? I don't think Donnie can manage more than a couple of hours sitting reasonably still—especially in a place like this. We'll have to visit outside though, because they don't let anyone under sixteen inside the facility. But they have plenty of covered porches and verandas if it's nasty out." We talked for several more minutes about what they'd been doing with Donnie before I glanced up at the clock above the nurses' station and realized how late it was getting. "Mama, I hate to do it, but I have to go. I need to give Geoffrey a call before dinner. Right after we eat is rest time, and they don't like folks to use the phone then. Listen, I'll give you a call later this afternoon to let you know what my results were and if the doctor still says it's okay to have visitors. Maybe Donnie will be around this afternoon, too, and I can talk to him."

"I'll make sure he's here, honey. He's gonna want to talk to you, too. Figure you can call around four?"

"Yes, that's a good time. Mama . . . thank you for everything. You don't know how much I appreciate what you and Daddy are doing. I love you so much and miss . . ."

She heard my voice break. "Darlin', it's gonna be okay," she quickly assured me. But I could hear the emotion in her voice, too. "You've got to have faith that you'll get through this. You've been through bad times before with the scarlet fever, and you came out of that okay. You're going to pull through this, too, Kathryn. You're a tough little gal, honey—always have been. Now, you go ahead and call Geoffrey, then call back here later. We'll be waitin' to hear from you, okay? I love you, darlin'."

"Okay. I love you, too, Mama." I couldn't seem to say it enough, or hear it enough these days. "Talk to you later." I set the receiver down in its cradle and stared at it as I let the sound of her voice linger in my head for just a moment longer. Then, after looking around to make sure no other patient was waiting to use the phone, I dialed Geoffrey's office number. His secretary put me right through to him.

"Kathryn, hello! I've been waiting to hear from you! How are you feeling?"

"I'm doin' all right, Geoffrey. It's so good to hear your voice! Are you doin' okay?" He confirmed that he was, then asked me what I thought of Pelham. "It's a good place," I could honestly tell him. "I like my doctor real well and everyone I've met so far." I repeated what I'd told Mama. "If I can have visitors, when would you want to come out?"

"I was thinking about a week from Saturday, if that'd be all right."

"That would be good. Mama said they'd come a week from Wednesday. Speaking of visiting; when do you think you'll go see Donnie? Being away from both of us has to be breaking his little heart. Do you think you can manage a trip out to Howling Cut pretty soon?"

"Maybe in a couple of weeks or so, Kathryn. Work has been especially busy. I've been working six, sometimes seven days a week. I just can't take more than a day or so away from it right now. I might just have to leave early one morning, visit with him for a few hours and head back that night."

"Oh, Geoffrey, couldn't you put work aside this once and spend the weekend with him? Just getting a few hours here and there with us won't be enough. It'll be hard on him."

"I'll try, Kathryn, honestly I will. Let's see how this week goes, and if I can get Walter and the new man, John Egan, to cover what I've got going on with three new patents coming through, then I'll take a weekend off soon. Okay?"

"I guess it'll have to be." I could hear the irritation in my voice, and I silently scolded myself for it. I wanted to sound cheerful when I spoke to my family, even if it was forced. On the other hand, I wanted Geoffrey to understand how important it was that he be the father Donnie needed him to be. This was a critical time in the foundation of their relationship, and depending on how attentive he was to Donnie's needs, and how selfless he was about his own, could either leave deep fractures in that foundation, or give it strength and cohesion. "Geoffrey, I need you—Donnie needs you—to be there for him now. This is a scary time in his life, and he's confused and sad. He needs your reassurance that no matter what happens to me, you'll always be there for him, and that you'll do whatever it takes to be with him. He needs to know that he's not secondary in your life, but the most important thing in the world, without question. He's your son, Geoffrey, and he's hurting right now." I was breathless and started to cough.

"Kathryn, you're upsetting yourself for no reason. Do you think I'm unaware of the role I play in my own son's life? I work as hard I do to provide all the good things in the world for you two; to give you both everything you want and need. And if my time is limited because of that, well, I expect you to understand the reason why. I assume as our son grows, he'll not only understand but appreciate all of the sacrifices I'll have made in order to give you both what you desire."

"Geoffrey, we *do* love you for all that. But don't you see? It's not what you can give us in the material sense that matters as much as your time and love. I don't know how to make you understand that. I know you're doing what you think is best for us, but at least for now, will you spend a little less time at work and a little more time with Donnie? Please?"

"I'll try, Kathryn. But I can't let the firm suffer because of it."

"But, Geoffrey, your son is suffering." I sounded tired, and I was more exhausted than I'd ever been before. "Listen, I have to hang up now. The nurse just told me it's time for dinner, so I have to go. I'll let you know what my test results are."

"Yes, please do. I want to know. And, Kathryn, I promise, I'll be there for Donnie."

"You need to promise *him* that, Geoffrey. Promise Donnie. I have to go now. I'll talk to you soon." I softly set the receiver down, and stared at it. How could a man who was blessed with a son as wonderful as Donnie choose not to spend as much time with him as he possibly could? I thought about all of the patients in this one hospital alone who would give everything they own to have the joy of spending more time with their families, doing those little everyday things that are so taken for granted. *Life is packed full of ironies*, I thought. And it seemed to me that most of them were just downright cruel.

CHAPTER 16

Spirits of the Darkness and Light

The light tapping of the rain awakened me from my afternoon rest period. I wasn't getting wet, though, as the light wind was blowing the storm away from my window rather than through it. Though the tapping of the rain was soft and comforting, it was not the usual sound filling the ward, so it disturbed my sleep. Ironically, the endless harsh, ragged coughing of others no longer kept me awake, staring at the ceiling, hour after hour; only my own coughing did. It was a world I was quickly becoming accustomed to in the week I'd been at Pelham.

It was only midafternoon, but the storm had muted the light. On sunny days, it was usually hard for me to sleep, lying next to the open window beside my bed. Above or beside all sixteen beds in the ward were windows. My bed was at the far end, and only one of two whose window was beside it rather than above it. I was glad I'd been assigned to that one because the window was low enough to look out while still lying in bed. From what I was told, the windows were always open, no matter the season, or the time of day. On colder days, additional blankets were piled onto our beds and on one particularly cold night, one of the women in the ward slept in her parka. Fresh air was supposed to accelerate "The Cure" for our battered lungs, and it helped to lessen the spread of our contagious disease by keeping the air circulating. Though it could be uncomfortably cold, I figured that come July and August, the cooling breezes would be a great relief. The damp air was another story, however. It seemed quite likely that it would kill us rather than cure us if we ended up with a bout of pneumonia, which was a common ailment among the tuberculosis patients. It was the deadliest and most feared complication.

Sighing with both frustration and resignation, I adjusted my pillows so that I could sit up a little higher and look out the window. If Nurse Silvers came in, she'd read me the riot act for not lying flat on my back. *Rest, rest, and more rest*, the thin, middle-aged night nurse was so fond of reminding us. Her other favorite saying was, *One needs a backbone not a wishbone to get well*. She reminded me of a little hen running from the ax in Mama's chicken coop. She moved quickly, no matter what minor errand or chore she was involved in, with her eyes darting this way and that. And she constantly pointed out the should-do's and the can't-do's for every patient under her care, no matter how limited or unlimited each one's daily activities might be. Nurse Silvers went by the rules in the hospital's rule book as if it were the Holy Bible, and the recitations of her favorite sayings were making us sick from their endless repetition.

But she wasn't the only one who irritated me. In just the short time I'd been there, I'd witnessed some of the staff treating the sane tuberculosis patients much as they did the insane ones. And no doubt some of the former had slipped over the line into a gossamer world of blissful detachment in order to escape the boredom, not to mention the constant worrying about death.

Staying positive was as hard to do as taking a deep breath without coughing. It wasn't just worrying about my own health, but also the health of the other women in my ward. I quickly learned that our moods were quite dependent on each other's progress as well as our own. When Peggy came back from her monthly X-ray after finding out that two more lesions had formed, and her large cavity had not decreased in size, we all suffered with her. That day left each of us quietly withdrawn, staring longingly from our windows at the world beyond the high fence. It wasn't a world that we were allowed to be a part of. To any passersby who caught a glimpse of us peering out, we must have looked like pitiful personifications of Rapunzel trapped in her tower.

I was drawn out of my melancholy thoughts by sounds outside my window. Dr. Ludlow had come out of the building and was standing on the porch, talking with a middle-aged couple I'd seen arriving earlier during visiting hours. Both the man and the woman were listening closely to what the doctor was saying, leaning in toward him as if they were hanging on his every word. To watch them, one might think the couple was hard of hearing, but I had witnessed that scene before: the look of great despair on faces belonging to the family of those being left behind. It was a look created partly by guilt and partly by sadness, with a pinch of hope in the mix, as well.

The couple spent several more minutes with Dr. Ludlow, then the man briefly shook the doctor's hand, while the woman could do nothing more than stare down at the tops of her shoes while wiping her nose with a handkerchief. They turned away from the doctor and then the woman clutched the man's arm as they walked down the front steps into the soft rain. Neither one had an umbrella, but neither did they hurry or even seem to notice that they were getting wet. Perhaps, they simply did not care. As they slowly made their way toward the visitors' parking area, the doctor watched them go. I could only make out his profile, but it was enough to see the grim look on his face. Even from the window, I could see the set of his mouth. There was anger there, or frustration, perhaps both, but it remained there even after he turned back toward the front door and walked away, out of my line of vision.

For the brief second I could fully see his face, I saw the weariness there. He had to be tired. But perhaps it was the victories of reuniting families with their loved ones that kept him going. Perhaps that made it worth it to him to keep going back through the front door. With nothing more to see, I lay back against my pillow and thought about all the people who had come and gone over the years, both the patients and their loved ones. I thought about my own arrival at Pelham, and the admissions process I'd had to go through, as countless others had before me and no doubt countless others would, long after I was gone. I also thought about the fact that I was not only one of the patients, but also one of the witnesses to the suffering of other patients; people who had become confidants, friends, members of the makeshift families we created. In many ways, watching their suffering brought the worst pain of all as we found hope for our own recoveries by watching theirs. And when they slipped away from us so did that hope—our most precious lifeline.

When it became clear the cavities in Peggy's left lung weren't healing, the doctors decided that it was necessary to perform an aggressive and painful procedure called an extraperiosteal thoracoplasty. Small sections of three of her ribs were removed in order to fill those areas with paraffin oil that would compress the diseased area of the lung. It all seemed more than the small, fair porcelain doll could bear. We watched her vibrant youth seemingly fade overnight, leaving her an even smaller, more shriveled-up version of herself.

Then, several days after the procedure, Peggy developed pneumonia. The doctors kept her sitting up in bed to help prevent her from drowning in her own fluids, and we sat quietly by her, watching her slipping and losing a hold on this world. After the pneumonia set in, it didn't take as long as it took the good Lord to create Heaven and Earth before Peggy breathed her last raggedly shallow breath and gently closed her eyes on a life that was cruel and unfairly short. Annabelle, realizing the end was near, had crawled into bed with her dying friend and had remained there, holding her and whispering words of comfort, until Peggy was finally released. The rest of us on the ward, having seen Annabelle get into bed with Peggy, realized what was happening and respectfully left them alone. We called no nurses or doctors, for this was a time that was to be shared among patients alone.

We knew the end had mercifully come when we heard Annabelle call out Peggy's name in a wounded sob. Quietly, we gathered around the bed, holding hands while shedding our last tears for her. I began to recite Psalm twenty-three, and the women joined in, then Marsha Beckley, who'd been admitted just two days before, led us in singing "Amazing Grace." When the last note died down, all was still. No one wanted to move, for when we did, Peggy would have to leave us forever. Finally, I broke away from the circle to press the nurses' button, saying a silent prayer of thanks as I did so that it was Dana who was on duty that day; then I rejoined the women as we waited in patient silence.

I heard Dana walk in a moment later. She walked over to us, peered between Roberta and me, and upon seeing Peggy, softly and sadly uttered, "Oh, dear." Then Dana asked us to please allow her to check Peggy's vitals to confirm what was so apparent to all of us, for her sunken chest no longer heaved in a fruitless attempt to trap a good lungful of air. I stepped aside to let her through, but no one waited for Dana's confirmation. Instead, we turned away and retreated back to our beds and our grief, except Annabelle, who went into the bathroom and threw up.

Lying in bed, I looked out the window. I wasn't watching anything, really. It was just my way of retreating into a small world of my own, cutting off everyone and everything around me for a little while. I had always needed time to myself, and I especially longed for it now. I needed time to digest the loss. Even though Peggy had been such a fragile, soft-spoken woman, there was a soothing strength to her. We had dubbed her "the balm of the ward." She never got angry, nor pitied herself and her situation, though she hated the fact that her illness separated her from the husband she so dearly loved, and hated the sadness it caused him. But Peggy always found something to smile about, even in her darkest days. Now, the balm was gone, leaving a noisy emptiness in her wake.

One of the doctors on duty was summoned to pronounce Peggy's time of death; then an orderly was called in to remove the body. With my back to the room, I shielded myself as best I could from the tragic scene playing out behind me, and focused on the activity below. The evening's visiting hours were nearly over and I watched people depart down the front steps of our building. As they descended the last step, umbrellas popped up against the light drizzle, and then they moved away from the glow emanating from the porch and the building's many windows, and out into the deepening gray of the parking lot. Headlights cut through the fog, creating ghostly pathways as vehicles navigated down the long drive toward the front gate. God, how I wished I was riding in one of them! I'd thought the same thing on Saturday as I watched the visitors leaving, Geoffrey being one of them.

He'd come every Saturday, and only missed one in the five weeks I'd been here, when he spent the weekend in Howling Cut. I was only too happy to give up that visit because it meant he and Donnie would finally have some time together. According to Donnie, they'd had a fun time, but *Daddy didn't like baiting the hook and asked Papa if there wasn't just a good seafood market to buy trout. Papa laughed so hard that he knocked the can of worms into the creek, so we had leftover meatloaf for dinner. Daddy took all of us to the ice cream parlor afterwards and we got milkshakes!* Lord, how that had done my heart good to hear him tell it. I wished it'd done the same for my lungs.

As planned, Dr. Ludlow had gone over my test results performed the day after I'd been admitted. Comparing them to the ones taken at the Flat Rock clinic less than a week earlier, Dr. Ludlow could see a slight enlargement of the cavity in my lung, and the development of two more lesions. He wasn't overly concerned with the changes at the time the two sets of tests were taken. He immediately started me on the antibiotic cocktail of streptomycin, para-aminosalicylic acid, and the newly discovered isoniazid.

At times, the side effects of the medications were more debilitating than the tuberculosis itself. I developed peripheral neuropathy because of the isoniazid, which caused severe pain in my feet and legs, making it difficult to walk. So I was given the latest "wonder drug," rifampicin, to combat the side effects of the other "wonder drug." There were times I was tempted to pack my bags and take the train back to Howling Cut, to seek out one of our mountain's herbal healers, whose ancient concoctions and remedies seemed to do as much good, if not more, than the standardized medicines enthusiastically prescribed by physicians in the modern world.

I was pulled away from my thoughts by some movement that caught my eye outside, at the edge of the tree line, just off to the right of the parking lot, where the evening's visitors were departing. The trees lined a pathway that wound around the facility and was used by patients as they attempted to build up the strength in their lungs by taking walks, or doing other mild forms of exercise. The movement was made by someone or something that seemed to flit from tree to tree as though he or she was trying not to be seen. As one of the cars pulled out from the parking lot, its headlights illuminated the person half-hidden behind one of the trees. I could just make out the blackness and wildness of the hair, as well as the body size, and thought it looked a lot like Mary Boone. From the stealthy way she was moving, it was apparent that she was not supposed to be there.

No psychiatric patient was supposed to be out alone at night. So, what was she doing? Trying to run away from the place? Trying to leave with one of the departing visitors? I pushed myself up to one elbow and shifted closer to the window so that I could get a better view. The woman moved to yet another tree and waited. Just when I was about to reach over and press the call button, she moved back toward the building and into the light, where I could see that it was definitely Mary. She was only allowed to wear the institution-issued green pajamas or overalls, but I could see that she had on a dark trench coat. I wondered if it was one she'd had with her when she was admitted, or if she'd stolen it from one of the staff members or even one of the visitors. Timing it so that she wouldn't be so noticeable, she reentered the building just as a group of visitors was exiting. Then she was gone from my line of vision.

I decided against calling the nurse. Mary was safe and back inside, and that was all that mattered. Lying back on my pillow, I wondered what her story was. I'd seen her several times over the weeks I'd been here, and for the most part, she was alone. No one seemed to want to have much to do with her, though maybe the reverse was true, too. She lived in a world of her own making, and I wondered if it was a comforting place, full of softness and light, or if it was a frightening place, filled with confusion and darkness. Judging by her actions, I was pretty sure it was the latter.

I had trouble sleeping that night. I couldn't stop thinking about the losses suffered by both Mary and Peggy. Who was the more unlucky of the two? I felt it was Mary. To lose the ability to rely on one's own clear, rational thinking, while the death of the body lagged behind the death of the mind, seemed the cruelest curse of all. I finally fell into a restless sleep toward daybreak, and even then, I dreamed that Mary and Peggy stood at the precipice of a great abyss, each urging the other to jump.

CHAPTER 17

An Inconvenient Truth

D r. Ludlow wanted me to spend as much time as I could outside in the fresh air. He thought it would be good for me both physically and psychologically, and there wasn't a shortage of places for me to do that. There were numerous porches and verandas attached to most every building. Many of the patients rested in rows of Adirondack chairs in those areas, but I preferred spending much of my "Sunshine Time" and "Reclining Time" in a chair near the enormous vegetable gardens. Even watching from the sidelines, I was able to get to know the personalities of the patients, and their relationships. I had a bird's-eye view of who interacted with whom, who fought with whom, and who was cousining with whom. It wasn't unusual to see two of the patients make up some excuse for going off together, whether for the purpose of finding tools or filling the water buckets. The list of reasons to go off in pairs was extensive and could get quite creative. Most of the gardeners turned a blind eye to the goings-on, for they could sympathize with each patient's loneliness. It took a terrible toll on the emotional well-being of many of them, especially the younger patients who were cruelly cut off from their lives, their loves, and their loved ones when illness demanded their complete isolation from the world they knew.

I understood how each patient felt, for I had those same longings; to be held and kissed and touched as intimately as I once had been, which was totally out of the question at this point. So, as most patients did, I resigned myself to the memories of those passionate days past, and worked hard at my recovery for the promise of regaining them in the future.

For some patients, memories and promises were not enough, so they took clandestine trips to the toolshed, or found the most deserted areas in the hospital and found physical, if not emotional, release. Many of us covered for them, explaining their suspicious absences, or confirming that they had, indeed, been on the errand which they claimed to have been on. I had never been one to lie, and still carried the memory of the acrid taste of soap on my tongue from the one I got caught telling as a child. Mama found a small carved wooden dog from the orchard's store tucked away in my dresser drawer, and knowing that neither she nor Daddy had given it to me, she asked me about it. It had seemed strange to her that I would hide it away.

I lied and told her Grandma Lydia had given it to me, but Mama quickly found out that that wasn't so. Mama had washed my mouth out with soap and told me that no truth could ever be as terrible as even the smallest lie. Then she withheld my weekly allowance for a month in punishment for stealing. As I matured, my own conscience dictated right from wrong, and I lived by the high moral standards that I'd been raised with as a child. So, when I first helped to explain why a couple of wayward patients were nowhere to be found, I not only felt guilty about lying, but I also saw how easily high morals could erode away, tiny lie by tiny lie.

Two people who concocted numerous excuses to go off together were low-risk psychiatric patients Lloyd Bishop and Maude Mosby. Watching the two of them plan, then implement their rendezvous was quite theatrical. Had they been in drama class, they would have failed the class miserably for they were comically overdramatic. One afternoon, for example, Maude, who was supposed to be weeding rows of carrots, fell down with a great flourish, claiming she'd twisted her ankle and needed help getting it bandaged. Lloyd, who conveniently happened to be in the next row over, gallantly leaped over the vegetables to rescue the damsel in distress. The two made their way toward the infirmary, but to no one's surprise, quickly skirted the building and were out of sight for some time. They returned before their gardening hour was over, and before the orderly sleeping in one of the Adirondack chairs woke up and noticed their absence. Maude came limping back, complete with a bandage to support her injury—and her story—with only one little detail overlooked: She, or Lloyd, or both, had bandaged the wrong ankle. No one batted an eyelash, except for Maude at Lloyd, who reciprocated by blowing her a kiss and mouthing, *My love.* Ah, life was certainly strange within the sanatorium, and yet, in some strange way, not so different from the other side of the high walls.

Just as I was getting comfortable in my lawn chair for my midmorning Sunshine Hour, and greatly anticipating another live episode of "The Lies and Loves of Pelham Place," one of the orderlies interrupted me. "Mrs. Cavanaugh, you got a visitor."

Looking up directly into the sun, I shielded my eyes but could make out that the dark silhouette was Mama. I had seen her just the week before, and as the trip was such a long one for my parents and Donnie, I'd requested that they start coming every third week. They had fought me on it, but because of the emotional distress the visits caused my young son, they reluctantly agreed. We'd learned after Donnie's initial visit that seeing me in this frightening and intimidating environment, looking more sickly pale and thin than when I'd left Howling Cut, had upset him terribly. It broke my heart to see them so infrequently, but it needed to be that way for all of their sakes. So I wrote to him often, and spoke to him on the phone even more frequently.

As I looked up at Mama in the blinding sun, my initial reaction was alarm. "Mama, what're you doing here? Is Daddy with you? Where's Donnie?" As I started to get up, a hacking cough erupted.

"Stay down, Kate, stay down!" She leaned over, firmly planting her hands on my collarbones. "They're both home and they're fine. Should I go get that orderly?"

"No, no," I gasped. Sliding my legs over on the chair, I motioned for her to sit down. She did but watched me with great concern while I tried to catch my breath. "What's wrong, Mama?" I hoarsely whispered.

"Honey . . . it's Grandma Willa. She passed last Friday." It was Monday, so that meant she'd been gone for three days.

"Why didn't you call me, Mama? You should have called me right away!"

"And what could you have done, darlin'?" Her voice sounded tired. I was finally able to clearly see her and she looked tired, too. "Since we couldn't come and get you for the funeral, we just thought it was better to let you know after it was over. At least we thought it was. I didn't want you to be here in the hospital, feeling sicker than you already do 'cause you weren't there with us. There was nothin' you could do, and I was worried it would just break your heart know-ing that the funeral 'n' all was going on, and you not there with us. I'm sorry if I did the wrong thing."

"Oh, Mama, you didn't do wrong! I'm sorry if it seemed like I was fussing at you." I took her hand in both of mine. "How you hold-in' up? I know losing Grandma has you all torn up." She merely nod-ded, not trusting herself to speak. "How'd it happen?" I softly asked.

Mama took a deep breath, trying to keep her composure. "She died in her sleep. Just the way she wanted to. She's with Sam now, and that gives me comfort. I miss her bad—real bad—but I miss the way she used to be, not the way she was in the last few months. She hated being confined to her bed and not able to do things anymore."

"I know the feeling." I smiled sadly. "I guess she's buried next to Sam." Though they'd married later in life, Sam had been Grandma Willa's one true love.

"She is." Mama nodded. "She's by him, for good this time. Kathryn, really, I'm sorry I didn't call you right away, I just didn't . . ."

"Mama, don't be sorry. Please. I know it's hard to know what's right to do anymore, under these circumstances. But please, promise me you'll let me know right away if anything happens to anyone else in our family. It's the only way I can stay connected. Otherwise, I'll start to feel left out. I'm already far away from y'all in miles. I don't want to feel that way emotionally, too."

"Oh, honey!" She pulled me to her, not caring how contagious I was. "You're close to us all the time. Why, you take up most of the space in our hearts! I promise, though, I'll call you right away if any-thing happens. Okay?"

"Okay." Hugging her felt wonderful, but after a few seconds, I re-leased her and sat back.

"Kathryn . . . honey, I need to talk to you about something else right now."

"What, Mama?" A sense of dread came over me.

She took a deep breath. "When Geoffrey spent the weekend with us, he started talking about Donnie going to school in the fall. But not school in Cabot, or Howling Cut—at that Penmire Prep School, down near Tryon. It's a boarding school, Kathryn, and he—"

"I know what it is, Mama." I should have been stunned, and yet . . . "Geoffrey went there as a kid and hated it."

"Then why in the name of the good Lord would he even begin to consider putting Donnie there? If he knows he'd hate it and—"

"Probably because it's convenient for him, Mama," I angrily responded. "Let's face it; it'd solve his daily dilemma about who's taking care of Donnie, and what time the nanny is leaving, and what days she has off. Think how that might interfere with Geoffrey's blessed schedule at work! Donnie's an inconvenience in Geoffrey's life when Geoffrey is the one having to look after him. His *own son* is an inconvenience!" I was fighting back tears. I didn't want Mama to see me crying. She was upset enough.

"I asked Geoffrey if he'd talked to you or Donnie about this yet, and he said no, but that he wanted to discuss this with you as soon as you were feeling a little stronger. I told him you were plenty strong enough to discuss anything that involved Donnie. I really had to watch myself, though, 'cause I was getting plenty mad, and I didn't want to give him any reason to pack Donnie up right then and there and take him back to Cabot with him. I don't know, Kate. I got the feeling that he might've already talked to the school, made arrangements or something. I asked him to let Donnie stay with us until you came home. I told him that Donnie could go to school in Howling Cut. It's where we all went."

"And that's the problem, Mama. He doesn't want his son going to some hillbilly school where he thinks the only things Donnie will learn are how to kill and dress a hog, and how to tell the difference between a thresher and a cultivator. What else did he say, Mama? Think real hard."

Her eyebrows drew together as she tried to recall any small details that had seemed insignificant to her but might mean something to me. "Well, we didn't talk too much longer 'cause Geoffrey said he had to be gettin' on back. Maybe he waited to talk about it until just before he left, fearing your daddy and I would have spent the whole weekend trying to change his mind. And he would have been right. Anyway, Geoffrey walked on out to the porch, where Donnie was shootin' marbles with Gabriel, one of the grandkids from the Lysander farm across the way, and told Donnie he was heading on back home. Said he'd had a good time spending the weekend with him, and that he'd see him real soon. Then the two hugged and that was that."

"Did Donnie seem sorry to see him go?" Mama's answer was important.

"Well, not particularly. He got right back to shootin' marbles," she responded. "Donnie's a lot more shook up when he's leaving you here. Lord, that child cried halfway from here to Howling Cut. Only thing that stopped the tears was sheer exhaustion. Poor little fella slept the rest of the way home."

My heart was breaking. It had suffered one assault after another: Geoffrey's desire to send his son away; the lack of emotion from Donnie when Geoffrey left him in Howling Cut; Donnie's broken heart after visiting me. However, none of it really surprised me. What did surprise me, though, was the ferocity building up inside of me over the boarding school news. I hoped that it wouldn't come down to me drawing a line in the sand, with Donnie tucked protectively behind me while Geoffrey stood on the other side. I didn't want a tug-of-war with our child being pulled apart between us. But if it came down to that, I'd pull with every ounce of strength I had left, because my child's happiness and well-being would depend on it. "I'm supposed to see Geoffrey on Saturday, Mama, but I'm going to call him later. I can't put off talking to him about this."

"Is there anything I can do to help?"

"Oh, Mama, you've done more than any mother should ever have to. I don't know whether I feel more guilty or grateful. I guess a big amount of both, really."

"Don't you dare feel guilty, Kate! You didn't ask to get sick and have your world turned upside down. I'm not doin' anything you wouldn't do for your own young'un, or anyone else in our family, for that matter. You're one of the kindest, most compassionate people I've ever known, and the fact that you're my daughter makes that blessing even sweeter."

"Well, Mama, then I guess the apple doesn't fall far from the tree." Smiling, I held my hand up to her cheek.

Laying her own hand over it, she said, "Now, I'm gonna ask you again: What else can I do for you?"

"Just pray, Mama. Pray that I get well enough to live long enough to raise my son."

She stayed until it was nearly time for me to go in for dinner. Aunt Harriet had the day off and Mama had plans to spend the night with her before heading home the next morning. The two women had grown up together and were more like sisters than sisters-in-law, and Mama needed her now more than ever. Mama's continuous worrying about me put enormous stress on her, and now, with Grandma Willa gone, so was one of Mama's greatest sources of strength. Though Willa would be sorely missed by us all, Mama would feel that loss as deeply as any she'd ever known. And there was the added concern as to where Donnie's future would take him. The stress of it all was beginning to show on her, bending her youthful, lithe body down under its weight. She needed a break from everything and everyone, and there was no better person to provide quiet refuge than Aunt Harriet.

I remained in the chair for a little while longer after she left. I knew I needed to call Geoffrey, but I wanted time to organize my thoughts first and work out exactly what I was going to say to him. The ward nurse, as well as my ward mates, would become concerned if I didn't return soon, but I just couldn't go in yet. I wanted to stay outside, feeling the cool breeze and the warm sun on my face. I needed to feel my hands in the dirt! I needed that warm, comfortable, familiar feeling again. God, how I'd missed it!

I missed the Cabot Children's Home, and working with the children in the enormous garden. I missed teaching them the proper way of preparing it, then planting and tending it. I missed taking my own son's tiny hands and pressing them into the dirt, teaching him that it was important to honor the earth and care for it. Longingly, I looked out at the garden. I had been put on limited activity by Dr. Ludlow, so I wasn't permitted to work in it yet, but at that moment, I didn't care what the rules were, or what I was and was not allowed to do. I knew what I needed more than a whole roomful of doctors did.

Pushing myself up from the chair, I took off my beige sweater, stepped out of my brown loafers, rolled up the sleeves on the yellow cotton blouse that I wore under a dark green jumper dress, and not caring in the least that they were about to become damp and muddied, headed for the farthest row in the garden, which was only now being prepped for planting. There were no tools around for me to use, but I didn't care. Kneeling down in the dirt, I buried my hands in it as deeply as I could. I needed to intimately connect with the soil. I needed to feel it and have it feel me. I needed its warmth and reassurance that it was still there for me. Using my hands as a sieve, I began clearing away small pebbles from the brown-black soil, and plucking away defiant weeds. Finally, my tears began to fall, moistening the soil as they did. Slowly, inching down the row, I sobbed, abandoning myself to my intense anger and sorrow, and the frustrating powerlessness I felt about so much of my life and, more importantly, the life of my son. Suddenly, my deep sobbing was interrupted by violent coughing, and I braced myself on all fours as my back arched and heaved with the desperate intake of breath and the forceful bloodied expectoration from my diseased lungs. Pulling a handkerchief from a large pocket on the front of my jumper with a dirty, shaking hand, I spit the nauseating phlegm into it and waited for the attack to subside. Once it did, I was left completely winded and exhausted, so I stayed still, giving my body a chance to return to its new version of normal. Then, very slowly, I resumed my digging, only this time I wasn't alone.

Turning my head to see who had found me out, I saw Philip McAllister kneel down in the dirt about ten feet away from me and begin sifting the soil just as I was doing. He looked over at me and I could see the deep compassion on his face. Then he softly spoke just two words: "I know." He said nothing after that, and I didn't speak at all as we continued working together in silent understanding until we finished the row, leaving it ready and ripe for the planting.

CHAPTER 18

The Great Divide

"Of course, I wouldn't, Kathryn! I wouldn't do anything if you were that opposed to it, and obviously you are about sending Donnie to Penmire. God, Kathryn, you'd think I was trying to sentence him to hard labor at Salisbury Prison!"

"To a five-year-old child, it will feel like you've done exactly that, Geoffrey." It was taking every bit of self-control I had to speak calmly to him. I'd actually taken the time to eat dinner before calling him. I was so angry or scared or both that I didn't trust what I would say to him, so I decided I would get some food into me and talk with my ward mates before I called him. Returning to my ward, I found that the women had already gone down for dinner. Quickly changing out of my soiled clothing, I joined them in the dining hall and told them about Mama's visit and the conversation she'd had with Geoffrey.

As I was quickly learning, our newest ward mate, Marsha Beckley, was a level-headed person, with two nearly grown children of her own. She was a tiny woman, but what she lacked in size, she made up for in courage. A widow who had lost her husband in World War II when his plane was shot down over Germany, she and the children had been stationed overseas in England with him, and upon his death, she'd pulled herself up by the bootstraps and promptly gotten herself and the children back to the United States. She'd raised them in her hometown of Spartanburg, South Carolina, on a secretary's small salary and large doses of good sense and love. Over dinner, Marsha readily offered her advice on the importance of staying calm, cool, and collected, especially given the fact that I was in a position of limited control.

"Remember, honey"—Marsha pushed her tray aside, rested her forearms on the table, and leaned in closer to me as if to emphasize her words—"your husband's not just a lawyer, with his own firm behind him, but he's the father of your boy, out there in the world, free to make whatever decisions he chooses without too much worry about you gettin' in the way. It's a man's world, unfortunately, and that's especially true when a man has the power that yours does. Stay calm, stay cool, and buy yourself and your boy some time until you can get back out there and have a real say in how things are gonna be." Her words rang true, and just underscored what I already knew.

"Geoffrey, you hated Penmire, so how could you even think about sending Donnie there? It's bad enough that I've been taken out of his life right now, but to remove yourself from his life for the most part, too . . . I'll tell you this: Donnie will think that you're removing him from your life because he's an unwanted, inconvenient part of it. That would be the cruelest thing you could ever do. And hear me when I tell you this, Geoffrey, you will live to regret it. For Donnie to come home only on holidays, or to just see his family on the weekends, would crush him. And it'd crush me." I stopped to catch my breath, and to stop myself from saying what I really wanted to say: *You're a thoughtless and selfish man, and not the person I thought I married.*

"Kathryn, why are we even discussing this? He's not starting school for almost four months. Hopefully, you'll be well, or at least well enough to come home and continue your treatment here, and then we can all resume our normal lives and this whole subject will be moot. Donnie will attend school here in Cabot, and you can personally take him and pick him up every day if you like."

"Don't patronize me, Geoffrey." My voice was deep, flat. I felt like a mother panther protecting her young from a circling predator. "September isn't far off, and prior to starting school, a child has to be enrolled, given the proper vaccinations, uniforms have to be ordered, et cetera. Schools will be closing for summer vacation in another month, so now is the time to enroll him for the coming year. Wherever Donnie's going, he's got to be enrolled immediately to start on time in September. You know it, Geoffrey, and I do, too."

"Fine, Kathryn." He was keeping himself in check, as always, but

I knew him well, and I could sense the anger simmering just below the surface. "Then you tell me where you think we ought to enroll him."

"Enroll him in either George Washington Primary, which is a wonderful public school and the closest to our house, or Chesterfield Academy, if you insist on sending him to a private school. I'm fine with either. Though, honestly, Geoffrey, if you truly want to know where I'd like him to go, it's Howling Cut Elementary. Let him stay with my—"

"Absolutely not! Under no circumstances will a child of mine attend a hillbilly school in the backwoods somewhere. That is out—"

"That 'backwoods somewhere' was my home, Geoffrey! And one I'm very proud of. I think we need to hang up now before we say anything more we'll regret." Taking a couple of deep breaths—as deep as I could at that point, anyway—I forced myself to calm down, and to stifle the cough that I could feel rising in my chest. I didn't want him to think I was too sick to make clear and rational decisions for our son. Swallowing hard in a useless attempt to hold off my cough, I added, "Geoffrey, I know this has been as hard on you as it's been on Donnie and me. For the sake of all of. . ." My coughing worked its way up and out. I held the receiver close to my body to mute the sharp bark-like hacking; it took a minute or so to pass, and another to catch my breath. "Are you still there, Geoffrey?"

"Yes, Kathryn, I'm here. You sound worse than ever! What are the doctors saying, and what are they doing about this?"

I didn't want to be sidetracked from our original conversation. "I'm all right, Geoffrey, and the doctors are doing everything they can. Getting back to what we were saying, let's try to resolve things by finding a middle ground and respecting each other's feelings. We've built a wonderful life together, and created a beautiful child. Let's not let my illness corrupt every aspect of our life together. Donnie loves you and needs you and I need you to be there for him. Please. I know it's difficult, but you have to carry the weight for both of us right now, even if it's an inconvenience." It pained me to even say the offensive word.

"First of all, Kathryn, Donnie is not an inconvenience. I'm just trying to do what's best for him and for all of us, and placing him in a school that will attend to him twenty-four hours a day, making sure all of his needs are met, seemed like a good solution."

"Donnie is not a problem, requiring a solution. And, no, Geoffrey, Penmire would not be able to meet every one of his needs. What he needs most is to feel loved and secure and wanted, and he won't find that at any school, much less one that cares so much about shoes being polished all shiny bright and knowing which fork one should eat one's ambrosia with!"

"Maybe not, Kathryn, but just like those shoes you mentioned, he'd be polished and shaped and groomed into becoming the young man we want him to be."

"No, Geoffrey, *you* want him to be. All I want for him to be is happy. Listen, I need to hang up now. The rest hour is starting and we aren't supposed to be on the phone. Please, call either Washington Primary or Chesterfield Academy and get him registered for the fall semester. Will you do that?"

"Yes. I'll take care of it. I'll see you this weekend."

"All right, Geoffrey, thank you. I'll see you Saturday . . . and I'll look forward to it."

"I will, too, Kathryn," he said, immediately followed by the sound of a click as he hung up the phone.

As I softly hung up my phone, too, I knew we were both lying.

CHAPTER 19

A Hobbyhorse Rodeo

The auditorium was not quite full, but staff members were standing along the walls just the same. They were to provide security, as well as assistance in case of any sudden health concerns during the show. Some of our biggest orderlies and aides had been assigned this shift with both purposes in mind. The auditorium's massive size allowed a maximum occupancy of 632, though there were probably no more than three hundred patients in attendance. However, the crowd included many low-risk psych patients, and losing control of even a fraction of them while gathered together in one large room with just three exits available was unthinkable.

Everyone looked forward to this event all year, if for no other reason than the diversion it provided from our everyday routine. From what I was told, the administrative staff had begun to have the annual talent show many years before, when Pelham was strictly a tuberculosis sanatorium, and it was still put on now for the same reasons as it was years ago. It was easy for depression to set in here, and that was especially true for the many patients who were never visited by anyone outside of the facility. Whether visits were impeded by embarrassment, fear of contagion, or mere distance was anyone's guess, but the fact remained that many a patient saw no one from their previous life from the day they drove through the sanatorium's gates until the day they drove back out. That fact resulted in widespread depression, which had to be treated as well as the patient's primary illness. Suicide was not unheard of, and occurred more often than staff or patients cared to think about. So, the sanatorium's administration did what it could to add enjoyment and variety to the patients' lives.

The show's lineup of entertainment included any patient who was deemed safe and sound enough to participate, and those same qualifications held true for the patients in the audience. The event was highly anticipated, talked about, planned, and practiced for. As might be expected, some of the acts were strange, to say the least, but entertaining they were, and everyone who planned to attend readied themselves with great gusto as they selected their nicest street clothes (if they were permitted to wear them), while the performers rifled through old stage costumes that had been provided decades before when money was more available. Women worked on each other's hairstyles and makeup, all the while discussing who would be performing in the evening's show, as well as gossiping about who would be necking with whom in the audience once the lights were dimmed. For some, it was the rare opportunity to have a "date" in a strange imitation of what they'd known outside the sanatorium's walls. It was not unusual to see a woman wearing the lovely linen suit she'd worn upon being admitted, while on the arm of some male patient wearing his worn overalls and farm boots because those were the only remnants of clothing that he had from the outside world. No one cared. Everyone was just happy for the chance to be happy for a night.

The TB patients were relegated to the balcony. The irony was not lost on any of us that those with the most severe pulmonary issues were being asked to climb a flight of stairs in order to stay as far away from the others as possible. There was an elevator, but only those in wheelchairs, or using canes or walkers, were allowed to use it. So, like the invalids that we were, we helped each other up the stairs. Marsha was recovering from a segmentectomy, the removal of a section of one of the lower lobes in her right lung, and had stayed in bed. As frightening as it was for her, it was commonly done, and as her doctor explained, removing this area where cavities kept recurring might prevent her from yet another relapse and might just send her into remission once and for all. Hearing those encouraging words had Marsha practically throwing herself onto the surgical table and personally handing the scalpel to the surgeon.

Annabelle and I found seats together. Three other women had been admitted to our ward in the last two weeks, and while two of them were given FBR orders, the other, Jane English, attended the talent show with us and sat next to Roberta at the end of the row below Annabelle and me. When Jane first arrived, she seemed nearly as meek and mild as dear Peggy. However, we quickly found out that unlike Peggy, Jane loved to gossip, much to the delight of Roberta, and the two became bosom buddies almost immediately. No one's reputation was safe where these two women were concerned, and it grated on my nerves, as well as Annabelle's.

I felt we had enough to worry about without having to concern ourselves over how such-and-such had happened to so-and-so. I couldn't keep far enough away from their mindless chatter, though I tried to by staying outside. Fortunately, the weather accommodated my desire for lots of outdoor hours, as did Dr. Ludlow through his approval. Another fortunate thing was that my cavity had shrunk in size, though by just a couple of millimeters; but still, I was improving.

The lights on the stage came up and our weekend nurse, Ida Silvers, began to play "Me and My Shadow" on the piano, which was set up on the far left side of the stage. Sounds of the tubercular chuckling and then coughing rolled through the rows in the balcony. The title of the tune was a little black humor for those of us whose lives were dictated by the shadows on our lungs. We all knew that if we didn't do a lot of laughing in order to keep a positive attitude, we'd end up doing a lot more crying, and dying.

At the end of the song, Dr. Theodore Sandell walked out onto the stage to enthusiastic applause and cheering. Tonight, he would be the show's master of ceremonies, but by day, he was the facility's assistant director. A wise man of great wit and unending patience, he was far more visible and readily available to patients and staff alike than was the actual director, Dr. Bernard Schwartz. The consensus was that Dr. Schwartz was not much more than an expensive empty suit, who was away from Pelham far more than he was in attendance. But no one seemed to miss him much, for the very capable Dr. Sandell handled the goings-on at Pelham with amazing skill and thoughtfulness.

"Thank you, thank you all." He held his hand up to quiet the crowd. He was not deaf to the increase of coughing, and wanted everyone to settle down. "All right, ladies and gentlemen, let's get this show on the road, shall we?" More applause. "First up, we have Betta Knowles doing what I'm sure will be a splendid version of Marlene Dietrich's 'Falling in Love Again,' from the movie *Blue Angel*."

The brightly illuminated stage dimmed down to a single blue muted spotlight. A woman walked onto the stage wearing a black, sequined evening gown, feathery purple boa, platinum-blond wig, and sporting a long black cigarette holder, complete with burning cigarette. Polite clapping was cut off by the piano as Nurse Silvers began to play an introduction. The audience was spellbound, caught up in Betta's transformation. Slowly, she took a pull on her cigarette holder for dramatic effect then began to sing in perfect imitation of the German-born actress's famous song in a low, husky, accented voice. She mesmerized the audience, and I looked around at people's expressions, as fascinated by their reactions as I was by the singer herself. Faces were softly illuminated by the spotlight. Some watched with mouths slightly ajar and eyes open wide, while some seemed overcome with emotion and wiped their eyes or quietly blew their noses. And some of the patients were gently smiling, including Philip McAllister, who happened to catch me looking over at him.

It startled me to see someone looking back. It especially startled me to see that it was he. I quickly turned my attention back to the stage as Betta, aka Marlene, finished her song. Loud and long applause, accompanied by cheers of "Bravo!" were her reward, and she shook Dr. Sandell's hand as she exited stage left and he walked back on.

"Wasn't she something?" he enthusiastically asked. "Well, that's going to be a hard act to follow, but if anyone—or any two—can do it, it's this couple: Lloyd Bishop and"—I was waiting for the name Maude Mosby to follow—"Linda Houser"—*who?*—"singing the ever popular Dale Evans and Roy Rogers tune, 'Happy Trails.'" *Oh, Lord! I bet poor Maude is fit to be tied!* She and Lloyd were our regular cousining couple during the afternoon's gardening hour, and I couldn't imagine she was thrilled with this duo now prancing out on the stage atop homemade broomstick hobbyhorses, and dressed in full cowboy and cowgirl regalia.

Suddenly, a woman stood up in the back of the main level. We were sitting above her and at a bit of an angle, but we could see her nevertheless. Unsurprisingly, it was Maude Mosby. Though her face was in partial shadow, I could still make out that she was mad just by the way she was standing: stiffly erect, with hands clenched into fists by her sides. Meanwhile, Roy and Dale had set aside their hobby-horses and were strolling side by side, arm in arm, gazing into each other's faces as they went on with their song. And as they did, Maude moved out of her row and down the aisle toward them. Her stomping added an accompanying drumbeat to Nurse Silvers's piano playing. Once Maude reached the stage, she climbed up the stairs, and grabbing one of the broomstick hobbyhorses, proceeded to swing it at a very startled and very horrified Dale Evans, who screamed and immediately ran off the stage, exiting through the curtain on the left, followed by Maude and the thick whacking sound of the mop-headed hobbyhorse. Meanwhile, the faux Roy did exactly what the real Roy would never have done: He ran the other way, exiting through the curtain on the right.

The audience went wild, with some of the patients actually coming out of their seats and excitedly jumping up and down. When they did, I wondered if the staff members along the walls were starting to mentally run through their plan of action in the event that the audience's heightened excitement turned into uncontrollable bedlam. Realizing that something needed to be done immediately to quiet them, Dr. Sandell disappeared backstage for several seconds then returned with a fedora in hand. He whispered something to Nurse Silvers at the piano as he passed her then, holding up his hand to silence the noise of the crowd, he set the hat on his head at an angle and began crooning a very decent imitation of Frank Sinatra singing "Night and Day," accompanied by Nurse Silvers at the piano. That was all it took to silence the audience. This was a side of the good doctor that we had never seen before, and would likely not see again, and no one wanted to miss a second of it. Somehow, we all felt privileged to be witness to it. The audience remained respectfully quiet through the last note of his song, then, as if in thanks for Dr. Sandell's gift, the crowd's behavior was perfectly polite as they applauded him, and it remained so for the rest of the evening.

When the show ended, the psychiatric patients were immediately assisted back to their wards, as were the other patients who were not ambulatory. Roberta and Jane had walked on ahead, while Annabelle and I were slowly making our way back toward building three when she abruptly stopped. "Durn! I left my sweater on the back of my chair. You want to wait for me or go on ahead?"

"I'll go on, if you don't mind. I'm ready for bed, to tell you the truth."

"You go, then," Annabelle said. "I'm in no hurry. I'll see who might still be hanging around. We don't get enough time to socialize, if you ask me."

I laughed. "That's because we're all sick, Annabelle! As the aide told me when I was being admitted, this ain't the Ritz. But go, and have fun. I'll see you back in the ward." We turned in opposite directions.

I took my time, savoring the beautiful night. I'd gotten as far as the old overgrown band shell when I heard footsteps rapidly approaching. Thinking that Annabelle had changed her mind and decided to come on back, I turned around. "You're fast . . ." But it wasn't Annabelle. It was Philip McAllister.

"So I've been told," he quipped.

I had to laugh even though the double entendre was a little bold. "I thought you were Annabelle."

"No doubt. Unless you're waiting for her, I'll walk back with you."

"She told me to go on. Good show tonight, wasn't it?" We started down the path.

"I'm still trying to decide which I liked better"—he mischievously smiled—"Sandell's singing, or the impromptu hobbyhorse attack."

"The Cubs could use someone who can swing like that," I pointed out.

"They could, indeed!" He laughed. "But the whole team would be afraid of her." We walked on for a moment in comfortable silence. The night was clear and cool. It felt wonderfully refreshing after being in the stuffy auditorium. Even with all of the windows open, it had been too warm.

"Do you have a minute to see something magical?" He saw my hesitation. "It's just over at the koi pond."

Philip didn't strike me as the type to be overly dramatic, so I was curious as to what he found so magical, especially in a place like Pelham.

"All right," I said. We took our time getting there as we enjoyed talking about the evening's performances. We passed our building and the gardens, and the tree where Philip had talked Captain Crow down from his nest, then finally neared the pond.

"This only happens at night during certain times of the year, and is best when the moon is full. Tonight's one of those perfect nights."

"What is it?" I laughed, but Philip was giving nothing away.

"Patience, m'lady, patience." We had left the walkway for the path that led to the koi pond and then it came into view. "Look," he whispered in awe, sweeping his arm out in front of us.

All around us were thousands of flowers that had opened themselves up to the light of the moon. Even though their bright yellow color was hard to distinguish in the soft glow, their beauty wasn't. Their petals were softly rounded, and reminded me of a girl twirling in a circle skirt. The flowers' heads gently bobbed in the light breeze, as if nodding their approval of our being there as witnesses to their extraordinary nighttime outing.

"Night-blooming evening primroses," Philip softly, almost reverently stated. "Beautiful, aren't they?" I softly answered yes, awestruck. We just stood there, absorbing the wondrous sight.

Finally, Philip broke the quiet. "C'mon, let's sit for a few minutes and enjoy it." Taking a narrow trail that had been made by thousands of feet seeking the comforting refuge of the pond over the years, we made our way around to a bench on the opposite side.

"Back home, we use the oils from the plant for skin problems," I said as I sat down.

"Oh, you're familiar with evening primrose?" Philip sounded surprised and a little pleased.

"Oh, sure! Mountain folks have used it since long before I was born, and probably before my grandmother's grandmother was, too. I know the Cherokee have used it forever, and where I come from— Howling Cut—we use what the Cherokees use. Evening primrose is good for a lot of things. I know that my grandmother Willa once gave it to my father for his hem—" I caught myself in time, but was mortified by what I'd almost said.

With a smug smile on his face, as though he knew exactly what I was going to say, he urged me on. "Your grandma gave it to your dad, *why*?" His smile grew bigger as I grew more uncomfortable, and I could see he was trying not to laugh. When I didn't answer, he goaded me on. "C'mon. You've got me curious now. What'd your grandma use it for?" He definitely knew. "Okay," he said, "I'll tell you what. If I guess and guess right, you have to sit next to me Wednesday during movie night. If I'm wrong, then . . ." He was thinking. "Then—"

I jumped in. "Then you have to let me help in the garden. By the way, how do you know so much about gardening?" I changed the subject rather than respond to his request to sit next to him on movie night. Surely he realized I was married, because I never went without my wedding band. But perhaps he didn't care. I did, though.

"I'm the product of Illinois soy bean farmers. My parents had over a hundred acres of them, and we raised some corn, too. I learned a few things about crops over the years," he modestly replied. "And as far as you working in the garden, you're on restricted activity, aren't you? I've seen you outside, watching us work, and with this look on your face like there's nothing in this world you'd rather be doing than digging in the dirt. But I figured you must be restricted because I've only seen you do it that once." He was referring to the afternoon he dug next to me while I cried. "You have a connection with the earth, just like I do."

"I love working with it. And once I'm off restricted activity, you'll have to make room for me in the garden. You oversee some of the patients working in it, don't you?"

He confirmed that he did. "I guess the powers that be saw that I got along all right with most of the patients, including the not-so-all-right psych ones. And since there aren't a lot of extra orderlies and aides around to watch everyone, I was asked to help manage a few of the patients—a mixture of non-psych and low-risk psych patients—during some of the gardening shifts. Gets me out of my room and involved with something I love. It just makes the days go faster; otherwise time crawls in this place."

"If you don't mind my asking, Mr. McAllister, what did you do in Chicago, and what brought you here?"

"First, call me Philip. Secondly, I'll gladly answer those questions if you answer the one I asked a minute ago: What did your grandma use the primrose for?"

"Hemorrhoids," I blurted out. And we both laughed until I started coughing hard.

"Okay, easy there, lady. Easy." The smile on his face faded into empathetic concern, and he placed his arm around me for support. I turned away to conceal what I expectorated into a wad of tissues I pulled from my pocket. It took me several minutes to stop coughing and catch my breath, but for me, the laughter had been worth it.

"I'm okay," I said, moving forward slightly, and he removed his arm. I looked over and saw the kindness in both his smile and his eyes. "Why are you smiling?"

"You're a brave little thing, that's all."

"What makes you think that?"

"Oh, I don't know. There's just a determination in you. Not self-pity or resignation, but real determination."

"Well, that's the only thing that's gonna get us out of here, isn't it?" I laughed.

"That's exactly what I mean! You're a little fighter, Kathryn. Is it all right if I call you by your first name?"

"Well, considering we're in a sanatorium, fighting for our lives, I don't see the sense in polite formalities, do you?"

"No, not really." He smiled. But when we looked at each other, we could read the sadness in each other's eyes, born from the cruelly unfair situation we found ourselves in.

Awkwardly, I steered us back to the conversation which my coughing had interrupted. "Okay, I answered your question about the primrose's alternate purpose, so now you have to tell me what you did in Chicago, and how you ended up here."

"Well," he began, "I taught eleventh grade physics at the Mozart School in Chicago for a year. But after a particularly bad winter, I thought I'd see what the South might have to offer as far as employment. As luck would have it, the University of North Carolina, Asheville, was looking for an adjunct physics professor, and voilà, here I am."

"So you contracted TB down here?"

"Out West, actually. This ain't my first rodeo, kid." He glanced over at me. "I've been hospitalized before. The first time was when I was in the navy. I joined up fresh out of high school, barely eighteen, but the war was winding down and I wanted in. I was based at the Naval Medical Center in San Diego as a private first class. I worked alongside the medics; I was considering going into medicine then." His voice got softer as he remembered. "God, there were so many casualties coming in from the Pacific Theatre. We almost couldn't keep up." Philip stared off in the distance, past the beauty of the primroses, and I knew that he was seeing distant places and once-familiar

faces that had been the center of his world then, but were now re-
duced to small, fading memories.

"Anyway"—he shook it off—"there was an outbreak of TB, and
I was one of the unlucky twenty-three who came down with it. The
irony of it was that I didn't have to go overseas to almost get killed in
the war. Fifteen of the guys who got sick made it, including yours
truly, but eight weren't so lucky. I was in a sanatorium in California
for thirteen months. For a while there, I didn't think I'd make it out
either. And to make a long story short, I went back home and back to
school, got my PhD in physics at the University of Illinois, taught at
the Mozart School, and then at UNC Asheville. I loved that job, too,
and was only six months into it when I started coughing up blood
again. X-rays showed a recurrence of lesions and the beginnings of a
cavity. The veteran's hospital in Oteen was full, but Pelham was
close and had room, so here I am and have been for the last five
months. And that, dear lady, is it in a nutshell."

I nodded but said nothing. There was nothing to say other than
perhaps *I'm sorry*, or *That's too bad*, but I knew that wasn't what he
wanted to hear. In just the tiny fraction of time I'd been around him,
I guessed that he would hate being pitied, perhaps even more than
losing the battle to this persistent disease. I had the feeling that Mr.
Philip McAllister liked to look ahead, toward the future, at the possi-
bilities it might hold, instead of dwelling on painful faded photographs
of the past. I just prayed that there was a future to take pictures of.

CHAPTER 20

A Visit from Santa

I had been at Pelham for almost three months, and had had no visits from anyone other than family members. For some of my Cabot friends, the distance was too far. Others, however, were simply too afraid to come to a place like this, and I couldn't blame them. I wrote letters often, though, which helped to pass the time, and I received them on a regular basis, too. Each one I read was a precious little reminder that I had a life beyond my illness and that I was missed by those I had shared it with. So, it was an unexpected surprise when George Eisenhower, the director of the Cabot Children's Home, came to see me one Sunday afternoon. He would be attending a conference in nearby Asheville for several days that week and had decided to take advantage of his proximity to Pelham to visit me. The day was beautiful and not overly warm for early July, so we occupied two chairs on the veranda outside of the dining hall.

"Kathryn, you are sorely missed at the Home. For some reason the vegetables aren't growing as abundantly as they do when you're overseeing them, and I'd be willing to bet my bottom dollar that they're not going to taste quite as good either."

"You're prejudiced. I'm sure they're growing just fine. George"—the tone of my voice changed from one of light banter to seriousness—"have any of the kids come down with TB?" I was afraid to hear his answer.

"No, Kathryn, none have." His answer was straightforward. We sat facing each other, and he reached across, grabbed my hand, and gave it a reassuring squeeze. "And no one is on any preventive medicine either, so rest assured, good lady, that all is well."

"Oh, George, you don't know how relieved I am to hear that!" My eyes welled up. "I've worried myself sick over it." I closed my eyes for a moment. "Thank you, dear, sweet Lord! Thank you. Now"—I refocused on George—"tell me all the news. How everyone's doing—the kids, the teachers, et cetera!"

"Everyone's doing well, Kathryn, and we've actually had two adoptions since you've been gone."

"Oh, that's such good news, George! That's wonderful."

"Well, the bad news is that we've seen an increase in residents because of this new polio epidemic. If it's not one disease it's another; or another war, for that matter. First we're overwhelmed by orphans from the TB epidemic and World War II, and now orphans are coming in as a result of polio and the Korean War. This balding head of mine is the result of every one of their heartbreaking stories." Sadly smiling, he rubbed the top of his shiny head.

I smiled, too, but out of great love and affection for this man I'd grown so close to over the course of just a few short years. And for the thousandth time, I thought about how much he looked like Santa Claus. In many respects, he was a real life version of the holiday icon, for not only did he look like Santa, with his "broad face and a little round belly," he also gave so many children the wonderful gifts of love and security, not to mention a birthday gift for every child under his care, and little goodies at the holidays, as well.

"So what are you thinking, George? That you'll have to put on another addition?"

"Well, yes. In a way, yes," he cryptically answered, with a twinkle in his bright blue eyes. I'd seen that look before and knew my good friend had plans. And from the way his eyes sparkled, I figured they were mighty big ones. "My dear," he said, leaning toward me with his forearms resting on his short, thick thighs, "I have a proposition for you." I leaned in to hear it.

CHAPTER 21

A Birthday

I went to the early nondenominational church service that was one of two offered every Sunday morning in the small chapel next to the auditorium. It was the first time I'd been to the nine o'clock service, as opposed to the eleven o'clock, and I was a bit surprised to see both Philip and Dr. Sandell in attendance. Afterwards, some of the congregation milled about on the veranda, enjoying coffee and cookies, but mostly the socializing.

Dr. Sandell and I were standing off to the side of the snack table. He was munching on a ladyfinger. My appetite had been off even more than usual in the last week, so I just had coffee. The truth of the matter was that I was feeling worse these days, and I dreaded seeing what the new lab results would show. I was scheduled to have them done first thing in the morning, but pushing aside my troubling thoughts about what might be discovered, I turned my attention to the doctor. "Dr. Sandell, had I known you were going to sing Frank Sinatra at the talent show, I'd have made sure I had a front row seat. You did a wonderful job!"

He laughed. "Ah, Kathryn, you flatter me. I do appreciate your kind words, though, even if there's not a grain of truth to them."

"You nearly had her swooning, Doc." Philip had joined us. Reaching over to the refreshment table, he grabbed a macaroon. "Honestly, she reminded me of Lois Lane being overwhelmed by just the proximity of Superman."

"Ah, you two bolster one's ego, but I think your medications have affected your hearing. There was nothing 'super' about my singing, but I thank you immensely, regardless. By the way, Kathryn, happy birthday."

"How did you know?"

"A little birdie named Harriet told me. She's working this weekend because a couple of the nurses are on vacation, but she was hoping there were enough on duty so she could join you and your family later this morning. Coincidentally, my daughter's birthday is July fifteenth, too."

"Oh, is that so! Will you be seeing her today?" The doctor answered that he would love to, but seeing as how she was in Timbuktu on a mission trip, he would be sending her loving birthday wishes from afar. "Well, speaking of which, my family will be arriving in another hour or so. I think I'll head up to my room and rest until they get here."

He encouraged me to do so, then wished me a happy birthday again before heading off to mingle with some other churchgoers. Philip walked back to our building with me. The day was slightly overcast, cutting the summer heat by a few degrees, but thankfully, it wasn't raining. Because my family would arrive around eleven, not long before the dinner shifts began, the dining hall veranda would be busy, so I planned for us to visit out on the expansive lawn where picnic tables and chairs were set up. I looked over toward the area and admired the beautiful panoramic views of the distant mountains and the vegetable gardens in the foreground.

"Are you working in the garden today?" Our concept of "Sunday rest" was not always what the outside world's was. Many of the patients who gardened considered it recreation.

"Maybe later on. I'll see if any of our gardeners want to get outside and work it for a little bit. Hey, I'm sorry, I didn't know it was your birthday, Kathryn." I told him not to be silly. That it certainly didn't matter. "So, you turned forty today?"

"Gee, thanks." I laughed.

"Actually, you still look like a young lassie. How old are you?"

"Old enough to know that a woman should never be asked her age. I'm twenty-five, if you have to know, and this is a birthday I'm glad I reached." Philip stepped off the path to retrieve a thick piece of maple branch that had been carelessly left behind after some tree trimming the day before. "I can use this in occupational therapy class. We can always find a use for decent pieces of wood. It's got nice color," he said, inspecting it.

We'd reached the back door of our building and took the elevator up to the second floor. The nurses' desk was in front of us as we came out of the elevator, but was unmanned at the moment. Philip's ward was off to the right, while mine was off to the left.

"Well, I hope you have a good visit with your family, Kate." His use of my nickname surprised me a little, but didn't seem offensive or inappropriate in any way. Actually, for some reason it sounded natural coming from him.

"So what's yours?" I asked.

"What's my what?"

"Your nickname. You called me by mine, so it's only right I know what yours is."

"Oh, noooo. I'm not saying." He folded his arms across his chest and shook his head.

"Fine. Watch the primroses bloom by yourself from now on." I was enjoying the bantering. "I'll see you around." I turned to leave, but he gently grabbed my wrist.

"Shuggie bum."

"*What?*" I laughed.

"My mother always called me 'shuggie bum.'" He rolled his eyes and shook his head, embarrassed.

"Oh, good Lord." I laughed again. Philip had turned a lovely shade of dusty pink. Here was a man who could work on soldiers who were physically torn apart in battle; and had the brains to get his doctorate in physics; plus had the guts and determination to make it through not just one bout with tuberculosis, but now a second one, as well— with the nickname "shuggie bum." In truth, it was charming—both the name and his reaction to it.

"Well, shuggie bum," I said, trying not to laugh, "I have to go now. Enjoy the rest of your Sunday."

"You, too." He chuckled, obviously not taking himself too seriously. "And happy birthday, Katie Primrose."

Back in my room, I lay in bed while waiting for my family to arrive but couldn't sleep. There were too many people moving in and out of the ward because of the church services and upcoming dinner service. With the addition of several new tubercular patients, there were nine of us in the ward now, and while it was more interesting, it was also noisier. I felt sorry for several of the girls who were pretty bad off and really needed the quiet. Their doctors wanted them moved to semiprivate rooms, but until some became available, they had no other choice but to be housed in our ward. We tried to be quieter, but naturally, as some of the other women's health improved, their activities—and noise level—increased. Other than feeling bad about the noise, which at times interrupted the round-the-clock rest needed for these critically ill patients, I wasn't much bothered by the activity in the ward. It was a reminder of the busyness and normalcy of the outside world, and I much preferred hearing that noise than the painful, ragged sounds of the dying in their pitiful attempts to keep breathing.

I kept sitting up in bed to look out the window, anxiously watching for one of Daddy's vehicles to appear in the parking lot below. In celebration of my birthday, Geoffrey was driving over, too. Neither Donnie nor my parents had seen him since he'd spent the weekend with them, and I hoped there'd be no residue of tension left from the Penmire Prep School issue. Putting the worry aside, I thought about seeing Donnie again. Though I was anxious to spend some time with everyone, without question it was Donnie I was the most excited to see.

It had been nearly a month since his last visit, and I had missed him terribly. We'd planned for him to visit me the week before, but he'd had a cold, so I told Mama to keep him home. This was the longest we'd ever been apart, and I'd felt every lonely minute of it. Feeling too restless to stay in bed any longer, I changed out of my robe and into a comfortable light blue cotton jumper dress. My clothes all swallowed me now; even the old ones that Mama had brought over from Howling Cut were too big. Wearing the jumper helped to hide how much thinner I'd gotten, though there was nothing I could do to hide the dark circles under my eyes and the gauntness of my face. The fact that my cheekbones were naturally high only accentuated the deepening hollows beneath them. Makeup didn't help much, though I applied it anyway. I knew that each time Donnie saw me, I frightened him, and because I'd been feeling worse, I knew that I wasn't going to look any better to him on this visit than I had on the last. I started to put on my sneakers, but it hurt my chest and ribs to bend over to tie the laces, and it also started a coughing jag that lasted several minutes and used up even more of the little energy I had.

I'd lain awake the night before, flushed and dripping wet with the night sweats. It was a symptom of the fever that kept many of us awake throughout much of the night. The middle of the night was when it was the worst. Maybe it was because we were just lying there thinking about how hot we were, or how much we missed our loved ones, but we often went without a full night's sleep, and found some quiet activity to help pass the dark hours. It wasn't unusual to see a glow pierce the night as one of the feverish women switched on a small reading light attached to her bed's headboard. The small circle of light would illuminate her pale, sweat-soaked, glistening face. Hand towels were kept on each patient's nightstand, so after wiping the wetness away as best as she could, she'd pick up a book or maybe a pad and pen, and begin constructing a letter to one of those people she so desperately missed. The night sweats were a cruel, evil little beast that tortured us in our loneliest, most vulnerable hours, making sleep, which was our only means of escape, an elusive thing.

I finished putting my hair up into a loose bun at the back of my head. When I wore it down, its thickness and weight were especially hot in this weather, but it also made my face look that much thinner. Coming out of the bathroom, I took another anxious look out the window just in time to see Daddy's truck pulling into a space in the parking lot. "They're here!" I excitedly said to Annabelle, who was reading until it was time to go down to dinner. "We'll be over on the big side lawn. Stop by and say hello when you're done eating." She'd met my parents before and they were always glad to see her. It gave them a small amount of comfort knowing that I had companionship, and Annabelle was my closest friend.

"Are y'all eating down there, or what?" she asked. "I can bring something back up for you, if you want, and you can eat it later."

"No, don't worry about me. I have a feeling Mama may have brought some goodies for my birthday. Thanks, though."

I started to leave but remembered the little gift I had in my nightstand for Donnie. Twice a week, I went to a ninety-minute occupational therapy class, which provided a much-needed diversion from the everyday monotony. It was not the same pleasure that working out in the garden would give me, but Dr. Ludlow had restricted me from taking that step yet. Still, I loved working with my hands, so I took advantage of the various craft projects available in the class. One was making toys, and though I didn't do the actual building or carving of the toy trucks, wooden soldiers, and baby dolls, I loved painting and decorating them, and sewing clothes for the dolls. I'd painted a large wooden fire truck a deep red, and the truck's accessories, like the ladder and hose, a bright gold, then added "Donnie's Fire Truck" in bright blue on the side. His birthday was just three days after mine, and it broke my heart that I wouldn't be there to share it with him. In celebration of turning six, my parents were taking him and his marble-shooting friend, Gabriel, to the zoo in Asheboro. *God bless them*, I thought for the thousandth time, and had to fight not to curse God in the next breath for letting me be too sick to be the one taking them.

Grabbing the truck, I walked out of my building as fast as I could, then went down to the side lawn where we'd planned to meet. Daddy was just sitting down in one of the Adirondack chairs and Mama was standing next to Donnie, with one arm around his little shoulders, pointing to something in the woods. I looked to where she was pointing and saw the quick flash of white as a white-tailed deer disappeared into the trees.

"Hi, y'all!" I set the truck on the picnic table, and then hurried toward Donnie, spreading my arms wide. He rushed into me so hard that I nearly stumbled, but grabbed the back of one of the chairs in time to catch myself. *Thank you, Lord, for not letting me fall*, I thought. *I'll forgive you about the zoo thing.* The last thing I wanted was for Donnie to be afraid to touch me.

"Mama! Grandma and I just saw some deer! Two of 'em! Grandma said one was the father 'cause it had big horns, and the little one was the baby. I asked Grandma where the mother is but she said she didn't know, but maybe out grocery shopping!" He giggled. I was too choked up over finally seeing and touching my boy to say a word. All I could do was kiss the crown of his blond head and hold his little warm, strong body against my weak one. *Thank you, God. Thank you for him.*

"Hello, darlin'." Mama smiled, walking toward us. Daddy had gotten up when he'd heard me coming, and I turned to him after Donnie released me.

"I brought you a birthday present," Donnie announced, as I was finally giving Mama a hug. "I made it myself," he said, beaming, and rushed over to one of several wrapped presents on the picnic table.

"How you doin', honey?" Mama was scrutinizing my face closely, while gently tucking some wayward strands of hair back behind my ear. Her brows were knitted together and the look of concern on her face told me she could clearly see the physical changes taking place, and more rapidly now

"I'm okay, Mama. Better now that y'all are here," I said lightly, but looked away as I spoke. I was never able to lie to her. She knew my face well; my eyes, my expressions. I might be able to fool the rest of the world, but never her. And I knew that the way I was looking these days, I couldn't fool the world anymore either.

"Here!" Donnie held his gift up to me. I took it and held it to my ear, shaking it. It made no sound.

"Here!" I said, grabbing the truck off the picnic table. "I'm sorry, I couldn't wrap my gift to you."

Donnie loved it, especially since the gift was personalized, and inspected it thoroughly. From him I received a handmade walnut frame, which Daddy had cut and whittled and Donnie had glued together, and within the frame was a beautiful picture of Donnie, fishing pole in hand, on the banks of Bailey's Creek, back home. There was also a handmade easel to set the picture on. "How'd you know I needed a new picture of you?" I enthusiastically exclaimed.

"I dunno." He shrugged. "Just did."

"Kathryn, I brought a birthday picnic lunch, complete with yours and Donnie's favorites!" Mama announced. "As soon as Geoffrey arrives we'll eat, all right? Then you can open your presents from us."

I told her I wasn't sure I could hold myself back from her good food that long; that when it came to her cooking, manners took a backseat. Mama looked as pleased as Donnie did when I opened his present. Appetite or not, I would happily consume the dishes she'd so painstakingly and lovingly made, even if it meant I would be sick later on from the rich food. My body just couldn't take heavy foods anymore. At this point, it was hard keeping down anything that wasn't bland and light, and I could only eat small portions of those.

Geoffrey arrived within a half hour. Donnie ran to him, obviously happy to see his father, and in turn, Geoffrey scooped him up, just as happy to see his son. Carrying him in his arms until Donnie squirmed to be set free, Geoffrey closed the distance between us and hugged me hard.

"Happy birthday, Kathryn." He continued to hold me. "It's good to see you."

"It's good to see you, too, honey." I was moved by his unusual display of affection, but there was nothing usual about our lives these days. Terrible stress and strain were put on a relationship when a spouse was hospitalized for great lengths of time. Responsibilities shifted, and roles were reversed. I wasn't sure who the confinement was hardest on; the one infirm, or their family members who were stuck picking up the pieces and trying to keep some semblance of normalcy going when there was nothing normal about their lives anymore.

Everyone was ready to eat, so we put out the picnic. Not surprisingly, Mama had outdone herself. Her reasoning, she said, was that the lunch was in celebration of *two* very important people's birthdays. Included were deviled eggs, macaroni salad, potato salad, coleslaw, fried chicken, slices of maple-and-brown-sugar-glazed ham, biscuits, cornbread, sweetened iced tea, and lemonade. For dessert was a blueberry yum-yum, which was a concoction of whipped cream, cream cheese, and blueberries—one of Donnie's favorite desserts—and my favorite: yellow cake with double the amount of fudge frosting.

Aunt Harriet ended up having to work because of the shortage of nurses, but she was able to join us for dessert. As I looked around at each of them, I thought about the last time all of us had been together at Uncle Prescott's wedding. I shook my head in amazement over how things changed in the blink of an eye.

The late morning was overcast, keeping the temperature pleasant, and a soft breeze kept bugs away from the food. While we ate, we caught up on everyone's latest news, including Donnie's fast-approaching first year of school.

"I'd rather not go," he very seriously declared, then crammed another spoonful of yum-yum into his mouth.

"Why? You'll love it, son," I said. "You'll have lots of friends to play with, and you'll learn all kinds of new things. I bet you'll love your teachers, too. You'll get to go on field trips, and play on the playground. You're a big boy now, and will be doing all kinds of fun things."

Donnie was thoughtful for a moment. "Then I think I'd rather stay little." We all laughed. It was a good day.

After dessert, I opened presents, beginning with Geoffrey's, which was a beautiful ivory-colored cashmere sweater, with matching scarf and gloves. From Mama and Daddy came a beautiful butter-yellow robe, and a small but beautifully crafted gold and ruby cross on a gold chain. And Aunt Harriet gifted me with a handsome leather-bound book of O. Henry's short stories. The cover was richly embossed with gold lettering. "This is one book I'm going to be selfish with, and not pass around the ward." I laughed. I thanked everyone again for their wonderful gifts, but especially the gift of their visit. Silently, I wondered if I'd have another birthday to celebrate.

It didn't take long after gifts had been opened and lunch had been eaten that I could tell Donnie was growing restless, as well as sleepy, and I suggested that Geoffrey and Daddy take him to see the koi pond while Mama and I packed up the remains of our picnic. That way, they could get going before too long. She'd brought a large thermos of coffee, and she poured us both a cup.

"Let's sit for another minute before we clean up," Mama said. "I have something else for you." Reaching into her purse, she pulled out a white envelope and handed it to me. I saw that my name was written in familiar handwriting and immediately knew that it was from Ditty. I hurriedly pulled the card out and opened it. Below the standard printed text of birthday wishes was a note from my brother:

> *It stinks that you have to be in the hospital on your birthday, but I hope you can make it a good one anyway. I'm sorry I haven't been to see you. I guess I stink at being there when you really need me but I promise to make it up to you. Get well real soon, Kate. Love, Ditty.*

I looked at the envelope again and confirmed that there was no return address or stamp, only my first name written across it. "How did you get this, Mama? Have you seen Ditty? Did he give this to you?" I was very happy and relieved to hear from my brother, but also confused, and in all honesty, angry. Ditty was right. He *did* stink at being there when people really needed him.

"No, honey, we haven't seen him," Mama softly answered. She looked and sounded tired. "We got a large envelope in the mail from him about a week ago with no return address, but the stamp was post-marked Unicoi, Tennessee. Inside were birthday cards for you and Donnie, and a short note to your daddy and me. All it said was that he knew we were worried about him, but he was fine, and working, and figuring some things out, like 'how to settle down and be okay with it.' Your daddy about had a fit with that statement. Said he'd settle your brother down by kicking him in the rump all the way back from Tennessee. 'Course, your daddy's really more worried than mad. We all are." She shook her head in frustration.

"Well, Mama, the good news is he's alive." I covered her hand with mine. "He's a survivor. Always has been."

"I'll tell you one thing he may not survive, Kate, is the wrath of his mother once I get ahold of him." She tried to smile as she attempted to lighten the mood again. After all, it was supposed to be a birthday celebration. But the truth of the matter was that there was much more worrying going on than celebrating.

We sat in silence for a moment, lost in our own thoughts, though they were probably very similar: wondering where Ditty was, how and what he was doing and with whom. Closing my eyes, I lifted my face up to the sun as it poked through the clouds. Then I looked out at the fields and saw that the midafternoon gardening was underway.

The patients were busy at various tasks all along the burgeoning rows of vegetables. I pointed out certain people I knew, or knew of, like Captain Crow. "His most recent escapade was collecting bird feathers, lots of them," I said to Mama. "Every time he was out on the grounds, he found a few more, and explained to whichever orderly or aide was watching him that he needed them in his occupational therapy classes for children's toys, including a boy-sized Indian war bonnet. But his real intention for them was found out when three pillowcases full of the feathers were confiscated from his locker, and he came clean about his plan to construct massive wings to use in his latest attempt at flying, this time from the top of the giant tower on the power building! Disaster averted!" I laughed, shaking my head.

"How'd you learn about all that?" Mama asked.

"From that man over there," I said, pointing at Philip McAllister. "He's someone Captain Crow trusts, and Philip helps to keep an eye on him in the garden."

Philip was busy working among a row of cabbages, and as though he could feel our eyes upon him, he looked up at us and lifted a hand in greeting. "He grew up on a farm outside of Chicago," I said, waving back. "Grew soy beans, of all things!" That seemed like a strange crop to Southerners. "I'm hoping I can work in the garden, when I'm a little better."

"I know you're not feeling good, Kate. I'm your mama. It doesn't matter what you tell me, I can see it. I know. Mamas know their babies inside and out. And I can tell from the outside that my baby's insides aren't so good right now. But that's just 'right now,' Kate. You're sure to have ups and downs."

"I know, Mama. And you're right, I don't feel good, but don't tell anyone. Honestly, I've felt pretty bad this week. But I have labs tomorrow and I'm happy about it. Hopefully, they'll see what's different, and fix what they need to, to change things back around again." I smiled. "I have real faith in the doctors here, especially Dr. Ludlow."

Mama said nothing, just reached over and took my hand. We stayed that way for several minutes, staring out at the garden. As we did, I noticed someone working a little distance from the others, in the farthest row from us. It was Mary Boone. Just as I was starting to point her out to Mama, the rest of the family returned from the pond, pulling our attention away. Donnie proudly held up a tiny, multi-hued hummingbird's feather.

"Lord, Donnie, hide it quick! Captain Crow's around!" Mama warned. While the rest of the family looked confused, she and I laughed and it felt good. No matter what, Mama and I had a special connection, and no sickness or distance of any kind could ever cause it to weaken.

With everything packed up, we reluctantly left the picnic table and headed toward the parking lot, unaware as we did, that Mary Boone had caught sight of us and moved in closer. She stood frozen in place, watching us hard, straining to hear our voices and barely breathing in order to catch any of our words, but not daring to come any nearer. And as she stood there, watching us retreat, tears streamed down her face and her fractured heart beat as rapidly as a hummingbird's wing.

CHAPTER 22

Lungs and Tyrone

"So, Kathryn, what it boils down to is that you need to have a pneumothorax. With that cavity growing as quickly as it has, we need to collapse that lung in the hopes that it will obliterate the cavity. Deflating your lung will also allow it to rest. It's a frightening-sounding procedure, I know, but at least half of the TB patients here have had the same thing done, and lived to tell about it." Dr. Ludlow smiled, trying for a little bit of levity. "Honestly, it's so common that many of the patients have it multiple times. They're back home the same day. It's a wonderful method of fighting these cavities, but it should also help with your fever, your coughing and expectorating, as well as your appetite. I'm concerned about your weight loss. It should help you all the way around. It's such an easy procedure that it's done bedside, and it's absolutely painless. You'll be somewhat sore for the next day or two, and a little more winded, but your lung will inflate again on its own in about a week, so this isn't a permanent collapse.

"Now, on a brighter note, your lesions have decreased in size, thanks to the antibiotics. We'll keep you on the same regimen for now, and continue monitoring your progress. So, let's get this procedure done this afternoon, and see if we can't start making some real headway with your recovery. Does that sound agreeable to you?"

"I . . . yes, I'm . . . fine with it, Dr. Ludlow." In truth, I was a little shaken up to hear the size of the cavity and the treatment recommended. The idea that a needle was going to inject air between my ribs and lungs, causing my lung to collapse, was frightening.

Though I was frightened that my cavity had increased so much, it explained the way I'd been feeling, and I was grateful there was something we could do to try to help.

"All right, then." The doctor looked up at me after he'd finished writing notes on my chart. "We'll schedule your procedure for midafternoon. In the meantime, get some rest until you have to go down for lunch, I mean dinner. I'll never get it right, I'm afraid." He smiled. I thought highly of the man, and most importantly, trusted him with my life. "Speaking of rest, I hope you weren't kept awake last night with all of the bedlam going on upstairs. One of the patients had a psychotic episode. It took two good-sized orderlies, and one good sized injection to calm her down. We don't know what shook Mary up—she rarely speaks, and when she does she's often incoherent—but something set her off. I apologize if she kept you awake."

I figured the odds were high that he was talking about Mary Boone, but didn't feel right asking. "I wondered what was going on up there," I said instead. "I could hear her screaming. I was awake anyway, though—night sweats. They've gotten worse. At times, I couldn't be any hotter than if I were in the middle of the Sahara, wearing a full-length mink coat, gloves, stockings, hat, and all."

Laughing, he again jotted something down on my chart. "All right, we can do something to help reduce that a bit, but the pneumothorax should help that, too." Looking up, he smiled, "Get some rest and I'll see you this afternoon about two."

True to his word, Dr. Ludlow returned at two o'clock. I'd been quiet through dinner, and ate even less than usual, just picking at some chicken salad because Annabelle and Marsha encouraged me to eat at least a few bites.

Marsha was still recovering from her segmentectomy, but she seemed to be doing well. Her rebound gave me hope that I would be back on my feet very soon, too, and feeling better than I had for some time. On the other hand, one of the newer women in our ward, Kaye Moody, who had been on full bed rest since she'd arrived several weeks before, continued to spiral down, no matter what treatments, procedures, or medications were tried. The medical staff had reverted to using some of the old techniques, just trying anything at that point to possibly save her. They even tried sandbagging her, which was the laying of sandbags on her shoulders and chest area, and increasing the weight daily in order to restrict full inhalations of her lungs. The theory was that the restriction would allow her lungs to rest and that would give the enormous cavities and numerous lesions time to heal. However, the technique had had little success in the past, and wasn't helping any now, but her doctors had been desperately trying to save her, and trying anything in order to do so.

Finally, there was nothing more that could be done for the poor woman, who was all of thirty-eight, with a precious ten-year-old boy and a loving husband, both of whom came to visit twice a week. With great sadness, we watched their hope fade away along with Kaye's life. It broke everyone's heart. I'd noticed that during the last week only the husband had come to see her and I guessed that it had become too much for their son to witness his mother dying. So, while one patient's triumph over the disease gave me hope, another patient's succumbing to it left me feeling depressed. Feeling depressed was one thing, I told myself, but to feel hopeless was another. I didn't let myself dwell on how many poor souls died in their war against this horrific disease, but tried instead to focus my thoughts on what I could do to win just the next little battle . . .

Dr. Ludlow performed the pneumothorax in a matter of minutes. After injecting me with a localized anesthetic of Novocain, he performed the procedure without any complications. "All right; your lung is collapsed and all went well. Rest today and tomorrow. Stay in bed for the remainder of today, though you can get up for the bathroom, but have your supper sent up to you. Tomorrow, you're free to walk around some, but just take it easy. Remember, it won't take much to leave you winded. After tomorrow, you should start to feel better, both from the procedure and, hopefully, from the obliterated cavity. If all goes as I expect it will, you'll be working out in your beloved garden for short periods late next week. Sound good?"

"Yes . . . yes." My mouth felt thick and dry. I'd been given a light sedative and was feeling groggy now that the procedure was over.

"I'll check in with you in the morning. You're an excellent patient, Kathryn. Wish they were all like you." He warmly patted my shoulder, then left the room.

"Kate. Kate." My name was being softly called. I opened blurry eyes to find Annabelle leaning over me. "Do you want me to have a supper tray sent up to you? The rest of us are going down in about thirty minutes and I didn't know if the doctor said you could go down, or if you're supposed to have a tray sent up."

"Eat here." My mouth felt like I had paste in it. "Will you tell 'em?" I whispered.

"Sure, darlin'. I'll have a tray brought up. You want anything else?"

"Water." Annabelle poured a cup, then helped me to sit up and supported me while I greedily drank.

"Anything else you need?" she asked as I lay back down and she tucked the blankets securely around me like a doting mother.

"New lungs and Tyrone Power." I closed my eyes and drifted back to sleep to the lovely sound of Annabelle's rich laughter.

CHAPTER 23

Of Earth and Air

"So, Kate, after we've prepped these rows by clearing out the old squash and pumpkin vines, we'll plant the winter crops—the mustards, collards—you know, the different greens."

Philip and I were standing at the end of one of the rows as he explained what work I'd be doing. I didn't care what it was. I would agree to just about anything, as long as I was outside, in the fresh air and in the garden, feeling the precious earth. I hadn't felt this good in a long time—since Uncle Prescott's wedding. He and Glory had actually come for a visit the week before, and just seeing the two of them, and how happy they were together, had raised my spirits. I hadn't had a chance to talk to Glory very much at the wedding, but after seeing her again, I said a prayer of thanks that dear Uncle Prescott had finally found someone wonderful to love, someone who obviously loved him deeply in return.

It had been a month since the pneumothorax, and I was feeling stronger. I'd gained six pounds, as well. It was a toss-up as to who seemed happier about the success of the procedure—Dr. Ludlow, especially when he delivered the news that the large cavity was no more; or me. Adding to that wonderful news was that Dr. Ludlow had given me the okay to work in the gardens each afternoon. I'd worked an hour or so a day to begin with but had increased my time until I was working two hours most days. My progress in all areas continued, and now our hope was that the antibiotics alone could treat the remaining lesions, primarily in my right lung, and prevent any further cavities from forming.

"Before we get started with this, though," Philip continued, "let's go over to the greenhouse. You haven't been in there yet, have you?"

"No." I laid down my hoe and followed him out of the row, then fell in step by him as we skirted the rest of the garden and continued walking on the lawn. "In the couple of weeks that I've been gardening, we've always worked outside. I remember seeing the greenhouse when we drove past it on the way to admissions. Lord, that seems like years ago! It's so strange to think that it's only been four months. Time sure does drag in this place, especially when you're thinking about the folks back home, and all the things they're doing and you're missing."

"Well, at least you have a 'back home,'" Philip said as we reached the greenhouse. Opening the door for me, he followed me in.

"Where will you go when you leave here?" I asked as I looked around. The building was a white A-frame structure, primarily made of wood and glass. The floor consisted of wooden slats, spaced slightly apart to allow for easy draining, and the walls were simply banks of large, framed windows, as was the ceiling. The building was obviously old and had been painted repeatedly over the years to prevent it from rotting away due to the constant heat and moisture within it, and all of the elements battering it on the outside. But there was a true beauty to the building that could only be found in the architecture of bygone days.

"I'm not sure where I'll go," he answered. "My parents are both gone now. They were sick with different illnesses but died just months apart, about five years ago. Dad went first and then Mom. Guess she died more from a broken heart than from heart disease." He smiled sadly. "I've got some family left in Illinois—an aunt and a few cousins, but that's it. Actually, I sent UNCA a letter a couple of days ago, asking if there's a chance I might get my old job back, or if there's another opening that I'm qualified to fill. We'll see what they say." He was walking slowly down the aisle, checking different plants, including the degree of moisture in their containers and pots.

"You wrote them last week? Are you thinking you'll be discharged soon?" For some reason, I didn't feel the elation for him that I should have. Oddly enough, it bothered me that he might be leaving.

"I've had two completely clear sputum tests. When I have three, I'm good to go. So I need to figure out where I'll be going and what I'll be doing, 'cause when that time comes, the state won't be paying my room and board anymore. I'll be out on my own, kid. Isn't that a beautiful word, 'out'? I'll be saying 'hallelujah' all the way down that long driveway."

"So, you might be out in as little as a month? That's great news!" To my own ears, my enthusiasm sounded forced, but I hoped it didn't to his. After that, I didn't know what else to say. Usually, I had too much of everything to talk about around him, but I didn't feel like saying much of anything at the moment. He didn't say anything either. He watched me, and I watched him for a few seconds. I noticed that his gentle brown eyes had a real light to them. In them was awareness, and a sharpness that let me know he never missed a thing. Suddenly uncomfortable, I dropped my eyes and examined the tops of my old brown ballet slipper-shoes.

"I have something for you." He walked halfway down one of the long rows of tables that ran nearly the length of the room. On top of them were countless trays of different varieties of newly sprouting vegetables that would help feed the patients and staff through the winter and early spring. Underneath was shelving where empty pots and other gardening paraphernalia were tucked away. Squatting down, Philip reached in and retrieved something, then returned to me with a package wrapped in simple brown paper and burlap twine that was tied in a bow on top. "A happy belated birthday." He gave me a half bow.

"What?" I was totally caught off guard. "Oh, no . . . really . . . this isn't necessary!"

"Well, you should have told me that *before* I made it, then," he teased. "Go ahead, open it." When he saw that I was still reluctant, he added, "Listen, Kate, we have few enough pleasures in here. Please, take this gift."

I could see that he was getting a great deal of pleasure from giving it to me and I knew how he felt; I got more pleasure out of the giving than I did the receiving. "Well . . . okay," I said, and excitedly began working on the gift wrapping, untying the twine and then pulling away the paper.

What was revealed was a most exquisitely carved box, about the size of a thick book. It was carved from a beautiful piece of maple, with grain that had been brought out to its fullest beauty by superb workmanship. But what made it so special was the hinged lid. The wood had been carved out, creating three flowers that lay next to each other. They were incredibly delicate and amazingly lifelike. Each one was on its own stem and a different length than the other two. And each one leaned slightly away from the others as though they had been gently blown down by a breeze. The petals were round, and each flower reminded me of a girl twirling in a circle skirt—just like flowers I'd seen! Philip had carved evening primroses, and had done it quite perfectly.

"It's beautiful," I whispered, as though the beautifully crafted box deserved reverence.

"I hope you'll make wonderful memories in the years to come. And I hope you'll fill this box with little keepsakes and reminders of them."

"I don't know what to say." And I really didn't. "It's just . . . incredible. It's beautiful! How did you learn to do this and where did you get this fine wood?"

"Would you believe I learned to do this in my occupational therapy classes? Who knew I'd have a knack for it?" He chuckled.

"A knack! I'd say it's a little more than a knack. You're naturally gifted, Philip. Don't downplay it. This is beautiful; the carvings, the wood—it's perfect."

"The wood was that piece of maple I picked up on the way back from the primrose display. Remember? The grounds crew left it behind after they'd done some tree trimming."

"Yes, I remember! You picked it up. And you turned it into this? That's amazing." I turned the box around in my hands, studying every fine detail of it, then lifted the lid and inspected the fine craftsmanship inside, as well. I wished Uncle Prescott had seen it when he was here. Being a skilled woodcarver himself, he'd have appreciated the fine work.

"I know you like teaching, Philip, but you ought to seriously consider doing something with your woodworking skill, too. It'd be a shame to let it go to waste."

"I'll give that idea due consideration." He smiled. "Now, let's finish the greenhouse tour and then get back outside. Some of the other patients will be out there soon, including a couple of psych patients, and I need to get them busy right away. Otherwise, they tend to get into things they shouldn't." He smiled good-naturedly. He was patient and kind with the psych patients, and I knew that many of them were not used to such consideration.

"I admire you for helping with those folks. How'd you ever get involved doing that?"

"Well, the staff was shorthanded one day. I was already in the garden and one of the attendants asked me if I felt up to staying a little longer to help with the next group of low-risk patients coming out to work the grounds. I said yes and have helped out ever since. I don't mind. They're not dangerous, just . . . well . . . a little off. And honestly, I enjoy helping them. Too often they get overlooked, or were even abused in other institutions, as well as at home. They've been ignored, kept locked up, drugged, or all three. People don't want to be bothered with them. It's bad. So I'm happy to see they're treated fairly here, and to get them outside instead of locked up in their rooms."

"You're a good person."

"No, not really. I'm just grateful to be . . . well, mentally all there. I saw too many people come back from the Pacific Theatre who weren't just messed up physically, but mentally, too. Sometimes the injuries we couldn't see were far worse than the ones we could. I thought about how that could have been me if I'd been on the front lines and walked into a death camp like Bergen-Belsen, or Auschwitz, and had seen what the soldiers saw. It was enough to send the most stable guy over the edge. The numbers of dead were unimaginable, and bodies were scattered everywhere. It's really frightening how inhumane mankind can be. We're the cruelest animals on this earth." He was quiet for a moment, reflective. "Anyway"—the look on his face brightened—"we got vegetables to tend to. On with the tour."

Back outside, I began raking one of the rows of potatoes that had just been harvested. About six people were working in the garden, including the very troubled Mary Boone. From out of the corner of my eye, I watched her; not because I was afraid of her, but because I was curious about her and felt pity for her, as well. But I didn't want her to know that I was watching her.

Now that I was close enough to her—she was just one row over, working on old potato mounds, as well—I could see that she frequently mumbled to herself. It looked as though she was carrying on a full conversation, for the inflection of her voice would change, as well as her expressions, exactly as though she was reacting to something someone said and then responding to it. She'd smile or laugh out loud, the sound pleasing, lilting, almost like a young girl's. Then her countenance would change and the tone of her voice would, too; becoming harsh, curt. Her posture was always slumped, though. She seemed permanently beaten down, and she looked around often, ducking her head slightly as she did, as if she was warily on the lookout for someone or something and was afraid she was about to receive a painful blow.

While I was raking from the east end of my row, Mary was raking from the west of hers, and the distance between us gradually narrowed. As we worked, I noticed her casting furtive glances at me, but she never allowed her eyes to hold mine. Then, when we were maybe five yards from each other, Mary let go of her rake and tentatively came toward me. She kept her head down, but looked up at me through her eyelashes. Her manner was almost submissive, as though she didn't dare look at me. Finally, she stood directly in front of me, with head still bowed and shoulders hunched. Her once black hair was dirty and stringy, and had just a few gray strands threaded through it.

"Hello, Mary," I said softly, hoping to reassure her. "It's a pretty day to be in the garden, don't you think?" I didn't know what she was thinking, or what she might want, and though I was a little apprehensive, I wouldn't move. For one thing, I didn't want to walk away from her, as if I was rebuffing her, when it had obviously taken some courage for her to come over to me. Secondly, I wanted to understand this broken woman better.

Slowly, tentatively, Mary lifted her head, turning her face up to me. Though she was not an old woman, and had clearly been beautiful at one time, the lines and wrinkles and numerous small scars on her face told me that she'd struggled and suffered in the years she'd lived. Her eyes were almond-shaped, dark and exotic, but they were eerily bright, feverishly so. There was no telling what she was thinking, or how she processed what she was seeing, but there was no mistaking the fire in them. She reminded me of a cornered and injured raccoon that had crawled through a broken wooden slat in the wall of our barn one cold March morning when I was a teenager. The little thing hissed at us and tried to move out of the corner, first this way and then that, but there was no escaping. Daddy had to put the coon down because he'd gotten his back foot caught in a trap and it was torn to pieces. We didn't know where the trap had been set, or by whom, but the animal had escaped, nearly tearing his foot off in the process. The intense fear and pain were driving it to madness, which was clearly evident in the eerie brightness of the poor little thing's eyes. Now I saw those same eyes in the woman standing before me, feverishly lit and reflecting their own memories of pain and fear. Even so, I could see something else in them, as well: It was a tiny flicker of recognition.

Slowly, Mary lifted a trembling hand and laid it ever so gently against my sun-warmed cheek. "From the good one." She stared at me hard for a moment, and then the smallest hint of a smile turned up just one corner of her mouth. Finally, she dropped her hand and walked back to the row she was working.

"Mary? What do you mean?" I softly asked, following her as she turned away. There was no response from her, so I asked her again, but when there was still no response, I stopped. I wondered if she even knew she had spoken to me not a minute before. But I knew she had. And I had the feeling that her statement had not been born of madness, but had been prompted by a memory from some other time and some other place. Who was "the good one"?

CHAPTER 24

Yessiree, George!

"So, that's it, I think." Roberta closed the suitcase on her bed, then surveyed the area around it yet again. We were the only three in the ward at the moment because it was dinnertime. In just the last week, two more women had been admitted, making a total of ten in the ward, the most since I'd been there. But Roberta was being discharged, and Annabelle and I had stayed behind to say good-bye. We were her "oldest" friends at Pelham, and though she and Jane English had spent a lot of time together and seemed to have a tight friendship, I noticed that Jane had said a brief good-bye to Roberta, then headed down to eat with a couple of other women. Perhaps sharing gossip did not build the strongest of bonds between friends, I cynically thought, and then scolded myself for being critical.

"Did you double-check the bathroom?" I asked.

"Five times, but who's counting?" She laughed.

"You should have checked six." Annabelle returned with Roberta's bright green shower cap. "Is Jim picking you up?"

"Yep, the power company let him take the day off." Her smile was a mile wide. "He's a lineman," she added. "Now, I really think that's it." She slipped the shower cap in a side pocket of her satchel. "An orderly will be here any minute to pick up all my junk." She turned to both of us. "You know, I never had many girlfriends. Don't know why but just didn't. Never felt like I had much use for 'em, if the truth be known. But you two have taught me different. I'll never forget you." Her voice broke and all three of us hugged together.

"Don't come back!" Annabelle said firmly, leaving our little circle. "We love you, but don't come back." An orderly walked in and Annabelle directed him over to Roberta's waiting luggage, then went into the bathroom. When it came to expressing her tender side, Annabelle liked her privacy, and I had no doubt that she was shedding a few tears behind that closed door.

"Roberta," I began, "I'll never forget your kindness my first night here. You don't know how badly I needed some comforting and you were there. I hope you and Jim have a wonderful—and healthy—life together for a long, long time. Now, go!" I laughed, reacting to my own tears, and grabbed some tissues from Roberta's nightstand. I followed her toward the door. "I hope we'll meet again, but not in a place like this."

"You listen to me, Kathryn." She abruptly turned around and stopped. "You can beat this damned disease. And I fully expect you to. You got that boy to raise and he needs you, especially with a father like Geoffrey. Your husband will try turning him into somethin' maybe the boy doesn't want to be. Forgive me for saying that, but I'm just callin' it the way I see it. You be strong." She hugged me hard. "Stay strong for yourself and that son of yours." Then she abruptly let go of me and walked out of the ward without looking back.

I sat down on her bed, thinking about her parting words, and waited for Annabelle to come out of the bathroom.

"Did she go?" Annabelle asked, poking her head out of the bathroom door and looking around. "Lord, I hate watching people leave. At least she didn't go out on a gurney, though," she joked. She blew her reddened nose. "You know, I was thinking, why don't you come to my occupational therapy class this afternoon? We're starting a new quilt throw—we're giving them to the Korean War widows—and we need you to help oust Dottie Mendelssohn. She's that TB psych gal. Harmless, but annoying as hell. Just about every time someone asks a question, Dottie yells out, *Yessiree, Bob!* You'll say to someone else at the table, *So, Marie, was that your daughter visiting you on Sunday?* and before Marie can say yes or no, ol' Dottie yells out, *Yessiree, Bob!* She about drives us all nuts. So, if you get there before she does, that'll fill up the table and she'll be out."

"That's mean," I said, but couldn't help laughing as I did. "The poor ol' thing. However, her spot is safe for today. My friend George Eisenhower, the director of the Children's Home in Cabot, is coming to see me."

"Again? Isn't this his third visit? Whatcha got goin' on with him, gal?" she whispered conspiratorially.

"Oh, Lord, Annabelle! You are a true drama queen. Forget art history, go into show business!" I laughed. "Listen," I said seriously, "I need someone to talk to about a proposition George made. Can we take a walk after dinner? I only need your ears, not a dozen other sets of them."

"Ah *HA*! I knew it! A proposition! Oh, do tell!" She sat down on the bed near to where I was standing.

"It's not *that* kind of proposition, Annabelle! Lord! I just need a sounding board. So, can we take a walk to someplace quiet?"

"Yessiree, Bob!" Annabelle enthusiastically replied. And we laughed and coughed all the way to the dining room.

After we were through with dinner, we walked to the koi pond. The day was sunny with a nice breeze that made it comfortable enough for late August. Annabelle and I sat on the same bench Philip and I had sat on the night of the evening primrose display.

"So, what's the news?" Annabelle eagerly asked.

"Well, first of all, I got my sputum sample results this morning, right before Roberta left. Dr. Ludlow called me down to his office in Administration and told me it's clear. My sputum is blood-free, Annabelle!" I could feel my whole face smiling. And Annabelle's mirrored mine.

"Oh, kid! That's fabulous news! That's just great!" It was wonderful being able to celebrate with Annabelle, because earlier in the week, she'd received the news that her second sputum smear had been as clear as the one the month before. "Good for you, Kate! Good for you!" She repeatedly patted my thigh—slapped it, actually, quite enthusiastically, to the point that it stung. But I didn't care. The world felt too good at the moment to care, and I knew that my friend was just thrilled for me. We rooted for each other, constantly and loyally. "Okay, so you said *first of all*; now what's second of all? And what's this proposition you mentioned?"

"I've told you about the Children's Home, and that George Eisenhower is the director, and the one I work most closely with. Well, as you know, he came to visit me several weeks ago." I smiled at her, tickled at her for being suspicious of his multiple visits. "Well, he's planning on building another children's home farther outside Cabot—

like around Marion, or somewhere in that area. He says we need a rural outpost of the Home. See, a lot of our residents are what're called 'half orphans.' That's where one parent is still alive but unable to care for the child. Maybe the child's father was lost in the war, and the child's mother doesn't have the means to take care of him or her, so that child becomes a resident at the Home. We see quite a lot of them coming in from the rural areas because of the level of poverty there. Work is just harder to find. We want the kids to be as close to home as possible. If they have any family at all, we want to make it easier for them to visit these children, and have some kind of connection with them. If the child is in a place that's too far for family to come for just a few hours' visit, then most of the time they don't come at all. Anyway, George needs help with this new location; getting it started and keeping it going once it's up and running. He wants me to oversee the gardens, et cetera."

"What's the *et cetera* part?" Nothing got by Annabelle.

"I'm getting to that. See, I have a year's worth of college credits. Even though I wasn't there quite that long, I doubled up on classes in a couple of my semesters so that I could finish as soon as possible. It was expensive—for my parents and me. Then I met and married Geoffrey. However, George told me that with just one more year of college, I'd have my two-year degree, which would then qualify me for the assistant director's position at the new Home. Do you know that George only has a high school diploma? But when he became a director of a school in Albany, New York, back in the late twenties, that's all that was required. Anyway, it's the fifties now, so I'd have to have that two-year degree just to become an assistant director. I could do the courses by mail, or even take them part-time at a couple of the different colleges in the area. George said I wouldn't have to be at the Home every day, just go over several times a week. He'll hire a director, of course, but he wants me over there, too, since I'm so familiar with the running of the Home, and because I'm from the mountains myself, and can relate to the rural folks."

"Well, how do you feel about all this, Kate? And what's Geoffrey gonna say about it?" I'd never seen Annabelle look more serious. Her dark, exotic eyes were searching mine for the truth.

"I think I want to do it. With Donnie starting school now, I'll have more time. But Geoffrey would hate it. I know he'll tell me not to do it."

"Even part-time?"

"Geoffrey wants me to be his socialite wife, full-time."

"And what are you going to say to that?"

"I just don't know yet, Annabelle. I just don't know."

We sat quietly together, deep in our own thoughts. Neither one of us said anything for a while as we watched the comings and goings of staff and patients moving along the walkways, and patients sitting with visitors on the lawn. As I looked around, I thought how very ironic it was that the place I'd dreaded coming to offered such solace and peace, especially as I stood at the brink of certain unrest in the place that I used to call home.

"Life's never easy, is it?" Annabelle reflectively mused.

"Nosiree, Bob," I said as I tossed a pebble in the fish pond. "Nosiree, Bob.

CHAPTER 25

Promises Broken,
Promises Kept

The sun blazed down on our shoulders, though we knew that its days for baking us in the gardens were numbered, for it was already early September, and autumn was beginning to show signs of its approach. Some of the leaves on the buckeye trees were turning a bright red-orange, as were the poison ivy vines, which encased many tree trunks like fishnet stockings. I was glad to see the change. I loved the cold weather, even though it meant the end of working in the garden until the early spring.

"Grab that spade lying in those marigolds, would you, Kate?" Philip asked, as several of us wrapped up a couple of hours of working in the flower beds around the administration building. "Everyone, let's put the tools in the greenhouse instead of the shed 'cause we'll be working by the staff's dining hall tomorrow and it'll be more convenient if we leave them in there." Turning to me, he said, "I've got to check the greenhouse heater. I bet it hasn't been used since late last spring. I'd also bet that no one's checked it."

The tools were stored away on some shelving right inside the door. As everyone filed out, Philip pulled out a stepladder and climbed up to inspect the heater that was suspended over a set of cabinets where little-used, miscellaneous items were stored. "Geez, this thing's dusty. Would you hand me a few damp rags, Kate, and a whisk broom?"

Grabbing a handful of rags from the closet, I quickly wet them, then handed all of the items up to him. A radio had been left playing on one of the shelves in front of Philip, and he turned the volume up. The Alan Freed show was on; a repeat broadcast from Saturday night.

It was one of the most popular forms of entertainment for us, especially with the advent of the new rock 'n' roll craze. And one of the biggest breakthrough artists was Elvis Presley, whose wildly popular hit "That's All Right" was presently playing. Philip began to sing along, though it was more of a hum than actual singing. "That guy is good! I like this new music okay, especially ol' Elvis, here, but you can't hang on to your sweetheart with this new stuff like you can with doo-wop or jitterbug music."

Distracted by my own thoughts, I didn't hear what-all he said, so I answered with a noncommittal "Uh-huh."

He glanced down at me from the ladder. "You were quiet today, Kate. Something bothering you?" He turned his attention back to the heater again.

"I'm just worried about Donnie. Mama and I talked earlier, to confirm what time everyone'll be here. Tomorrow's the day my folks bring Donnie back from his summer stay with them, and Geoffrey's coming over from Cabot to pick him up. School starts in a little over a week. I spoke to the poor little fella and asked him if he's excited about starting the first grade and he began crying. Said he wanted to stay with my folks. I tried to convince him that he'll love his new school, and told him he'd have fun bein' home with his daddy again, but I knew I wasn't convincing him. Shoot! I'm not convinced myself! Anyway, when Mama got back on the phone, she said he'd been crying all week. Said he keeps sayin' he doesn't want to leave. I'm just sick about it. The worst part is that I promised I'd be there to take him to his classroom on the first day of school, and now I'm gonna have to break that promise. It's the first time I won't be keeping a promise to him!" I choked up. I turned away from Philip and pretended to busy myself with the plants on one of the long tables, trying to pull myself together.

"If this is the first time you've broken a promise, then you deserve the Mother of the Year award, Kate! Listen, when a promise isn't kept because of reasons beyond the control of the one who made the promise, then it's forgivable. Yeah, it's a bitter pill to swallow, but you have to forgive yourself. Donnie will, too. There's nothing pretty or easy or kind about being institutionalized while the rest of the world—especially your family—goes about the business of living. I have so little family left, Kate, and honestly, it's a blessing sometimes, at least for the time I'm in here. Donnie will be okay once he gets back home and busy with school. He'll readjust to living with Geoffrey. Kids are very resilient. You know that."

"Yeah, I guess," I answered, though I wasn't convinced.

Philip finished cleaning the heater and handed the rags and broom down to me. I put them in the sink to wash later as he put the ladder away. "Kate," he said as he came out of the closet and stood in front of me, "there's nothing you can do about the situation at home right now. But you're getting better, so stay focused on that and you'll be home again soon."

As he spoke to me, I noticed that his brown eyes had a lot of gold in them, much like my father's, actually, and his hair was thick and wavy like his, too, though it was a much lighter brown and longer than my father's. The Drifters' song, "Money Honey," began playing on the radio. Its unmistakable bluesy sound spilled from the speakers like warm honey. "Now, *that's* a song," he said, turning away from me to turn the volume up, and interrupting my study of him. "We shall end this day on a lighter note, with a dance!" he declared, pulling me toward him by my wrist.

"Oh, no, Philip, I don't feel like dancing. Really." I started to pull away.

"And that's exactly why you should! C'mon, you'll feel better. Just this one." He looked like a little boy and I couldn't help but laugh.

"I think it's *you* who's gonna feel better . . . All right—but just one."

He set the pace and we began a slow jitterbug. Closing my eyes, I could imagine being in a smoky, stale-smelling juke joint, surrounded by bad whiskey and even worse company. The heat in the greenhouse helped create the sultry illusion. The driving, heavy rhythm lifted you up and eased you down, rolling and building like waves on the ocean, playing and pushing you, until it fully pulled you in with its sensuous pulse, touching something deep inside and intentionally causing a reaction.

Philip pulled me closer so that the jitterbug turned into a slower, closer dance. With the side of his face resting against mine, he breathed in my scent. I could feel his intake of breath and then the slow exhale. He pulled away and looked at me, and then he gently reached out and took a wayward lock of hair, which had escaped my low bun, between his fingers, lightly rolling it back and forth, as though he'd wondered what my hair felt like. Then, slowly, softly, he touched his lips to mine . . . and I responded. The kiss intensified with our tongues meeting, moving together, finally tasting each other, and at last knowing. It felt natural, when I knew it should feel all wrong. Holding me firmly, he pulled away just slightly, but was still so close that I could feel his breath against my mouth. Then, he whispered, "Kate . . ." It was a soft plea, but emotionally charged, asking for more. And I wanted to answer it, completely and fully, but I couldn't. I had made promises and I had always done everything in my power to keep them, including the one I made to Geoffrey, in front of God, many years before. And now I was starting to take the first step toward breaking it. I stepped back and touched my fingers to my lips as if to stop them from saying something they shouldn't, or from doing any more damage than they'd already done.

I shook my head vehemently, and my eyes welled up. "I have to go. I have to . . ." I hurried out of the greenhouse, and he stood in the doorway watching me go, figuratively and literally. He knew that he had no choice, for the decision had to be mine, and I'd made it.

I waited until the last minute to go to supper that evening, telling Annabelle and Marsha to go on without me, that I needed to make some phone calls. But the truth was, I didn't want to see Philip, and he was usually in the dining room about the same time that I was, even though he was on the other side of the room. Right now, though, even that was too close. I needed to think about what had happened, what could have happened had I not stopped it, and how I felt about it all.

Later on, lying in the darkness, knowing that sleep would never come, I heard that inner voice, the one that whispers the truths that one can't hide from. And the truth it whispered frightened me.

CHAPTER 26

Divided We Fall

"So, have him try his old ones on to check what still fits, then get what he needs. I'm so sorry to leave all of this to you, Geoffrey. I wish you'd let Mama take him shopping for his school clothes."

"It isn't necessary, Kathryn. I'll take him to get whatever he needs. We have better shopping in Cabot. Your mother means well, but let's face it, the shops in Howling Cut leave much to be desired." I let his little jab slide. I was never going to change his feelings about the place.

"Well, please let Donnie help pick out what he wants to wear," I continued. "Guide him, of course, but let him think he's helping to make the final decisions. He's growing up and he needs to have a voice in things that concern him, even if he does try to pair stripes with plaids." I smiled.

"When are they all getting here?" He impatiently looked at his watch. This was the first time Geoffrey was early and he was getting anxious to head back to Cabot.

"They'll be here any minute. We said eleven o'clock, and it's just five of. How are things at work?" I changed the subject to something I knew he could talk about forever.

"Actually, everything's going quite well. We'll be adding another partner next week, and Kathryn, you'll be impressed to know that it's a woman, Gina Omar. However, she *is* a Yankee," he said wryly and smiled. "She's from New York."

"New York? Then why does she want to come to Cabot?"

"She did some freelance work with our firm several months ago and fell in love with the mountains. She's top-notch, and we're fortunate to be getting her."

"The business has expanded quite a lot since you've taken over, Geoffrey. I know that's been your goal, and I'm proud of you. I know it makes you happy."

"Thank you, Kathryn, and it should make you happy, too. It just means having more of the finer things in life."

We already have them, Geoffrey. We have so much! Look at your son, your health, your wife who is still alive. Look at us, Geoffrey! I sadly thought but did not bother to say. He would never see it that way.

"Look, there they are!" I said. Shielding my eyes from the sun, I saw Mama and Donnie coming down the lawn toward us. I was immediately struck by the fact that Daddy wasn't with them and felt a surge of panic. I got up and walked toward them.

"Where's Daddy, Mama?" I said as I hugged Donnie to me, and then hugged her.

"At home with a broken leg!" she said, turning to hug Geoffrey, who was just setting Donnie back down. "Your daddy's an ol' fool." She laughed, shaking her head. Just by her smile, I knew he was all right.

"What happened?"

"Well, you know that stray cat that adopted us a couple of weeks ago? Well, he got up in one of the apple trees and couldn't get back down. So, that fool father of yours gets up in there to get the poor little thing down, only *he* comes down—hard! Broke his leg, and the cat ran off! Your daddy will be all right, but he can't do much more than complain and keep me running from hither to yon, getting this and that for him. He's got a cast that goes all the way to mid-thigh. Lord, honey, they'll have to put me in Pelham before long, but in one of the crazy wards!"

"Well, Mama, you'd get to see Aunt Harriet real often." I laughed, relieved that no more harm had come to Daddy than a broken leg.

"All right," I said, "y'all come on and sit down. And, Donnie, you come tell me all about getting ready for school, and what you're most excited about." I pulled him over to my lounge chair, and we sat down, with him straddling the end of it, facing me.

"So, Daddy's going to take you to meet your new teacher at Washington Primary next Thursday. Isn't that exciting?"

He shrugged then mumbled softly, "I guess."

"Honey, you're going to make so many nice friends. You know, I remember when I started school. My teacher's name was Miss Mays. I was scared to death, but I remember we started to play this—" I stopped talking as Donnie burst into tears.

Leaning over toward me on the chair, my sweet, frightened, broken-hearted son buried his head in my lap, and sobbed, "I wanna stay at Grandma's!" His little shoulders shook with his wrenching sobs, and it took everything I had to not start sobbing with him. I was glad he wasn't looking up at me or I wouldn't have been able to hold myself together. "Oh, darlin'! Oh, goodness!" I ran my hand up and down his back, stroking him, trying to comfort him. "It's gonna be okay." I looked at my mother, then over at Geoffrey. My mother was softly crying, too, and was digging in her pocket for a handkerchief. Geoffrey, on the other hand, looked like a deer caught in a car's headlights. His eyes were big and round, as if he was stunned, with no idea whether he should say something or just stay quiet. And then Donnie said the one thing that broke my heart. "And you won't be there to take me the first day!" I laid my head down against my son's and cried with him.

"Oh, for God's *sake!*" Geoffrey walked away, moving some distance from us, obviously disgusted, and perhaps hurt, though I'd have bet my last dollar that it was only the former. He stood there with his hands on his hips and his back to us for a couple of minutes, then he took a deep breath and returned.

"Son," he said curtly. "You need to pull yourself together. You're making everyone upset, not to mention that you're making an enormous fuss over the most ridiculous thing. You're coming home to go to school, and that's a fact. And your mother won't be there to take you, but I will be. Sometimes life is cruel and unfair, but that's life, Donald. You're old enough to understand that."

Donnie had sat up and turned toward his father as he was talking to him. When he heard what Geoffrey was saying, he lay against my chest and closed his eyes. I wrapped my arms around him and gently rocked him, softly whispering to him as Geoffrey lectured that everything was going to be all right. I didn't quite believe it, though, and I was sure that my very bright and very sensitive son didn't believe it either.

I held up my hand to stop Geoffrey from going on any further and making matters worse. He stopped talking immediately, probably because he was taken aback that I would have the nerve to cut him off. He marched away from us again, but this time walked as far as the overgrown band shell, which was at least fifty yards away. He needed to cool off.

"Donnie, look at Mama. I need you to look at me so that you know I'm telling you the truth." Slowly, he got off my chest and looked at me, still trembling and winded from his sobbing. "Son, I've never broken a promise to you until this one—about taking you to school on your first day, right?" He thought for a second as if trying to recall another time that I might have let him down, but unable to, he nodded. Then, relying on one thing that had always comforted him, he slipped his thumb into his mouth. I didn't stop him.

"I need you to know that I didn't break this promise on purpose. You're big enough to understand that I was sicker than we thought I was, and though the good doctors have tried their best to make me well in time to take you to school, they just weren't able to. But, I *am* feeling better. I'm able to do more things now than I could for a while. See that garden over there?" He looked to where I was pointing. "I just planted mustard greens in it a couple of weeks ago, and I thought of you 'cause I know how much you love 'em!" He hated them, and I tickled his ribs, making him giggle. Thank God. "So, even though I'm doing better, I'm still not as good as they want me to be. They can't let me out of this place, even to walk you to school. You know why?" His hands were now planted down on my thighs and he was listening intently. "Because they want to fix me up to where I'm feeling so good that I will never, ever have to come back here again. They want me to be able to walk you to school, even when you're in college! You think your girlfriends will mind your mama walkin' you to school?" He smiled broadly and shook his head. "Well, I say that's just too bad for them 'cause you're my boy and will always, always be! Whatcha got to say about that? Huh?"

I tickled him again, and then he let out a big sigh, as if in resignation that things were not going to be just as he and I wanted them to be—at least not for a while. "Okay, so here's the plan." I was stroking his hair. "You go on and be with Daddy, 'cause I'm gonna tell you a secret, Donnie; he needs you, real bad. And if you go with him, you'll really be helping me because I won't worry about him so much knowin' you're there to watch out for him. Would that be all right with you? Can you do that for me?"

He thought for a few seconds, then nodded his head and softly said, "Uh-huh."

"That's my boy," I said, leaning down slightly and kissing the crown of his head. As I did, I smelled his hair. It was a mother's favorite perfume. "You take care of Daddy, he'll take care of you, and the doctors will take care of me, and we'll be together before you know it! Does that sound like an all-right plan to you, little buddy?"

"Uh-huh."

I looked him straight in his eyes, and said very seriously, "It's going to be okay, son. We'll all be okay." Then I hugged him hard and prayed that what I said wouldn't turn out to be another broken promise to my son.

They left soon after, before anyone, but especially Donnie, could get upset again. I walked them to the edge of the parking lot and fought back the tears as I said good-bye to each one of them. Donnie held on to Mama, not wanting to let her go. The only reason he finally did was that she promised to come see him in a few weeks and bring the tree-climbing cat back for him. Geoffrey had agreed then and there to allow the cat to come live with them. I believe he would have agreed to most anything at that point to keep the situation under control, and to prevent anything more from delaying their departure.

I watched them drive out of the parking lot and all the way down the long driveway. Mama was going to spend the night at Aunt Harriet's, to break up the drive home, and Uncle Prescott and Glory were spending the night with Daddy. And Geoffrey and Donnie were going to Donnie's favorite restaurant in Cabot for chili dogs. There was nothing more I could do for any of them at that moment.

Suddenly, I felt exhausted. I was mentally and physically worn out. Knowing that I had absolutely no energy left in me, I decided to have a tray of supper sent up to my room. I couldn't sit at a table in the dining hall and talk about superficial things, things that had no meaning to me at all. Besides, I didn't want to see Philip, because the truth of the matter was that I wanted to see Philip—badly, so I had to avoid him, especially that evening. My emotions were too raw, and I was too vulnerable. I might say things and allow things to be said that shouldn't be said or even thought of. I knew what I was feeling, and I didn't need to be reminded of Philip's emotions.

I started back toward my building and glanced up at it. But when I started to look away, a lone figure standing at a window on the second floor of the building next to mine caught my eye. It was Mary Boone. The sun acted like a spotlight on her, making her clearly visible. I could see that she was watching me, but it was the look on her face that brought me to a standstill. It was one of absolute despair. Her mouth was slightly ajar, making it look like an eerie, slanting gash in her face. And her hands were closed into fists up at her throat, as if she was tightly clutching the material of her robe together. She stood there sobbing, hard; hard enough that I could see the slight jerking motions in her shoulders. There she stood, deep in her unreachable pain. And as I watched her dissolving in it, I couldn't help but think how well her feelings mirrored mine, and those of my family.

CHAPTER 27

Parting Paths

It had been over three weeks since the emotional visit with Mama, Donnie, and Geoffrey. Donnie had been in school for over two weeks and, thankfully, seemed to be enjoying Washington Primary. Though Chesterfield had been Geoffrey's choice of the two schools, they'd had an overabundance of students register and had had to turn down quite a few, including Donnie. Geoffrey had been indignant beyond reason. As far as he was concerned, his son should have been enrolled regardless, especially since the headmaster was on the board of trustees with Geoffrey at our church. But he complained to no avail. Their limits were their limits, he was told, and Geoffrey had attempted to register Donnie too late.

Geoffrey had hired a part-time nanny, Nell Lewis, to pick up Donnie at school and stay with him until Geoffrey returned about six each evening, and so far, their routine seemed to be working for each of them. Apparently, the smooth running of my household was the best medicine I could have been given because my second sputum test had come back clear, too, and my X-rays showed that some of my lesions were completely gone, while the ones that remained were much smaller, and no new cavities had formed. The miraculous antibiotic cocktail was working well, and I couldn't have been more grateful to the doctors and the incredible people who had never given up the research until they found success with these amazing, curative medications and procedures. *If only the breakthroughs could have happened sooner, before two billion people were destroyed by this disease*, I thought.

My daily routine at Pelham had changed in the last three weeks, and it was entirely due to my fear and shame: I was afraid to see Philip, ashamed of the episode in the greenhouse, and ashamed of my strong feelings for him. Though the kiss was far from cousining, I had to be honest with myself. I knew that I could have given in to that moment and allowed us to go down a road where there could be no undoing what was done. I did see Philip around the grounds and in the dining hall, but it was always at a distance and I kept it that way, knowing it was far safer for both of us.

I had stopped working in the garden for the most part, and only spent time in it for short periods, when I was sure Philip wouldn't be there. But as the growing season was winding down, so was my time in the garden. Instead, I spent most of my active time working on different crafts in the occupational therapy rooms. I'd busied myself working on a queen-sized quilt for my parents for Christmas (which was still several months away, but I'd need every bit of that time to finish it), as well as a toy sailboat for Donnie and a beautiful model ship for Geoffrey. He'd been in the sailing club while in college, but now that we were landlocked in Cabot, he'd traded his sexton for a tennis racket. However, I knew he loved ships of all sorts, and I hoped he'd be pleased with my gift.

I was trying to think positively about Geoffrey, and our marriage, which was the main reason I'd avoided Philip. I couldn't be distracted by a temporary infatuation when I had a long-term, committed relationship that needed my attention. However, I kept having to push aside the fact that whenever I thought of Geoffrey, I felt a heaviness, whereas when I thought of Philip, there was only lightness. So, to lessen my inner turmoil I avoided Philip, hoping that the old saying *out of sight, out of mind* would prove to be true. But getting someone out of your heart was another matter altogether.

One Wednesday evening after supper, Marsha and I were taking a walk along the pathway leading to the koi pond. It was movie night and we were killing time before the film started, to enjoy the touch of fall in the air. More and more leaves were beginning to turn magnificent shades of bright orange, red, and yellow, while some had already fallen. Somewhere on the grounds, a pile was being burned, and the seasonal smell drew most everyone into reflective moods, thinking of home and the upcoming holidays. Homesickness and loneliness were felt more this time of year, and the fact that Annabelle had been released from Pelham late that morning made Marsha and me a bit more melancholy than usual.

We were thrilled that Annabelle had been given a clean bill of health. From now on, her treatments of antibiotics could easily be taken while living an everyday, normal life. But because there was nothing at all "everyday normal" about Annabelle, we already missed her in just the seven hours she'd been gone. Her vivaciousness and energy set her apart from the other women in the ward, and we'd thrived on it. She'd kept ward life fun—as fun as it could be in an institution—and certainly interesting, and for those reasons, we loved her and would feel the void that her absence created.

"What are they showin' tonight, anyway?" Marsha asked, interrupting my thoughts of Annabelle.

"*The Quiet Man*, with John Wayne and Maureen O'Hara. It's set in Ireland, and it's good. Geoffrey and I saw it last year when it first came out."

"Oh, you don't want to watch it again, do you? We could go back to the room, if you'd rather." As usual, Marsha was always thinking of others.

"I don't mind seeing it again, and it sure beats going back to the room." I checked my watch. "It's starting in fifteen minutes. We'd better head on over if we want to catch it from the beginning."

The movie was shown in the auditorium, the same one used for the talent show, and because it was a popular diversion, as well as a chance to socialize, it usually drew a good crowd.

One of the orderlies immediately directed Marsha and me toward the tuberculars' section up in the balcony. The whole back row was empty, so moving a few seats in from the aisle, we sat down.

"Want one?" Marsha held out a brown bag of peanut butter cookies that she'd brought from the dining hall.

"Lord, no! No, thanks. I swear, Marsha, I've put on five more pounds, and if I'm not careful, I'll start gettin' a little too plump."

"From your mouth to God's ears, m'dear! That means you're getting well, and to gain a good amount of weight is your meal ticket out of here—no pun intended." She chuckled.

The lights came down and the screen came to life with a news short. Black-and-white images of a smiling Brazilian president, Getúlio Vargas, showed him just days before he committed suicide after being accused of conspiracy to murder his chief political opponent, Carlos

Lacerda. Next, scenes of the Soviet Union's military practice drills flashed before us as we were informed of the growing tension between Russia and the United States. Finally, as if to end the news on a good note, the scene shifted to more soldiers, but these were our own, walking down the stairs from a plane and out onto the tarmac as they returned to the homeland, waving, smiling, and triumphant, after winning the Korean War. As we watched, "God Bless America" played softly beneath the voice of the newscaster, and everyone in the audience cheered, while several military veterans stood and saluted the images on the screen. It reminded me of sitting in the only movie theater in Howling Cut, the Galaxy, when I was a teenager, clapping and cheering as the men returned from Europe at the end of World War II. There was nothing like home; and the returning soldiers knew that. So did those of us institutionalized around the country. My melancholy grew a little, and I tried to focus on the next story coming up, but it was an advertisement; a cartoon box of popcorn and one of candy strutted across the screen, urging audience members to go to the lobby for a treat. *Maybe in the real world, I thought, but in this surreal one, the only thing in the lobby were the orderlies to ensure that the Captain Crows and the Mary Boones did not just go out to the lobby for a treat, but out the door and the facility's front gates, too.* After watching the news briefs, though, I wasn't sure which was the crazier world—the one I was in at the moment, or the one beyond the walls.

The Quiet Man started, and I laid my head back and closed my eyes. I was tired. I hadn't slept well the night before. The night sweats were barely an issue anymore, but my worries about the future were. I was hopeful I'd be leaving Pelham before too long, but when I did, what then? Could Geoffrey and I pick up the pieces where we'd left off? And, if so, would our former life be enough for both of us? I'd never had thoughts like that before, but I had a lot of time to think about things, and see them from afar. Being removed from the life I once knew gave me a chance to see things a little more objectively, giving me a different perspective on things.

Utmost in my mind, of course, was Donnie's happiness and well-being. And while I realized that the thing that would make Donnie the happiest in the short term would be my returning home, I wondered if my little boy was unhappy in other ways. When he had cried in my lap the day Geoffrey had come to take him back to Cabot, the intensity of his unhappiness stunned me. I wondered if the emotional distance between Donnie and Geoffrey had created fissures that were becoming increasingly harder to close. And, perhaps, widening that chasm even more had been the physical distance between them over the last several months. I told myself that once we were all back home again things would get back to normal, and maybe even be better than they had been before, including their father/son relationship and our husband/wife one, as well. As I sat there thinking, hardly even hearing Maureen O'Hara's lilting Irish brogue emanating loudly from the auditorium's speakers, I gave myself a hundred different reasons why things at home would change when I returned. And when I got to number ninety-nine, I wondered if coming up with a hundred more might actually convince me that they would.

"You were snoring!" Marsha laughed. She'd had to shake my arm to awaken me when the movie ended. Apparently, I'd been asleep for a good part of it. "And you snore like a sailor, too," she teased as we got up to leave.

"Oh, I do not!" I laughingly denied, following her down the stairs. Though, if the truth were known, I'd been accused of snoring before. I'd broken my nose when I was about eleven, playing base-ball. As I'd looked up to make the catch, the sun blinded me, and the ball nailed me, leaving my straight nose just a little offset. *Gives her character*, my father had said. *It gave her a broken nose!* my mother had replied, and promptly replaced the hardball with a softball.

"Oh, phooey!" Marsha laughed. "Why, heck, if someone didn't know any better and walked into our ward in the black of night, they'd think they were in the men's bunk room on board the *SS Snoresalot*." She walked out into the lobby.

"Hey," I heard a deep voice say from a small shadowed alcove where the restrooms were. Startled, we both turned to look, and out into the light stepped Philip, unable to hide a grin. "Sorry, ladies, I didn't mean to scare you." He looked nice, dressed in gray flannel pants and a dark blue buttoned-up long-sleeved shirt, with a light blue vest over it. He was usually wearing blue jeans and flannel shirts, or T-shirts if he was working in the garden.

"You most certainly did intend to scare us!" Marsha accused with a good-natured laugh.

"Hi, Kate." His mischievous expression faded when he turned to me. "If you're not in too big a hurry, could I talk to you for a few minutes?"

"I'll see you back at the ward," Marsha promptly said and hurried away before I could object.

"Philip . . ." I turned to him. "It's getting late and I—"

"I'm leaving tomorrow, Kate. I was given my walking papers today." He smiled slightly, trying to keep it light. But I felt like I'd had the wind knocked out of me, taking all of my words with it.

"C'mon, let's take a walk. It's a nice evening." I didn't object, and started down the auditorium steps with him and out to the walkway. "Oh, look, the moon is full! Too bad it's a little late in the season for evening primroses," he said as he admired the brightly lit orb. I tried to say something, anything, but my mouth was bone-dry. I licked my lips, trying to moisten them.

"Philip, I'm happy for you." My words sounded stiff. I tried again. "So, all of your tests are clear?"

"Yep. I'll stay on my meds for a while, but that's it. I'll get checked every few months, of course, but with my medications, I should be fine. Amazing what they can do today, isn't it? You know, you're looking good. How're you feeling? What did your latest tests show?"

I caught him up with my positive news. "So, I'm hopeful I'll be going home soon. Speaking of which, where will you go now? Did anything open up for you at UNCA, or anywhere else you applied?"

"No, nothing yet, but I have a couple of irons in the fire. First, I'll head down to Atlanta for a little bit to see a couple of navy buddies of mine. One of 'em has a construction company and got a government contract for building VA housing—you know, modest housing with really low interests rates for veterans. He said he'll put me to work if I want, and though it's not quite my choice of a career, it's a job, at least until I can find a teaching position somewhere. So, I'm taking the 11:05 train out of Asheville in the morning."

We were near the koi pond. "Let's go over there and sit down for a few minutes," he said. "I need to say a couple of things to you." He saw my hesitation. "Lord, Kate, relax. I'm not going to bite you." He smiled at me as tenderly and patiently as a parent would a child.

Once we sat down on the bench we'd shared before, he jumped right in. "Listen, I'm sorry about what happened at the greenhouse." I started to tell him that he didn't need to apologize, but he held his hand up to stop me. "Let me finish. Now, don't get me wrong, Kate. I'm not a damn bit sorry I kissed you—on the contrary. But I *am* sorry it upset you so, to the point that you've kept your distance from me."

I was uncomfortable discussing this, so I looked out at the pond. The moon and the light breeze created an iridescent shimmer on the water. "I only want you to be happy, Kate, and the fact that I've upset you so much upsets me even more. But it was one kiss, and it's not going to happen again. I know you have strong morals and that you're a woman of integrity, and also one who keeps her vows, but I'll be gone tomorrow, so let's part today as the good friends that we've become. Working in the gardens with you was a happy time for me. I looked forward to those days, and spending hours with you. And, I'll, well . . . I'll never forget you. I never want to, either."

"I'm going to miss you, Philip." I looked directly at him. It was time to be honest. "I'm thrilled for you that you're well and can leave, but I'm going to miss you. You've . . . been a good friend." *You've become more to me than that*, I thought, but could never say.

He was watching me hard, as though he was trying to decide something. "Kate, I can promise you this: If the circumstances were different and this was another time, in another place, that kiss would have been the first of many. I'll remember the taste of you and the smell of you for a long time to come. As a matter of fact, it's going to take a whole lot of time and determination to get you out of my head, and keep you out. But the circumstances are what they are. Just promise me one thing, Kate: Make sure that the rest of your life is the happiest part. You deserve that, and your son does, too. I know there's a real sadness and disappointment about your life that you try to hide, and you hide them pretty well, but I know they're there. Don't spend the rest of your life wishing for more and settling for so much less. You deserve to be loved, in every way—passionately and thoroughly. And if you won't let me love you, then make sure that someone else does. Just promise me you'll do everything you can to make the rest of your life really count."

"I promise. I promise I will." *But I want it to be you loving me*, I thought. "Will you please write to me, just let me know you're okay?"

"No. There's no reason to." He didn't mince words. He was straightforward with everything he said. It was one of the things I admired about him.

My head hurt. And my heart hurt. It literally hurt. Feeling like I was made of wood, I stiffly stood up. "I understand. You're right." I could feel my eyes starting to fill. I couldn't let him see it. He couldn't know. I could never admit to him what I'd finally admitted to myself a moment ago, that I had begun to love him. "It's getting late," I said, needing to be away from him. "Nurse Silvers will have a fit if I'm not back in the ward soon."

As we walked back, we talked about the possibility of my release in another month or so. "And what will you do then, Kate?"

"Go home, raise my son, and try to pick up the pieces with Geoffrey."

"Then it'll be hard keeping that promise." He smiled, but it didn't reach his eyes.

"What do you mean?"

"That you'll make sure the rest of your life is the happiest part." We had come to the front of building three. "You go on in. I'm gonna walk for a little longer."

"Are you sure?" I said, deciding to let his remark go. I could clearly see the intensity of his eyes and the firm set of his mouth as we stood underneath one of the tall street lamps that lined the walkways.

"Yeah, I'm sure." Philip took my hands as he looked up at the building; the place he had called home for many months. "If they get sore about me coming in late, well, they can just kick me out of the joint!" He smiled, and I forced one, too. Then, he gently leaned down and whispered, "Bye, Kate," before softly kissing my cheek. His lips lingered there for a moment, and my eyes closed as they did. How I wanted to turn my mouth to his, to be physically and emotionally connected to him just one more time. But instead, I whispered goodbye and forced myself to turn and walk away from him. And quite possibly the one chance at fulfilling my promise.

CHAPTER 28

Lost and Found

"... and he's playin' it for everything it's worth!" my mother said, though she was trying not to smile.

"Well, that's the biggest bunch of hogwash I ever heard!" my father responded.

We were sitting on lounge chairs out on the lawn under the weakened rays of an early October sun. We were all enjoying the beauty of a perfect fall day, but I was particularly enjoying the bantering between my parents. It was the first time I'd seen Daddy since he'd broken his leg, and aside from the cast, he looked like his usual, wonderful self. I knew that Mama was finally at ease and enjoying the volleying between them, too, as Daddy had given her a real scare when infection had set into his leg and the doctors were concerned about it getting into the bone, and possibly spreading from there. But just as in my case, antibiotics had saved the day. They had stopped the infection from spreading, and then had stopped it altogether. There was concern that his leg might never be the same, and that he would limp as a result, but in typical Jack Harris fashion, he made light of it, saying that with his bum left leg and Mama's bum right foot, between the two of them they'd have one perfect pair of extremities. He also said that if they leaned against each other, they'd both walk strong and straight. When he said it, I thought to myself that, figuratively speaking, they had done exactly that for the better part of three decades.

"How was your visit with Donnie and Geoffrey last weekend,

honey? Donnie sounded like he's enjoying the first grade when I talked to him on the phone a couple of weeks ago," Mama said.

"He seems to like school okay. It'll take a little gettin' used to, of course. The little boy sitting in the desk next to his is in his Sunday school class, so at least he knew someone right off the bat, and he said he likes his teacher, so that's a big help." I was still hurting from not being able to take him to school on his first day, but Geoffrey had filled in for me, and I hoped and prayed that with him doing more for Donnie, the two might find a comfortable rhythm together, bringing them closer because of it.

"Still no sign of the cat, Mama?" The tree-climbing cat still hadn't been seen.

"No, but when I talked to Donnie, I told him we'd keep looking. I asked him if he wanted to go buy one at the pet store, but he said no, that he wanted that particular cat and would wait for it to come around. Too bad that cat had such unusual markings, or I'd just go buy a substitute and hope he'd be none the wiser."

"Oh, he'd know." I laughed, nodding my head, confident my bright little son would immediately recognize an imposter.

"Well, we have news about Ditty," Daddy announced, almost dejectedly.

"Oh, what, Daddy? Is he all right?"

"As all right as someone can be, sittin' in the county jail over in Unicoi. He called us on Monday morning. Said he got nabbed at the Carolina-Tennessee line while runnin' a batch of hooch over from Lost Cove. Ditty was only about twenty yards into North Carolina when he got pulled over. But bein' that it was a Saturday evening, and just about quittin' time for the Bantam County deputies, not to mention that one of 'em had a daughter he had to walk down the aisle that night, they didn't want to be bothered. So they radioed the Unicoi County Sheriff's Department, and said they were holding a boy at gunpoint for 'em right at the state line. Told them they knew who he was when they saw him comin' and that they'd stopped him just before he could cross over onto the North Carolina side because they knew that the Tennessee boys would like to have him. Said to come get him and they'd hold him till they got there. So, one of 'em held a shotgun right at Ditty's nose, while the other one got in his car and backed it right up into Tennessee. They held Ditty next to his car until the Unicoi deputies showed. Nice knowin' how our tax dollars are paying for such fine, upright guardians of our fair state," Daddy sarcastically added.

"They had no business deciding which side of the law Ditty was on—literally," Mama said. "I asked him if we could come to see him after we leave here but he said no, that he was too embarrassed to see us right now. We're worried sick 'cause Ditty said he could get up to five years in the state prison over there. Lord, it's a terrible mess. We told him we'd hire a lawyer for him, but he wouldn't hear of it. Said he got himself into this mess and he was gonna get himself out. All we can do is pray at this point." No one said a word for a moment as we mulled over the situation and the possible consequences. Finally, Mama broke the silence. "Well," she said, standing up and walking over to the picnic table, "it won't do any of us any good worrying about it to the point that we starve. How 'bout we have ourselves a little picnic?" She put on a brave face, but I knew she was scared to death for her only son. I got up to help her unpack a large basket of food they'd brought. Daddy stayed on the lounge chair where he could sit comfortably, keeping his leg elevated in its big, heavy cast.

"Are those collards they've got there?" Daddy was watching half a dozen patients as they worked in different rows of the garden.

"That and mustard greens. They're pickin' 'em for tomorrow's dinner." I felt a stab of pain that I wasn't working out there with Philip, and never would again. Time was not lessening the pain, although it had been almost a month since he'd left. "With it bein' warmer down here, the growing season lasts a little longer," I said, trying to get my mind off of him. I looked back at Mama. She was holding out a plate to me, filled with deviled eggs, ham biscuits, and homemade pickles.

"Give this to your father, would you, Kate. Jack," she called over to him, "you want coffee yet? I remembered the sugar this—" She stopped mid-sentence and I turned to look at her from where I was standing next to Daddy.

Mama had a stricken look on her face and was white as a sheet. The coffee cup she was holding in her hand was tilted and some of the coffee she'd just finished pouring had spilled out. "Mama?" I tried to see what was causing such a reaction in her. "Mama, what's wrong?" I moved toward her as Daddy was attempting to get up with the aid of his crutches. "Are you sick? What is it?" She was standing stock-still and didn't utter a word. Again, I turned to see what she was staring at.

There, in the middle of a row of greens was Mary Boone. She stood frozen in place, just like Mama, and was staring back at her. Her arms hung limply at her sides, and a spade dangled from her left hand. Suddenly, Mama whispered a name so quietly that I wasn't sure I'd heard her correctly. It was a name that she had not spoken in a long time: Merry Beth. As if on cue, both women dropped what they held in their hands and began to slowly walk toward each other. Not a word was spoken by either one as they continued to lessen the distance between them. Finally, they stood directly in front of each other. For a moment, neither woman moved. Then Mama lifted a shaking right hand and tentatively laid it against Merry Beth's face. That small action was all it took and the two came together in an intense embrace; one that seemed to suggest that at last, someone had been found who was thought to be forever lost.

CHAPTER 29

The Ties That Bind

"She was found wandering the streets outside of Asheville almost six years ago, and was taken in by the Benedictine nuns at the Convent of the Holy Trinity. They could see that she had been beaten and that she needed far more help than they could provide. Mary . . . rather Merry Beth, had no identification and just kept mumbling incoherently. When the nuns asked her what her name was, it was hard to understand her nonsensical ramblings, but what they thought she said was Mary Boone. That's a little off from Merry Beth Coons, but that's what they thought she'd said, and maybe she did. Perhaps she didn't want to give her real name for fear of being found by someone she was afraid of," Dr. Sandell suggested from across his desk.

Earlier, out in the garden, Mama and Merry Beth had clung to each other and cried for the better part of five minutes until a couple of nervous orderlies had insisted that Merry Beth be returned to her room until it could be verified that we were indeed her family. We were quickly taken to the administration building in search of Dr. Sandell, or the chief psychiatrist, at the very least. Fortunately, Dr. Sandell was there and we were immediately ushered into his office, where the details of the surreal reunion and background information about Merry Beth were explained to him. We requested that Aunt Harriet be present if she was working that day. She was quickly located and joined us in the director's office. Now he had Mary Boone's thick file laid out before him, explaining her illnesses, and what little they knew about her past.

"She's been diagnosed with schizophrenia and dissociative amnesia. With her schizophrenia, Merry Beth displays what are called 'negative symptoms.' These diminish a person's abilities, and often include being emotionally flat or speaking in a dull, disconnected way, if at all. The patient often struggles to remember things, organize their thoughts or complete tasks. Genetics is a big factor," he explained. "Schizophrenia occurs in roughly ten percent of people who have a very close—or what we term 'first degree'—relative with the disorder; such as a parent or sibling."

"Our mother wasn't right—right in the head, I mean," Mama said. "She lost several children to different illnesses, and she thought she was cursed and responsible for their passing. She actually tried to give our brother Prescott, Merry Beth, and me away for fear we'd die, too. Mama ended up killing herself when we were teenagers. I was always afraid that Merry Beth was cut from the same cloth as poor Mama." My mother's pocketbook was sitting on her lap, and her hands kept opening and closing on the top of it as though it was a life preserver and she wanted to make sure she had a good grip on it. She had to be in shock from the day's turn of events. And while I knew that she was overjoyed to find Merry Beth alive, her illness was just one more layer of worry for my mother to bear.

"The other illness that she's been diagnosed with is dissociative amnesia," Dr. Sandell continued. "The distinctive feature of this disorder is the patient's inability to remember important personal information. In many cases, it's a reaction to a traumatic event, either one involving them personally, or one they have witnessed. They may develop depersonalization or trance states as a result. Merry Beth displays these symptoms regularly. Sometimes she just stands still for long periods, until one of the nurses or orderlies guides her to a chair or her bed, where she'll passively sit down or lie down, according to the caregiver's direction. She's never been violent, but she *is* dissociated—disconnected from the world. and perhaps even her own feelings. I feel certain that the beating she suffered close to the time that she was found wandering the streets wasn't the first—not by a long shot. My opinion is that she was brutalized and traumatized over many years."

"Ray Coons." Mama practically hissed his name.

The doctor looked perplexed. "That's the man Merry Beth married back in her teens," my father explained. "He was beyond no-good. He was evil. That bastard—excuse me, ladies—liked to hurt women. Does anyone know where *he* might be?" he disgustedly asked. Dr. Sandell said no. "That figures," my father replied. "You know, he tried to kill Rachel, when he was robbing her family's sawmill and Rachel happened to walk in on him. Merry Beth was party to the robbery." It was obvious my father hated the man, and had been angry with Merry Beth for many years.

"She's been ill her whole life, Jack," Aunt Harriet said, leaning forward in her chair and gently laying a hand on my father's shoulder. She and I were sitting next to each other behind my parents. She knew the pain my parents had been through on account of Merry Beth and Ray. And she was shocked to find that her sister-in-law's sister had been at Pelham for years, unbeknownst to her. However, as Harriet explained, she'd never worked in the same building where Merry Beth was housed, nor did she eat in the same dining hall, and she wasn't involved in any of Merry Beth's activities, such as the gardening. Also, Merry Beth had left home when Harriet was a young girl, and she'd not seen her since.

"She looks so . . . different than I remember." Harriet shook her head, comparing the institution's photo of Merry Beth, taken on the day she was admitted, to a small, worn, and creased photo Mama had, tucked away in her wallet. The photo had been taken when her sister was about ten. She was at a lake near Howling Cut, and written on the back of the photo was "July 4th picnic, '22."

As they talked, I thought back to the time I'd seen Merry watching me from the window and crying on the day that Geoffrey had come to pick up Donnie to take him back home. She'd obviously seen Mama. And maybe she'd seen Mama, or was hoping to see her, the night she was hiding in the trees, watching the visitors leaving Pelham. We would probably never know. But what I did know was that Merry Beth had some understanding of a connection between her and our family, and most definitely with Mama. As they stood there crying, holding each other, Mama heard Merry Beth softly moan "Rachel" a couple of times.

"Yes, Merry Beth! I'm Rachel," Mama had confirmed. But other than those two utterances, Merry Beth had said no more.

"It's highly unlikely that she'll ever be capable of living outside of this facility," I heard Dr. Sandell say as I tuned back in to their conversation.

"I've bet on worse odds, Doctor." My mother smiled, and a little twinkle sparked in her tired eyes.

PART THREE

CHAPTER 30

The Betrayal

It was about six in the evening and I was on my way down to supper when the nurse at the desk stopped me just as we'd opened the door to the stairway to walk on down. "Call for you," she said, handing me the receiver across her desk. Startled, I took the phone.

"Kathryn, we found Donnie's cat!"

"Oh, Mama"—I laughed, relieved that's all it was—"that's wonderful! I know that he'll—"

"Wait!" Mama cut me off. Now I could hear the real urgency in her voice. "Listen to me. I called Donnie about ten minutes ago to tell him, and to let him know we'd bring it to him when we come to see you next Wednesday. That maid Genevieve answered and said that Donnie was at school. I asked her why he was so late gettin' home, and wasn't that new nanny person supposed to collect him at school about midafternoon. She said that the new school he started would be keeping him all week now, and the nanny was let go late last week! What's going on over there, Kathryn?"

My heart was beating fast and there was a ringing in my ears. Obviously the night nurse saw that something was wrong and reached out to me. "Mrs. Cavanaugh! Here, let me get you a chair. You're white as a sheet!" Pushing her own chair out from behind the desk, she wheeled it around to me, then carefully pushed me down onto it.

"Kathryn! Are you there? Did you hear what I said?"

"Yes, Mama, I'm here. I heard what you said." It was hard to breathe, much less talk. "Geoffrey must have enrolled him in Penmire. Oh, dear God!" My voice cracked and I started to cry. I could hear Mama trying to reassure me and making suggestions on what we might do, but my mind was racing. *Donnie's at Penmire! Oh, Lord, Lord, Lord! Now, what? Think, think! I have to pull myself together.*

I took a few deep breaths, forcing myself to breathe evenly. "Mama?" She immediately stopped talking when she heard my voice. "Okay, Mama, I'm gonna have to call you back. I need to make a phone call, but I'll call you back in a few minutes, so don't go anywhere. Wait right there, okay?"

"I'm not going anywhere, Kate. Call me right back."

I pressed the button down in the receiver's cradle to disconnect our call, then asked the nurse for a phone book. While she located it, I blew my nose and tried to breathe more naturally. I needed composure to pull off this phone call. The nurse handed me the phone book and I rifled through the pages with trembling hands. Finding the number I was looking for, I dialed nine to get an outside line and then dialed the number. It was picked up on the third ring.

"Hello? Yes. This is Mrs. Cavanaugh. My son, Donald, started at Penmire this week. Unfortunately, I couldn't accompany him as I'm down with a nasty cold." I sniffed. "Anyway, my husband, Geoffrey, brought him in, and, well, you know how well-meaning but lacking men can be when it comes to the little details. Geoffrey forgot to find out Donald's room number and I've got a little care package all ready for him, but without a room number, it has no place to go." I laughed, hoping I sounded a little flighty.

"Oh, dear, Mrs. Cavanaugh." The older-sounding woman at the other end laughed along with me. "I have one of those well-intentioned husbands at home, too. I know exactly what you mean! We would have made sure Donald got his package, even without the room number, but let me take a look at the room assignment chart. Ah, yes, here he is! Donald's in room 303. Is there anything else I can do for you tonight, Mrs. Cavanaugh?" She oozed helpfulness. It was amazing what the hefty tuition at a boarding school could buy.

"No, thank you, not at this time, except please don't tell Donald that I called. I don't want him to have any idea that a care package might be en route." I didn't want Donnie mentioning to Geoffrey that I'd called. I didn't want Geoffrey to know that I'd found out that

Donnie was there. Angrily, I wondered when my less-than-honest husband was planning on telling me.

"Oh, no, I won't mention a thing about your call, Mrs. Cavanaugh. It'll be our little secret."

"I appreciate your help." I sniffed, using my congested nose to my advantage. "Good night." I ended our call and then promptly called Mama.

"Mama? He's there. I'm gonna get him out, but I'm not sure how yet. I'll know more by tomorrow afternoon."

"Kate, why don't you let your daddy and me go get him?"

"You may have to, but I'm not sure you can. They may only allow a student's parents to withdraw a child from school. I don't know what their policies are, and I didn't want to start askin' too many questions about that right now. It might have sent up a red flag. I definitely don't want Geoffrey, or even Donnie, knowing that I'm going to take him out of there, so the fewer questions asked, and the less said, the better. You and Daddy have done enough already, Mama. Lord, I've about worn you and Daddy out, not to mention your car. But there is one thing I'm going to have to ask of you."

"Anything. Anything at all!"

"Can Donnie stay with y'all once he's out? Would that be all right?"

"Do you really need to ask, Kate? That's ridiculous! Of course he can stay here. Of course."

"Thank you, Mama! Thank you. I don't know what I'd do without you and Daddy. I'll never be able to pay y'all back for everything you've done."

"Well then, it's a good thing we never put you on the books. Call me as soon as you know what's going on."

"It'll probably be early afternoon before I'll know anything. Will you be there?"

"We should be back by then. We've got an appointment in Marion to get your father's cast off. But, Kathryn, if you should decide you need us to go pick Donny up, you call me early so that we can do that instead. We can always reschedule the doctor's appointment."

"You go on, Mama. You need to take care of Daddy. I'm glad he's gettin' that heavy thing off."

"Yes, indeed," she enthusiastically agreed. "With bustin' Donnie out, then hiding the little fugitive away, the law's likely to come a'callin', and we'd all better be able to run like hell!" She started laughing, and I did, too. It was the small dose of levity that we both needed. It helped everything. It helped to calm me, which helped me to think more clearly. Besides, I knew that it might be the last time we had anything to laugh about for a while.

CHAPTER 31

Declaring Victory

"Mrs. Cavanaugh, Dr. Ludlow is ready to see you in his office now." I was sitting in the administration building's back waiting room, which was reserved for patients only so that visitors wouldn't be exposed to our illnesses any more than they had to be. I'd been there since seven thirty that morning, and it was now a little after eight. I hadn't been able to sleep at all the night before because I'd been too wound up after the phone call with Mama. I was anxious to talk to Dr. Ludlow, and the minutes had dragged on like hours.

I hurried down the hallway to his office, but stopped just outside the doorway when I saw Dr. Ludlow was on the phone. He turned from gazing out the window and waved me on in. I quietly sat down across the desk from him.

"Well, you tell her I said that I don't have the class's pile of penmanship practice sheets, and that she hasn't been teaching for the last thirty-one years. But tell her that I'll stop by to see if I can't help her find them after I get done at work. Tell her I said to lie down and rest until I can help her search." There was silence as he listened, then, "Okay, Helen, that's fine. Yes, ten milligrams is fine. Okay, I'll see you then." He replaced the receiver in its cradle. "Heaven help every person with dementia and every child of a parent with it. I have to wonder what she did in her life to deserve it, or what *I* did." He shook his head and chuckled, but there was no masking the sadness in his eyes. "Mother's in a nursing home in Asheville. Moved her down soon after I came down. We're about all the family each other has anymore. Half the time she recognizes me and half the time she thinks I'm Gary Cooper."

"Well, in all honesty, Dr. Ludlow, you do kind of look like him."

"Your eyesight is shot, Kathryn, but thank you. Now, how can I help you? What's going on?"

"Dr. Ludlow, I need to leave Pelham for a couple of nights and I wondered what the institution's policy is about that."

"Do you mind my asking why?"

I trusted the man with my life, so I trusted him with the truth. "Because my husband enrolled our son in a boarding school last week, even though he promised he wouldn't. I know my child is confused and scared, and I need to go get him."

"Where will you take him from there?"

"To my folks' place in Howling Cut."

"I see." Dr. Ludlow was thoughtful for a moment; then he rose and walked over to a set of filing cabinets that lined one of the interior walls. He rifled through the top drawer and pulled out a file. "All right; let me have a look here," he said, sitting back down at his desk and putting on a pair of reading glasses. He turned to the last page in the file. "Kathryn, you do know that you're not due for your next X-ray and sputum sample for another ten days, don't you?" I said that I did, and that I was praying the results would show that my lungs were healed. "Let's go on over to the lab. Considering your progress thus far, I think we can turn a blind eye to those ten days, don't you?"

After the tests, I sat down on the bench outside to wait for my results. It was the same bench I'd sat on my second day there, where I'd watched the patients working in the garden, including Philip and Merry Beth. It was the day they'd sung "I've Been Working on the Railroad." So much had happened since then. Philip was gone, and in a sense, Merry Beth had been found. So many of the women in my ward had come and gone, too, and a few had left us in the way we prayed none would. Even with all of the miraculous advances in the treatment of tuberculosis, the disease still took prisoners, and some didn't come back alive. The minutes dragged. But finally, I heard steps coming toward me on the walkway and looked up to see Dr. Ludlow approaching.

"Come with me, Kathryn." I couldn't read his face and he didn't say another word as I fell in behind him and we returned to the administration building. Entering his office, Dr. Ludlow shut the door behind me, then told me to have a seat as he went back to the filing cabinet. Pulling out another form, he returned to his desk and began filling it out. "So, how are you going to get there?" he asked as he continued to write.

"I'm sorry?" I was sitting on the edge of my chair, and I leaned in toward him as if that might pull my test results out of him.

"How are you going to pick up your boy and then get back to Howling Cut?" He looked up from his writing and smiled broadly. "I'm releasing you today, Kathryn. Permanently. Your X-rays are clear with the exception of one old lesion that has diminished quite a bit in size. Continuing to treat it with antibiotics should heal that up, and most likely, it'll be completely gone by the time you have your next X-rays. As you know, it'll take a few days for us to get your sputum sample results, but I'd be willing to bet it'll be streak-free. You're going to call me next week to confirm that, though. So, how are you going to get to your boy's school?"

If it hadn't been for the fact that I had a six-year-old son feeling abandoned and unloved, I would have danced around the room at that moment, pulling Dr. Ludlow around with me. However, I needed to stay focused on what I had to do. "Actually, I need to get to Cabot. That's my home, and my car is there. My parents are down in Marion right now getting the cast off Daddy's broken leg, but I'd really like to get out of here as soon as possible. Otherwise, they'd have to drive all the way over here to pick me up, then drive me to Cabot, then return to Howling Cut. It's too much to ask. Do you know if Aunt Harriet is here today? Maybe she—"

He held up a finger to interrupt me and dialed his secretary. "Grace, who's in the garage right now? Good. Patch me through to him, would you?" He listened for a moment, then, "Who's this? Ah, yes, Harold, do you have any pick-ups or drop-offs scheduled over the next several hours?" As he waited for the driver to check his schedule, Dr. Ludlow put his hand over the mouthpiece on the receiver and said, "Go get packed, Kathryn. I believe we've won this war!"

CHAPTER 32

The Feeling of Home

"Harold, let me at least pay you *something*," I said as he set my luggage by my front door. He was the same driver who had picked up Aunt Harriet and me at the train station when I was admitted to Pelham.

"Mrs. Cavanaugh, it's Pelham's policy to ensure that our guests have transportation to and from the facility whenever it's needed," he insisted. "This is protocol, so please, put your money away. Besides"—he smiled—"it's absolutely my pleasure."

"Well . . . thank you, Harold. I can't tell you how grateful I am for your help."

"Mrs. Cavanaugh, seeing you leaving in a car rather than a hearse is a joy. God bless you, kind lady. I hope never to see you under sad circumstances again." He pumped my hand enthusiastically. Chancing the fact that it might embarrass him, I leaned over and kissed his cheek. "Thank you, Mrs. Cavanaugh." He looked embarrassed but mostly pleased. Then he turned away and walked back down the front steps.

With shaking hands, I worked my house key into the lock. Hearing the deadbolt click, I slowly pushed the door open and took in the sight of the grand foyer with its black-and-white tiled floor, and the eighteenth-century southern Queen Anne mahogany table sitting in the middle of it. An enormous crystal vase sat on the table, artfully displaying a medley of berry branches. Stepping inside, I continued to look around at all of the finery that had been so tediously and painstakingly picked out, with the help of a couple of different interior designers. The opulence of it brought dear Annabelle to mind. This home seemed more suited to her taste than mine. I thought of her often and wondered how she was doing, but as was often the case when patients were released from Pelham, they didn't follow through on their well-intentioned promises of staying in touch. Life thankfully went on.

Refocusing on the task at hand, I left my satchel and small suitcase at the foot of the large sweeping staircase, which was built in the shape of a wishbone, with one set of stairs on the right side of the foyer and another on the left. Taking the stairs on the left, I hurried up to the second floor and down the hall to Donnie's room at the end. Opening the door to his walk-in closet, I retrieved one of his larger suitcases from a top shelf. Taking clothing from hangers and shoes from the rack, I then turned my attention to articles of clothing in his drawers. I didn't take too much, but I figured that at Penmire he was undoubtedly wearing uniforms and dress shoes, so I took what he'd need in order to shed, both literally and figuratively, that rigid lifestyle. Finally, I grabbed Donnie's teddy bear, the one he'd had since he was a baby, which Geoffrey insisted should be included in the next trash pickup. However, I'd held firm that Donnie's childhood was short enough, and if he found some sense of comfort and security with the bear, then so be it.

Moving down to the other end of the hall, I entered the master bedroom and then my own walk-in closet. Geoffrey's was on the other side of the bedroom and far more meticulously organized than mine. Reaching up to a long shelf that spanned the length of the closet, I pulled down a large suitcase that Geoffrey had brought back from the sanatorium for me. Pressing the buttons on the latches, I confirmed that it still held the clothes I'd taken to Howling Cut for Uncle Prescott's wedding. After adding just a few other articles of clothing, I snapped my suitcase shut and then grabbed Donnie's. Hurrying down the stairs, I set both suitcases next to my other luggage, and then went into Geoffrey's home office.

There were several exceptionally fine and rare original pieces of artwork on the wall. However, one painting was just a reproduction of Van Gogh's *Wheatfield with Crows*. Lifting it off the hanger, I set it down, then focused my attention on the safe that was hidden behind it. The combination was easy to remember: our wedding date. Opening it, I reached into its dark interior and pulled out several velvet-covered jewelers' boxes. After selecting several pieces of my best jewelry, I pulled out a large leather envelope-style pouch, with "First Imperial Bank of Cabot" embossed in gold on the front. Sitting at Geoffrey's desk, I counted out the money that it held, and finding that it totaled $4,300, I divided it exactly in half and slipped some of the money into my suitcase, and some into the zippered lining of my pocketbook.

Then, replacing the pouch and painting over the locked safe, I took one last look around the room to make sure that there was nothing out of place and exited the room. As I hurried out into the foyer, I ran smack dab into Genevieve, who had just come back from the market.

"Oh, Lord!" I shrieked, and just as startled, Genevieve shouted, "Save me, Jesus!" As soon as we recognized each other, we tightly embraced, laughing until we cried, or perhaps crying until we laughed.

"Good God a'mighty, missus! Whatcha doin' here!?"

"I'm not here, Genevieve. You haven't seen me."

"Then who's ya supposed to be?"

"No one; a ghost, a specter. I haven't been here. You haven't seen me," I impressed upon her.

"No'm. I ain't seen ya. Shoot, I been to the store. We musta been like two ships that passed in the night." She smiled. This woman, this friend, was one I could count on.

"Here, Genevieve." I reached down into my purse and pulled out $200. That was exactly a month's wages for her. "You take this." I pressed it into her hand, closing her fingers around it.

"What's that fer, missus? You don't got to pay me a thing for not seein' ya!"

"It's not for that, Genevieve. It's for the wrath you'll have to put up with when Geoffrey finds out I've been here and gone. And it's also because you've been a good friend to me these many years. Now, I have to go." I reached up and kissed the tall, broad woman's plump, warm cheek. "Thank you for everything."

"You ain't comin' back, missus?" She hugged me tightly to her. I whispered that I didn't think so, at least not for a while. She firmly held me away from her then and looked me directly in the eyes. "You go be happy somewhere—you and your boy." She was definitely no one's fool.

"I will—*we* will," I tearfully whispered. "You take care of yourself, Genevieve." Then I picked up our luggage and left the house. I stopped for a few seconds and looked up at the massive structure. This place had never been a true home to me. A home should create a feeling of comfort and safety, and most of all joy, for everyone under its roof. But this house had not been much more than an enormous, elaborately decorated symbol of wealth and prestige that held our belongings and kept us dry from the storms outside its walls. But never from the quiet, unspoken ones within.

Go, I thought. *Go!* So, hurrying over to the garage, I bent down and grabbed the horizontal handle at the base of the door, holding my breath as I raised it, and praying that my 1953 red-and-white Pontiac Chieftain was still inside. And it was. Just patiently awaiting our escape.

CHAPTER 33

The Power of Love

"**B**ut Mrs. Cavanaugh, usually we receive some kind of advance notice that a student is being withdrawn. Are you sure Mr. Cavanaugh approves of Donald's removal?" Mrs. Caldwell, the director of Penmire, condescendingly asked as she stood on one side of the counter in the front office, while I stood on the other. She had a hard look about her, especially her eyes. Adding to it was her unnatural jet-black hair, which hung straight to her shoulders, framing a face that was wrinkled enough to give away the fact that her hair was naturally gray.

The administration building was one of a dozen handsome cream-colored stucco buildings with dark green colonial shutters that made up the very large and prestigious boarding school. Aside from the buildings were a pool, tennis courts, athletic track, shooting range, and archery field. To the average observer, it must seem a child was certainly privileged to be attending such a place, participating in as many recreational activities as academics. But if the school was stripped of its façade of expensive perks, what would be left were the bare bones of rigidness and strict discipline, with very little room for error and even less forgiveness for such.

Originally built in 1873, the facility had first been used as a military school with the purpose of grooming young men for dedicated and lengthy careers in the armed forces. The school's original mission statement still hung in its place of honor, within a thick gold frame, high on the wall above the director's desk. Even from where I stood at an angle to it, I could still make out the school's ambitious intentions:

> *The mission of Penmire Military School is to provide each cadet with a strong academic foundation, a healthy mental and physical environment, and leadership training for a better understanding of the obligations of honor, citizenship, and self-discipline, all deemed necessary for a successful and beneficial life of service and selflessness.*

Apparently, too many people had found that the school was just a little too severe for even the most devoted military-minded families. A new tactic was adopted. Penmire was advertised as a boarding school that offered the highest quality education. Soon the school was able to charge a hefty tuition to parents of "high-strung" children who had plenty of resources to pay for their children's direction and discipline, but not the time nor the interest to administer it themselves. So Penmire Military School became Penmire Prep School, and even though the uniforms were a little less militaristic, the school's protocol and code of conduct remained the same and were strictly enforced. Anyone who strayed off course was quickly and harshly reminded not to do so again, and most students didn't make that error twice.

"Maybe the better question, Mrs. Caldwell, is not if Mr. Cavanaugh approves of our son's withdrawal, but whether I approved his enrollment in the first place," I said evenly, using every bit of self-control I had in order to do so. "Now, let me have whatever forms are needed to formally withdraw my son, and we'll be on our way."

"I can assure you, Mrs. Cavanaugh, this is against Penmire's protocol. Just as we have certain guidelines for the enrollment of the students in our school, so do we have them for their withdrawal. Perhaps I should call Mr. Cavanaugh, and we can discuss this. It's highly unusual for—"

"I'll tell you what," I said, interrupting her. My words sounded clipped and had dropped an octave as I was getting angrier. "While you call my husband, I'll call the police and explain that you're refusing to release my son to me. That's kidnapping, Mrs. Caldwell, and I tend to believe that your school's board of directors, not to mention its trustees, will be none too pleased to find themselves tangled up in a mess like a kidnapping charge. But we can certainly do it your way. Just hand me the phone, please, and we'll both make our calls." My hands were gripping the counter tightly as I leaned halfway over it, ready to go over the entire thing to get to the director if she didn't release Donnie immediately.

"Mrs. Cavanaugh, I'm quite sure that won't be necessary!"

"Then go get my son!" I hissed in a deadly low voice. The director motioned for her secretary to go retrieve Donnie. Then she walked to a filing cabinet, pulled out release forms, practically threw them at me, and I filled them out. As I continued to wait, the silence was heavy in the office. I was too tense to sit down, so I remained where I was while Mrs. Caldwell went into her office and found paperwork to pretend to be involved with. The minutes dragged like hours until, finally, the door opened and Donnie was ushered in.

Apparently, he had no idea why he was being brought to the director's office, and his little face was drawn and frightened looking. Donnie hardly glanced up until he heard me say his name, then his head snapped up and he looked totally stunned as he saw me kneeling there, with my arms wide open, waiting to encircle him like a living life preserver. He blinked hard once, as though he didn't quite trust what he was seeing, then finding that I was still there, he didn't make a sound or say a word as he threw himself into my arms.

I held him tightly, then lifted him up while whispering to him that everything was going to be okay, that we were going home. I felt the familiar trembling and heard the raw sound of his sobbing, just as I had at the sanatorium when Geoffrey had come to take him back to Cabot. But this time, his sobbing was out of relief; relief that his abandonment among strangers in this frighteningly rigid place had finally come to an end.

CHAPTER 34

Prodigal Sons

"Manchester? *That's* what you're going to name the cat? Well, that's a good strong name, son, but what made you think of it?" I laughed, looking over and drinking in my son's sweet, up-turned face. Penmire was an hour and a half behind us, and Howling Cut was about the same amount of time ahead. Before Donnie could explain the reason behind the cat's name, I spotted one of his favorite restaurants. "Hey, there's a Bob's Big Boy. It's late, pal. We need to eat." I whipped the Pontiac into the parking lot. It was a little before 1:00 p.m., and the place was still busy with its dinner crowd. As we walked across the parking lot, I admired the low-lying foothills that were still bright with autumn colors. High in the mountains of Howling Cut, the colors would have mellowed to rich, rustic hues by now, and the temperatures would be falling along with the leaves.

We entered the restaurant and I steered Donnie over to a couple of empty stools at the counter. A waitress brought menus over, but we knew what we wanted and ordered hamburgers with fries. Then, because we were celebrating freedom from our respective confinements, Donnie ordered a chocolate shake, while I indulged in a peppermint.

We were nearly done eating when I remembered our conversation about the cat. "So, go ahead and explain its name," I said, before taking the last bite of my burger.

"Mrs. Manchester was the nice teacher I had at that school," he replied, then noisily sucked up the last bit of milkshake through his straw.

A feeling of foreboding crept in. "Don't you mean 'nicest'? As in, the other teachers were nice, but she was the nicest of all?"

"No. I mean she was the *only* nice one. The others yelled, or made us do extra stuff, and sometimes sent us to the director's office to be hit."

I tried to keep my voice even. "Did they ever punish you, honey, or hit you?"

He looked ashamed. "Mrs. Caldwell hit me with a paddle three times. I mean, she hit me three times one time. I talked during a test." He looked down, whether from humiliation that he'd been paddled, or because he felt guilty for being disobedient in class, I wasn't sure. And I also wasn't sure if I was glad or sorry I hadn't known about this when I was just two feet from Mrs. Caldwell.

"Look at me, son." He slowly raised his head and his little face was flushed. "No one, *no one,* has the right to hit you, for *any* reason. Do you understand? No one! She's not going to touch you again. Ever. No one is. Okay?" I could see that he was trying not to cry. I reached over and gently pulled his little head toward me and kissed the crown of it. "You want another shake—to go?" I whispered next to his ear. He nodded. I ordered two more shakes and we hit the road. And that, I swore to myself, would be the only thing getting hit in my son's young life for the rest of the time I had anything to say about it.

The roads continued to carry us upward into the looming peaks beyond. As we traveled, we talked about the many things that had gone on while we were away from each other. In just six months' time, much changed in the life of a five- turned six-year-old little boy. While I loved hearing about all of the goings-on, it also saddened me that I hadn't participated in his activities, many of which he'd done for the first time.

We were only about five miles from Howling Cut, and heading up the curving Timberland Road when Donnie spotted a hitchhiker up ahead. He was wearing a hooded sweatshirt and we could only see the back of him. He was walking in the direction we were going, with his left thumb sticking out. "You gonna pick him up, Mama? Papa always does."

"Well, that's because Papa's a man. Women shouldn't pick up people they don't know. And I'm not sure anyone should, really." We had just pulled alongside the man, but I didn't want to make eye contact with him because I didn't want him to think we were stopping. We carefully passed him on the narrow road, and I continued explaining the potential hazards of picking up a stranger as I glanced at the man in my rearview mirror. "Most people are nice, but . . . Oh, my God!" I slammed in the clutch and the brakes, then eased the car over to a small space between the road and the mountainside. "Stay here!" I said, switching the ignition off and setting the parking brake. Then I ran back as fast as I could to the hitchhiker—the stranger— who wasn't really a stranger at all, but my brother, Ditty.

CHAPTER 35

Fight or Flight

"So, they let me go on account of the dispute over which side of the state line I was really on," Ditty continued, explaining why he'd been released from jail. "I told the judge what happened—about those North Carolina deputies backin' my car up over the Tennessee state line so that they didn't have to deal with me—and they all said I was lyin'. But the judge knew that the one deputy had a daughter gettin' married the night of my arrest because he'd been invited to the wedding. And he figured there was no way I could have made that story up 'cause there was no way I'd know about that wedding unless the story had played out the way I said it did. So he let me go. I drove out of there as fast as I could—without speeding—and got all the way to Red Hill before the engine blew. Guess I'd run the thing too hard too many times." He sheepishly smiled, his innuendo not lost on any of us.

We sat around the kitchen table until well into the evening, long after Donnie had gone to bed. Only after he was out of earshot did Ditty and I give detailed accounts of the confrontations each of us had just faced. Needless to say, it had been a day where emotions ran high, and no matter how tired I was, I knew that it would be hard to sleep.

One of the most emotional scenes was when Daddy and Mama came home after a lengthy afternoon down in Marion. Their appointment with the orthopedic surgeon had been delayed by several hours when he was called into emergency surgery. They'd almost rescheduled their appointment, worrying about me and afraid that I might need them, but since they'd not heard from me, they decided to wait for the doctor. Daddy said they were so worried the whole time they were there that they nearly asked the doctor for two sedatives once they got in to see him. I knew he was joking, but still I figured it wasn't too far from the truth.

By the time they got home, Ditty, Donnie, and I were already there. We'd been watching for them, and as soon as they pulled into the yard, we walked out onto the porch. Daddy had just gotten out of the passenger's seat with the aid of a cane, and Mama was coming around the front of the car. When they saw all three of us at the railing, they froze. Donnie rushed down the steps, shouting "Grandma!" and threw himself into Mama's arms, while Daddy remained where he was, but lowered his chin to his chest, closed his eyes, and began to softly cry. Ditty walked down the porch steps to him and, without saying a word, wrapped his arms around Daddy. They stayed that way for a minute or two, with my father leaning on my brother, just as my brother had leaned on our father throughout his life. I'd stayed on the porch, watching them, absorbing it. Finally, everyone came up the steps, and as my parents hugged me, with both of them crying now, I knew, without question, that this was where Donnie and I needed to be. It had been my home for most of my life, and it had never stopped feeling like home, even when I lived in my own house in Cabot. And I knew that Donnie felt the same way.

Finally, with exhaustion winning out, I got up from the kitchen table, washed my coffee cup in the sink, then kissed everyone good night and made my way upstairs. Walking into my old bedroom, I realized that the night air had shifted from refreshing to chilly, and the one blanket on the bed wasn't enough. I lowered the window until it was open just a crack, then went into the closet and grabbed the blue and yellow Sunbonnet Sue quilt that Grandma Willa had made for my fifth birthday. After gently laying it on top of my sleeping child, whose small body hugged the far side of the bed close to the wall, I slid beneath the covers, careful not to wake him. Lying on my left side, I studied his face. In looks, Donnie was becoming a combination of Geoffrey and me. *Geoffrey.* He'd called several times already, at least I was quite sure it was he, for my parents' phone never rang that much. But I wasn't ready to talk to him, so it was just easier not to answer the phone at all. I knew, however, that first thing in the morning, I'd have to call him, and it was going to be a difficult call, at best.

Carefully, I moved some of Donnie's blond hair away from his closed eyes. I wanted to—needed to—touch him to assure myself that he was really there, and apparently he needed those same little reassurances, too. Normally, he would be in the spare bedroom, but he wanted to sleep with me, at least for this night, and I understood. It was almost as though we were afraid to lose sight of each other for fear one of us would vanish again. Rolling over onto my back, I stared up at the ceiling. The light from the front porch below illuminated the room enough that I could still make out the old familiar watermark that resembled a man on horseback. Growing up, when I couldn't sleep, I used to make up stories about who the man was, and where he was riding to. As a little girl, the stories involved the man saving me from monsters; as a teenager, he saved me from human bullies.

About thirty minutes after I'd heard everyone come up for bed, including Ditty, who'd decided to spend the night with us instead of going over to his apartment, the shrill ringing of the phone shattered the quiet stillness. Leaping from bed, I hurried out to the hallway and answered it in a hushed whisper. I knew it would be Geoffrey, but I couldn't have him disrupting the household all night long.

"Kathryn! Where the hell have you been? I've called your parents' house a half dozen times and no one's answered until now!"

"Geoffrey, it's twelve thirty in the morning. Can't this wait until tomorrow—later today, actually?"

"Listen! I'm going to be there in the morning and I'm taking Donnie back with me. And you sure as hell better be there with him. How dare you take him out of school without discussing it with me! And *surprise, surprise*—my wife is out of the state hospital without even telling me that, too! How very thoughtful of you, Kathryn."

"Geoffrey, don't come tomor—" The line went dead. I tried to call him back but the line was busy and I knew he'd left the receiver off the hook.

It was tempting to pick Donnie up, quilt and all, and take off, but there would be no more running. I wasn't going to do it to myself, and especially not to my son. Besides, this was the only place that I would run to. And no one was going to run me out of my home,

Geoffrey included. I looked over and saw Mama standing in the doorway of her bedroom. "You okay?" she whispered.

"Mama, with y'all picking apples this time of year, I know Donnie would be a big help to you and he'd love it. Why don't you take him out there first thing in the morning—and pack a picnic lunch, 'cause you might be gone for a good while. And, Mama, take him to the farthest part of the orchard; that back thirty acres, okay?" She didn't say a word. Her smile said it all.

As I quietly crawled back into bed, I could hear Donnie's even breathing. If the phone had disturbed him, he had fallen back to sleep. Rolling onto my back, I stared up at the man on horseback, and oddly enough, felt an overwhelming sense of peace come over me. Enough so that I silently told my longtime defender that he was finally free to go save other damsels in distress, because I was strong enough to fight my own battles now.

CHAPTER 36

Ends . . .

Mama and Daddy left with a tired and grumpy Donnie in tow a little after 8:00 a.m., and Geoffrey pulled into our yard, with gravel flying and engine running hot, exactly an hour and twenty minutes later. The car had barely come to a stop when he got out and started to charge up our front porch steps, but was stopped short when I walked out the screened door to meet him.

"Hello, Geoffrey," I said evenly, and walked over to the porch railing.

"Either you can pack your bags, Kathryn, and Donald and I will follow you back to Cabot, or you can choose to stay here and I'll take Donald without you. Your choice." He was carefully controlling the tone and volume of his voice, and because of that, it sounded tight, as though it was painful to speak. He turned and walked back to his car.

"We're not going, Geoffrey. We're staying here, at least until I can sort some things out."

"There's nothing to sort out! You're out of that damned hospital and Donald's been discharged from Penmire. What the hell more could you want? Seems to me you've got the world on a string." His control was beginning to break down as he realized he was no longer in control of me.

"Geoffrey, what has made you so angry? Is it because I took Donnie out of Penmire without discussing it with you first?"

"It would have been kind of you to do so," he snapped.

"But, Geoffrey," I calmly replied, "you didn't discuss his enrollment with me."

"You were ill!"

"I wasn't dead!" Now I was starting to lose my own self-control. "What were you thinking, Geoffrey—that I'd be okay with it once it was said and done?"

"Actually, yes! I figured once he was settled and happy there, you'd be fine with it. You'd see that it was the right place for him. That other school wasn't challenging enough for him, Kathryn. I knew he'd be far better off at Penmire."

"But he wasn't happy at Penmire! *You* were happy he was there! But Donnie was miserable, and most of all, he was devastated that you left him there."

"Oh, for the love of *God*!" He slapped his thigh out of frustration, then put his hands on the edge of the roof of his car and laid his forehead down on them. "You're going to make sure he grows up to be nothing more than an addle-minded hillbilly," he mumbled in a low voice, but loud enough to make sure that I heard him.

"Go back to Cabot, Geoffrey," I said in a low, flat voice. "We're staying here."

"I swear on a stack of Bibles, Kathryn, I will fight you for custody of my son, and I *will* win. You forget that I have a whole law firm behind me. Not to mention that I've got quite a few great litigation attorneys who are close friends. You try to fight me, Kathryn, and I'll crush you in court. You'll be begging to see Donald twice a year. Be very, *very* careful. I'm warning you!"

Ditty came around the corner of the house, but I couldn't tell from his face whether he'd been listening or not. Very casually, he leaned up against the porch, with his left leg bent so that his cowboy boot was braced against the house, supporting his weight. He didn't say anything as he chewed on a toothpick that jutted out from the corner of his mouth.

"This is a private conversation between your sister and me, Andrew."

Ditty pulled the toothpick from his mouth. "Oh, I wasn't gonna interrupt y'all, Geoff," he drawled, knowing Geoffrey hated being called by that nickname. "But I had a question I wanted to ask you—while I thought of it, ya know.

"Why is it that the men you run with—you know, the fifty-dollar-cigar-smokin' kind of guys—have such a thirst for white-trash whiskey, and white-trash joints, like the Back Alley Club, outside of Cabot? Ya see, Geoff, a couple of times when you and some of your pals were there having your private parties, well, hey, I was there, too! On one of those nights, me and my partner at the time were runnin' late on bringing in a crate of that apple brandy that sells faster'n we can hardly make it. The owner of the joint hates it when we're there at the same time as all his ritzy clientele, but hey, when you've had a flat with no spare, it slows ya down some. So there we were, storin' the stuff in a little spot where the ATF agents can't find it, and I can see y'all out the window of this special little storeroom, a-huffin' and puffin' on those ritzy cigars, and entertainin' some high-priced 'ladies.' And I thought to myself, *Man oh man, my brother-in-law is sure havin' a hell of a good time!*

"Kind of hurt my feelings you never asked me to come along to one of those little parties, Geoff, but then, my sister here might have found out what all goes on. And knowin' her the way I do, I think she'd be especially sore that some of those high-priced ladies aren't quite ladies yet. They still got a few years to go. And you know, I was thinking, Geoff, I bet the North Carolina Bar Association, not to mention the ol' police chief and the district attorney in Cabot, might be fairly interested in learning about these little goings-on, too.

"Now, seeing as how you're a big high-class lawyer and such, you could probably worm your way out of all that mess. But you know, it just might tarnish that sterling reputation of yours. And who wants to do business with a crooked lawyer?

"Personally speakin', I think the whole lot of you is a bunch of no-goods, and I bet a few more people might come around to my way of thinkin' if they were to find out what really goes on behind closed doors. And you know, Geoff, even if you were to try to take me down by claiming I'm just a moonshinin' ol' jailbird, it's gonna take quite a bit of your time and money convincing folks not to listen to me and continue believin' in you. And, hey, I don't have much else to do right now, so I'm game to get into it with you. Shoot, why not?

"Either that, Geoff, or you get the hell out of here right now and don't come back. I have a great memory, and what I saw goin' on with you and your buddies won't fade from my mind for a long, long time. And who's got sharper memories than young'uns? I bet those little gals can remember real well, too. Ya think maybe our apple brandy helps to keep the mind clear?"

I held on to the porch railing in front of me with a death grip.

Hearing what Ditty had witnessed made my stomach turn, and I kept swallowing hard and taking deep breaths to keep myself from being sick. As shocking as Ditty's allegations were, I thought back to those nights when Geoffrey claimed he was working but his explanations just didn't quite add up. There'd been too many times he'd come in late, with whiskey on his breath and poor excuses for it. I didn't know whether I had chosen to turn a blind eye to what might have been going on, or whether I had just put too much faith in my husband to believe he would ever do anything to hurt me or jeopardize our marriage. Either way, the realization of what had been taking place during some of his late evenings may well have devastated me at another point in our marriage, but it didn't now. It just confirmed what I already knew: The marriage was over.

Geoffrey was standing stock-still, but his face was beet red and his hands were clenched into white-knuckled fists. "You're a lying son of a bitch, Andrew! Do you really think you can get away with trying to blackmail me?"

"No, no, Geoff," Ditty said, sticking the toothpick back into the corner of his mouth. "Like I said, you'd probably win, but the fun of it all is playin' the game. Shall we have a go at it? I can make a couple of phone calls and get the ball rolling."

"Go to hell, Andrew."

"Go to Cabot, Geoff. And leave Kate and Donnie be."

Geoffrey stared at Ditty as though he was weighing the likelihood that my brother would actually follow through with his threat. Then, obviously deciding it wasn't worth the risk to find out, he opened his car door and moved around it to get in. "I'll see you in court, Kathryn. I'll be damned if I'm going to let you raise our son in this hillbilly backwoods town—around these kinds of people! I'm going to fight you for custody with everything I've got!"

"No, you won't," I evenly stated. "No, you won't, Geoffrey, and I'll tell you why: because Donnie's too much of an inconvenience for you. He's a disposable child in your eyes. He's never held much importance in your life, or value. And if you do try to take him, just to spite me, I'll fight you with every ounce of strength I have left in this body, and I'll make it a very ugly public affair. And even if I don't win, legally speaking, I'll make sure you lose, professionally speaking. The public will see me as the pathetic wife, stuck away in a state sanatorium, close to death from tuberculosis, heartbroken at being away from her husband and little boy, only to learn her husband tired of the inconvenience of raising their son alone and selfishly sent him away to boarding school. Can you imagine the reaction when folks learn the reason the father chose boarding school was because his son interfered with the man's extracurricular—and illegal—activities?"

I walked down the porch steps and stopped about six feet away from my husband. He was absolutely stunned by my defiance. I looked closely at him before speaking again and could see the anger and fear on his face. Despite all of the betrayals, and the lies and deceit, this man standing before me had been someone I once loved. He had tried to love Donnie and me in the same way he had been shown love by his own father and probably his father before him. It was a skewed love, both crippling and cruel, though its destructiveness was unintentional. Suddenly, all of the intense emotions—both good and bad—that I'd ever felt toward my husband were gone, replaced in an instant by one emotion only: pity.

"Let us go, Geoffrey," I said, taking a couple of steps toward him. "You know that I'm not what you want in a wife. I never was. First, I was an amusement, then a conquest, and finally, an embarrassment to you. You've never liked my humble beginnings, or the fact that I'm proud of where I came from and have always refused to pretend that I'm something I'm not. It embarrasses you that fifty percent of Donnie comes from that same stock, and that he tends to be more like me than you, and feels comfortable here. He's happy in Howling Cut, and I will be again, too, once I heal some.

"Let's part quietly and gently from each other, Geoffrey, for your sake and mine, but most importantly, for our son's. Then we can each be who we want to be, comfortably and freely, without worrying that we're hurting each other, or forcing each other to be someone or something we're not." I laid my hand on his hand, which was bracing the car door open, creating another barrier between us. "Please, Geoffrey," I quietly said, "go live your life and let us live ours. He'll always be your son, and you'll always influence him. I promise you, he'll grow up to be a wonderful man. We'll both see to that." I waited. Geoffrey still said nothing, but I knew his mind was busy processing all that had been said, and what he stood to gain or to lose should he fight me on this.

"Kathryn . . ." The anger and the fear had left his face, leaving him looking tired and resigned. "I never meant to hurt you, or Donnie. Nor did I mean for things to turn out this way."

"I know that, Geoffrey." I nodded, squeezing his hand. "I know."

He stood there for a moment as though weighing what to say next. Then, obviously deciding that there was not much more to be done, he ducked into the car. "Have your attorney call my office," he said, searching my face for a moment. I wondered if he was waiting for me to change my mind. I stood there, saying nothing. "Good-bye, Kathryn." He turned the key to start his car.

"Good-bye, Geoffrey." I turned away to start the rest of my life. And the first step in doing so involved calling George Eisenhower.

CHAPTER 37

. . . Another Road Begins

I sat in my car at the far end of the school's dirt driveway and watched the different scenes of activity going on along the ridge in the distance. It was remarkable seeing how much had been accomplished in just the ten weeks since I'd called George, telling him I'd take him up on his offer to be involved in the building and running of the new rural branch of the Cabot Home for Children. It had taken us little time to break ground, partly because my parents had donated ten acres of land to the project. As a result, George had been able to put all of the government funding into the rapid building of the school.

Several construction crews were hard at work on the first two of five permanent wooden structures that would make up the facility. There would be a four-story school building, housing first through twelfth grades; two dormitories, one for each gender; plus the administration building, and a gymnasium that could double as an auditorium when the need arose. And because Guinn Timber Products was supplying much of the materials, construction was moving along at lightning speed. The mill was also building the school's desks, tables, and chairs, so many of the buildings would be furnished nearly as soon as they were completed.

One of the people helping to move things along was Ditty. He'd thrown himself into the work at the sawmill, and at least for the time being, seemed enthusiastic and grateful about the positive turn his life had taken. He'd settled back into his apartment above the mill's garage, and though everyone was happy for his return, none of us was willing to bet that his return to his old life was permanent, or that he wouldn't disappear again one morning. There was no disputing the fact that every now and then, a restlessness, and perhaps a discontentment, pushed my brother out the door and on to parts unknown. It was a part of Ditty that fought conformity, and found the day-in and day-out routines of responsibility painfully monotonous and suffocating. In that regard, he had never quite grown up, and I wondered what calamitous thing might have to happen to finally settle him down. I prayed that nothing would; that the change would simply come with the passage of years, and perhaps through the satisfaction of seeing how his hard work greatly benefited so many people. Only time would tell, though.

Over and over again, I was amazed at how quickly things could change and *had* changed for all of us. How seemingly overnight, one thing could be torn down, like my marriage, while another thing could be born, like the school and my new life, all of which seemed to be changing shape with the passing of every hour.

Checking my watch, I saw that it was almost 7:20 a.m. I needed to get a move on. I had a physics test in one hour at Vance State College for Women. After I'd called George two months ago, my second phone call had been to Vance to get information on enrollment. After reviewing my standing credits, the dean of admissions had informed me that if I carried a fairly heavy load, I could complete a two-year degree in about nine months' time. By the following week, I was a student there. I had enrolled Donnie in Howling Cut Elementary, as well, and it tickled me that the two of us were study buddies in my parents' kitchen every evening after supper. Life was certainly full of strange twists and turns.

Following the test, I had to drive all the way to Cabot to interview three prospective teachers for our new school, which, we prayed, would be open for the summer semester. We knew the dormitories would be ready for our little residents, but we hoped the school would be ready then, too. Because I would still have a couple of months of schooling to complete at that time, George would come and go between the Cabot and Howling Cut locations, until I had my certificate in hand. But once I had it, I would be the official onsite assistant director, and George would only need to come to Howling Cut once a week or so.

It would seem strange being back in Cabot. It would be the first time since I'd stopped by to pack up some of Donnie's clothes before taking him out of Penmire. I wondered if I'd feel as separated from it now as I did from my husband. Our divorce was almost complete, due in part to the fact that I'd only asked for child support for Donnie; half of the money from the sale of our house, which was set to close the following week; and for Geoffrey to pay for my tuition. I wanted nothing more from him, though I was determined to make sure that Donnie received all that he needed and was entitled to from his father. Fortunately, Geoffrey wasn't fighting me on it; obviously he realized that I was asking for far less than the courts would have granted me. And in all fairness, I knew that Geoffrey wanted to provide for Donnie. Just because they weren't close didn't mean that they didn't love each other, and because I would raise Donnie, I made a vow to myself that I would work alongside Geoffrey to ensure that their relationship grew stronger over the years, not the opposite.

About thirty minutes later, I pulled into the parking lot in front of Vance's fine arts building. Early though it was, the lot was already filling up. More and more women wanted a college education these days. In the past, our professional career choices had been fairly limited to being a nurse, teacher, secretary, cook in a restaurant, or airline stewardess. But it was a new day and age in 1954, and the opportunities afforded to women were becoming far more numerous, with more and more doors opening up for us all the time. We were taking advantage of them with great enthusiasm and determination, too. But we were well aware that it was still a man's world, and that no matter how well we performed in our studies or our work, we would be judged more critically than a man. We knew we would suffer resentment at times. But we knew that we were ready and willing to put up with it all in exchange for a better future. And not just for ourselves, but for every girl and woman who might follow, who dared to set even loftier goals for herself, and who aspired to climb to even greater heights than we could ever imagine.

As I walked through the breezeway, the cold mid-December wind cut through my dark green wool suit, lifting the hem of the flared skirt dangerously. I pinned it against my body with a beige-gloved hand and was glad that I'd not worn a hat that day. I wished I'd taken the time to put on my coat, which sat uselessly on the front seat of the car. Increasing my pace as much as the crowded breezeway would allow, I wove in and out of a throng of female students and finally reached my physics classroom at the very end. Entering the classroom, I saw that there was as much of a commotion going on in there as there was out in the blustery hallway. School would be out for the Christmas holidays in two days, so everyone was excited.

Finding an empty desk toward the back, I looked up at the wall clock above Dr. Toomey's desk, and saw that it was 7:56. There were just a few minutes to go before the class bell sounded. Opening my book, I took one last look over some highlighted areas. As I studied again the material I'd read at least a dozen times throughout the semester, I couldn't help but overhear a conversation between two young women who sat in front of me.

"He's cute as a button!" the redheaded girl whispered.

"I'd call him handsome, not cute," the blond one corrected.

"Either way, I'd take him," Red responded.

"And I'd let him take me!" Blondie replied, which caused an eruption of laughter in their immediate circle.

A new arrival sat right next to the blonde. "Who're you talking about?" She jumped right into the conversation.

"Our substitute teacher. Some of us had him in our Fundamentals of Physics class last night and he said he'd be here this morning. Too-long-Toomey is out for a while." Someone snickered over the use of our physics teacher's moniker, which described the man perfectly; he was long-winded and known for putting students to sleep.

Smiling as I listened to them, I felt a small spark of envy for their unclouded enthusiasm over all that life might throw their way. I was seven years older than many of them, though in some ways I felt old enough to be their mother.

Suddenly the piercing blast of the bell sent the students who were still standing scurrying for an empty seat. Just as the bell stopped, the door opened and our substitute teacher walked in with a cup of coffee in one hand and a briefcase in the other. Unlike most of the male teachers, he wasn't wearing a dark, conservative wool suit, but instead was casually dressed in a pair of light gray slacks and a soft blue turtleneck sweater. There was no fedora covering his thick, rather long wavy hair, and it was quite obvious why this man had the undivided attention of the entire classroom.

"Good morning, ladies." He smiled a rather rakish smile, though it wasn't meant to be such. It was just his laid-back, easy style and the ladies loved it. "Dr. Toomey is a bit under the weather today, so you're stuck with me—and still stuck with your test, I'm afraid."

Good-natured booing ensued. He laughed as he turned to the black-
board, selected a piece of chalk, and began to write his name across
it. But I didn't need him to write it or to say it. I knew his name well:
Philip McAllister.

I could feel the smile spreading across my face, and I had to keep
myself from laughing at the sheer joy of seeing him again. Suddenly,
I felt as young and giddy as one of life's-little-hopefuls sitting all
around me.

Philip turned back to the desk, pushed the buttons to unlatch his
briefcase, and pulled out a thick sheaf of test papers. "Would one of
you mind—" he began, but stopped short. He finally saw me sitting
toward the back. "Well, Mrs. Cavanaugh," he smoothly stated, but
the smile that broke out on his face was as broad as mine. "Would
you please help me pass these out?" As I walked to him, I was aware
of every student's eyes upon me. It was obvious we knew each other.
They were just trying to figure out how and why. I moved to within a
couple feet of him, and we both stood there, frozen, unsure what to
say or do, how to react. I could tell he was as shocked as I, for the
sheaf of papers in his hand trembled slightly.

"Hello, Dr. McAllister." I smiled as our eyes met. "It's good to
see you again." I reached for the papers.

Handing them to me, he softly responded, "Stay after class."

"What'd she do?" joked one of the students who was sitting near
enough to catch his words.

"She survived," he said, so softly that only I could hear.

"We both did," I said. "Thank God."

Three hours later, we finished our third cups of coffee and second
pieces of pumpkin pie at Mahaffey's Diner, just off campus, and finished giving each other an overview of all that had happened since
we'd parted ways at Pelham.

"So my irons in the fire had pretty much gone cold," Philip continued, "and I took this job at Vance until something else more permanent came along. Actually, I'm subbing both here and at UNCA. I
just couldn't deal with the construction job anymore. It was okay for
a while. I enjoyed the physical labor, but I felt like my brain was
withering away. So I took my pay and headed back this way. I love
the mountains. They . . . well, they get in your blood somehow. Anyway, I found an apartment that I could rent by the month, and put job

applications in all over the place, and that's my story." He grew quiet, staring at me for a moment. "God, you look good, Kate. You look . . ." His words fell away. "It's just . . . so damn good to see you."

"Philip, let me ask you something. It's an important question, and I don't know if you can answer it right now or not," I said, pushing my coffee aside and resting my forearms on the table.

He rested his forearms on the table, too, and leaned in. "Try me."

Fifteen minutes later, the bill was paid, and Philip and I were on our way to Cabot to meet with George Eisenhower.

EPILOGUE

"I know darn well they're gonna do it," I said over my shoulder as I stood at the second-story bedroom window of Grandma Willa's first home in Howling Cut, which was now my own. "Shoot, I know how they'll do it, too." I continued to suspiciously scan the dark yard below and the road beyond, watching for any pinpricks of light that were moving and out of place. "And I know exactly who'll be leading the pack!"

"So let 'em come, Kate, and you come back to bed." Philip chuckled.

"That's exactly where they want to find us!" I laughed, but the temptation of loving my new husband again was too great, so double-checking that the two buckets next to the window were full of water, I went back to him. He lifted the covers for me and I slid in by him, resting my chin on his chest. Slowly, sensuously, I felt his large, strong hand slide up the back of my thigh and beneath my nightgown, rubbing and stroking me as we lay in wait for the midnight shivaree to commence. I had no doubt that Daddy and Ditty would be out in front of the makeshift parade, with Donnie riding high on the shoulders of one of them.

"I can't believe you were almost late to the wedding," I said, lifting my head and gazing at the man I loved so deeply.

"You were the one who said we had to stay out of the way all day. You said I wasn't allowed to see you in your wedding dress beforehand, and you wanted us to keep Donnie occupied. So really, it's your fault," he teased, lightly slapping my bottom.

"But you could have come in a little earlier, you know."

"Well, first we had to stop by the school. Some of the science books arrived today, and I needed to make sure that the teachers will have what they need when school starts next week." Philip was thrilled to be head of the high school math and science departments, and George and I were just as excited. It had also been suggested that upon George's retirement in just several more years, Philip would be the ideal candidate to take over as the director of the Howling Cut branch of the school. Having a doctorate, he was more than qualified.

"Then we went fishing," Philip continued, "and they started biting just when we were packing up to leave. First one bass hit, and then another. It became a feeding frenzy! Donnie was thrilled, especially since he caught the biggest one of all."

"I have one question: Did you cringe when you had to put the worms on the hook?" I laughed.

"What? Uh . . . no," he answered, confused by the question. "How else you gonna catch a fish?"

"There's another reason Donnie loves you. He does, you know."

"Yeah, I know. I kind of like the little guy, too." Philip chuckled, pulling me up toward him and kissing my lips, gently at first, then far more deeply as I responded.

"Wasn't the wedding beautiful, Philip?" I sighed, laying my head down in the crook of his neck, but immediately lifting it again as another thought struck me. "I can't get over Annabelle and Marsha showing up! I was standing out in the alcove, ready to come down the aisle, when the two of them walked in. I started to cry but held back as best I could 'cause I didn't want to mess up my makeup. They said they almost missed the wedding after getting lost on one of the back roads. Lord, it was good seeing them again. They look so well! Thank you, sweet Jesus," I added as I laid my head back down.

"The only thing that would have made it perfect was having Aunt Merry Beth there, too, but Dr. Sandell said she's just not able to leave Pelham yet. And like he told Mama a while ago, she probably never will be. I hate that for her—and I hate it for Mama, too."

"But at least your aunt is safe there, Kate. She doesn't have a husband pounding on her, and she's not cold and starving out on the street somewhere. Did they ever find out where her husband ended up?"

"No, unfortunately not. Honestly, I wish we'd heard he was dead and gone. God forgive me for saying that, but it's the truth. Hey," I said, changing the subject, "wasn't that something, seeing Dr. Ludlow escorting Aunt Harriet to the wedding! I thought something was up when she brought him here for Christmas dinner. She said that he just didn't have any family around anymore since his mother died right before Thanksgiving, but I kind of thought there was more to it than that. Strange the way life goes, isn't it?" I said softly. But Philip barely managed an "uh-huh" as he began to drift off to sleep.

Lifting my head, I studied his face again. I would never tire of looking at Philip, or tire of loving him. I sighed with deep contentment and laid my head back down on his chest as I waited for the night to erupt into fireworks; first, the shivaree kind, and after that, our own loving kind. As I lay there, I was lulled into a half sleep listening to the strong beating of his heart, and the gentle, life-giving rhythm of his breathing.

Don't miss Janie DeVos' haunting novel BENEATH A THOU-SAND APPLE TREES, available to order now!

As the 20th century dawns, the world is transformed in dizzying ways. But nestled in North Carolina's Blue Ridge Mountains is a place, and a family, out of time—where one young girl will grow to face the challenges of each generation before her—and discover whether she has the strength to overcome them . . .

The eldest surviving daughter of Anna Guinn, Rachel rarely ventures far from her home in the Appalachians, aside from an occasional trip into town to trade a penny for a peppermint stick. Sometimes she yearns for more, but as much as she fears her mother's unstable mind, she is anchored by the strength of her grandmother, Willa. Freed from an abusive marriage, Willa holds the family together through hardship, all the while fulfilling her role as keeper of her neighbors' carefully guarded secrets—the most painful of which may be her own.

In this isolated, eccentric world where people depend on moonshine to put food on the table, hang talismans to chase away ghosts—and tragedy can strike as suddenly as a coiled copperhead—Rachel wonders what life has in store. Most of all, she worries whether she and her sister have inherited the darkness that lurks inside their mother. Her one respite is the town's apple orchard, the ally she finds there—and the revelation that she can take her destiny into her own hands, decide what to leave behind—and what is truly worth carrying into the future . . .

CHAPTER 1

1916, Howling Cut, NC

I wasn't born with a bad right foot. Instead, I'd been dealt a bad hand when an accident at Papa's timber mill crippled me. The man known as the *off-bearer* was busy stacking boards that had just been cut by the spinning, sharp-toothed saw and didn't see me walk up beside him. With his mind a million miles away, he was simply repeating the tedious pulling-off-and-stacking motion of yet another board when he turned and dropped it on my foot.

It seemed to happen in slow motion. The off-bearer, who was a stoic Irishman named Rusty Flaherty, saw me standing there just a fraction of a second after he'd let the board go, and the look of horror on his face was one I would never forget, and which froze me in place. I was lucky, they said, because it had narrowly missed my head. But I wasn't lucky *enough*, for even though Papa immediately threw me in the wagon and hauled me over to Doc Pardie's house, my foot had never healed right.

The doctor wouldn't operate because I was only four and "still had growin' to do, and there ain't any use but to wait 'til she's done a-doin' it," he'd told my father. I heard Papa tell Mama later that he wouldn't have let Doc do it anyway, since he smelled like he'd "dived into a bottle of one hundred proof. Maybe it'll just straighten out on its own," he'd said, without too much conviction in his voice. And it had healed, just not straight enough or strong enough, and there'd never been enough money to do anything to correct it.

I walked with a pronounced limp, and the fact that I was short and small-boned only helped to accentuate it. I'd been given the offensive name of Laggin' Leg early on, and each time I was called by it, I wished the darn pine had, indeed, clobbered me in the head. But, as Grandma was quick to remind me when I came home in tears, I must have been saved from certain death for a reason, and "that which doesn't kill us makes us stronger," she'd point out, while pointing at *me* to emphasize *her* point.

That's all well and good, I thought, *but I just wish the good Lord had warned me to stand on the other side of Mr. Flaherty, and found someone else to make a point with.*

The first time someone referred to me as Laggin' Leg was when I was six. It was during Sunday school class as I walked back to my seat after reciting the first five verses of John. I'd proudly made it through my recital without omitting one word, and Mrs. Jacobson was in the midst of telling the class that I was "a true disciple of the Lord's," when nine-year-old Ray Coons deliberately stuck his foot out in front of me. Suddenly, I went from walking proudly with my chin up, to lying on the floor with a split in it. The whole class—all thirteen of them—fell into fits of laughter, while stars danced before my eyes as though they were having a celestial recital on the scuffed pine floor where I lay staring in dazed confusion.

"Ray Coons!" Mrs. Jacobson scolded as she quickly walked over to me. "I saw that!"

"Why, Miz Jacobson, I didn't do nothin'," Ray innocently objected. "She's just a cripple, that's all. She can't walk too good. She's got that laggin' leg o' hers, and she falls all the time, don't ya, girl?" Ray looked at me as though he'd cut my throat if I didn't concede that the fall had been my fault. I didn't—couldn't—say a word, however, as I was too busy trying to refill my lungs with air; the fall had knocked all of it out of me. And the wracking sobs that had followed only made the possibility of my breathing again that much more unlikely.

The episode left me with two things: a scar on my chin from the gash that required four stitches (which Doc Pardie sewed during a rare moment of sobriety), and the cruel new nickname. I hid in the back of the loft in the barn after receiving my stitches until Grandma coaxed me out with the smell of a cheese biscuit. I think she'd given me time to process the event—and to get hungry enough to make cheese biscuits more important. I came down the ladder and turned around, facing her.

Looking at her was like looking at an older version of myself, except for the fact that she had thick, medium-length, coal-black hair, with just a few streaks of gray blended throughout. My hair, however, was long and curly, and the same insignificant color brown as a withered maple leaf, just like my father's. But Grandma and I had the same build, same face, and the same brilliant blue eyes; "Carolina blue," she always called them. As we stood looking at each other, she pulled pieces of straw from my hair, then rather roughly rubbed away the telltale tracks of some dried up tears. I knew she wasn't mad at me for crying, but was angry with whoever had been the cause of it.

The wind whistled through the gaps in the plank siding on the north side of the barn, creating an eerie tune and causing me to shiver. Our town, Howling Cut, had been named for just that very reason—the eerie, howling sound the wind made when it rushed down the mountains and through one of the logging roads or "cuts" in the forests which surrounded us. And the place was living up to its name at the moment Grandma handed me the biscuit and pulled the collar of my worn-out brown coat closed, trying in vain to keep the cold out.

"I can't keep life from hurtin' ya, Rachel," she said. "Alls I can do is learn ya to be tough enough to stand up to it."

She pulled me close to her and I could smell the smoke from our wood stove when I laid my face against her breast. She sighed after a long moment, held me away from her, and I caught the glint of tears that threatened to spill over from the reddened pockets of her lower lids.

"C'mon. We're gettin' as cold as our supper is." Turning, she led the way out of the barn.

JANIE DeVOS

BENEATH A
THOUSAND
APPLE TREES

Janie DeVos, a native of Coral Gables, Florida, worked in the advertising industry in the late 1980s, but left the field in 2000, to turn her love of writing into a full-time career. DeVos started her freelance writing company, Rainy Day Creations, and became a copywriter for several greeting card companies. In 2002, her national-award-winning poem *How High Can You Fly?* was published as a children's picture book through River Road Press, and a second hard cover picture book, *The Path Winds Home*, soon followed.

In 2007, Ms. DeVos's third children's picture book, *Barthello's Wing*, was published through East End Publishing, and was included in Scholastic Books' North American school book fairs. To date it has sold over 90,000 copies.

Ms. DeVos gave up city life to live in the beautiful Blue Ridge Mountains of North Carolina, in 2007. And though she continued to write for children, including the publication of her fourth children's book, *The Shopkeeper's Bear*, in 2012, she found her writing interests began to change as she became more embedded in the lives and the traditions of the mountain people.

Ms. DeVos has made numerous appearances in schools, libraries and bookstores, and has been a keynote speaker as well as a selected author for special events, including the Miami Book Fair International, and the Carolina Literary Festival.

Janie DeVos has begun writing the first book in a new three-book series, *A Corner in Glory*.